TEXAS TOUGH

**Center Point
Large Print**

**This Large Print Book carries the
Seal of Approval of N.A.V.H.**

TEXAS TOUGH

Hascal Giles

CENTER POINT PUBLISHING
THORNDIKE, MAINE

This Center Point Large Print edition
is published in the year 2004 by arrangement with
Golden West Literary Agency.

The text of this Large Print edition is unabridged. In other
aspects, this book may vary from the original edition. Printed in
Thailand. Set in 16-point Times New Roman type.

ISBN 1-58547-479-7

Library of Congress Cataloging-in-Publication Data

Giles, Hascal.
    Texas tough / Hascal Giles.--Center Point large print ed.
      p. cm.
    ISBN 1-58547-479-7 (lib. bdg. : alk. paper)
      1. Texas--Fiction. 2. Large type books. I. Title.

PS3557.I3443T495 2004
813'.54--dc22

                                                        2004004296

ONE

They came out of the rock hills onto the flatlands west of Clayfield in late afternoon, walking their horses in single file with Ray Beemer in the lead and Wyatt Kirk keeping a watchful eye on him from ten feet behind.

Beemer sat slumped in the saddle of his black mustang, a thin and seedy-looking man, his sullen face covered with a stubble of black beard and his lips pinched in a tight line. His arms were bound at the wrists below the cuffs of his threadbare flannel shirt, leaving him free to fan out his palms far enough to grasp the mustang's reins. The battered holster on his skinny right thigh was empty, as was the rifle scabbard next to his saddle.

Wyatt Kirk was well-armed. As his body swayed in concert with the buckskin's stride, sunlight struck pink and purple sparks from the mother-of-pearl butt plates on the short-barrel Peacemaker in his tied-down holster. Another six-gun, an iron-handled Colt .45, was stuffed into the waistband of his Levi's, a Remington 12-gauge was in the saddle boot, and a Winchester rifle was tied down atop the bedroll behind his saddle. All of the weapons were not his; the iron-handled Colt and the Winchester were the weapons Wyatt had taken from Ray Beemer when he cornered the man in a box canyon that morning at daylight.

Squinting his china-blue eyes in the shadow of his gray Stetson, Wyatt Kirk looked past Ray Beemer at the town that lay ahead of them. Heat waves wriggled like fleshless fingers above the prairie grass, creating an illusion of sun-seared storefronts floating in space. Distances were deceiving in the clear Texas air, but Wyatt estimated they still had three miles to go before they reached Clayfield.

Ray Beemer turned his head and looked at the man who trailed him. He cursed, and spat over his horse's rump. "You know what you are, Wyatt Kirk? You're no better'n a damn renegade Comanche out liftin' scalps for the pure hell of it. You got no right to truss me up and herd me in to the law. You ain't got a badge, you got no legal authority, and you—"

"I've got a faster gun than you," Wyatt cut in mildly. That's enough. Now shut up before I bend it around your head."

Beemer faced forward again, but his bearing changed. He straightened in the saddle, his neck stiff while he flexed his shoulder muscles. Wyatt Kirk had observed the body language of men when their mind toyed with a decision, and he became wary and suspicious. He slid his hand closer to the Peacemaker, wondering if there was any way the bound man could make a move against him. He called to Beemer to pick up his horse's pace, and was not surprised when the man twisted in the saddle and began to swear at him again.

"You're a damn bloodsucker." Beemer's voice was a snarl of disdain, but his wet lips revealed the nervousness he was trying to conceal with defiance. "You're a damn prairie vulture livin' off the miseries of other people. I hope somebody blows your brains out someday."

Wyatt shrugged indifferently. "You ain't the best com-

6

pany I ever rode with, Beemer. I'm glad I'll be rid of you as soon as I can find a jail to put you in."

Ray Beemer continued to sneer and swear, feeling secure in the knowledge that Wyatt would not shoot an unarmed man. A bland smile settled across Wyatt's lips and he jogged on in silence until Beemer exhausted his supply of insults. The man's words cut deeper into Wyatt's conscience than he would allow his expression to reveal, and it aroused thoughts of the vow he had made to himself on many such occasions.

He had become a bounty hunter almost by accident, stuck to it as an interim job while he looked for other work, but as weeks turned into months and months into years, he knew he was making excuses to himself to avoid taking orders from another man. The money he received was not worth the risks, and he disliked the way he earned his living. He wanted to quit chasing outlaws and go home before he died in some badlands coulee from a bushwhacker's bullet or on some cowtown street from a faster gun.

Each time he collected a reward, Wyatt promised himself it would be his last. His determination waned, however, when he thought of the bitter disagreements with his brother, Justin, which had caused him to ride away from his half interest in the Keyhole Ranch three years ago. His father's death had cast a pall over the ranch four months before Wyatt left, and it should have drawn Aaron Kirk's two sons closer together, but instead it had created a breach between them that might never heal.

Even if he was able to arrange a truce with his brother,

he was not sure he would ever be able to tolerate Justin's proud, domineering wife, Wilma. Wyatt doubted that he could find any more contentment and sense of worth at the Keyhole than he could in tracking down thieves and killers for the price on their head. However, the longing to make the most of his heritage and live on his own land remained strong within him.

Preoccupied with his thoughts, he watched Beemer's back with a fixed, unseeing stare until he noticed the man's arms and shoulders twitching with frantic movement. Instantly alert, he sidestepped his buckskin to get a better view. Despite the ropes on his wrists, Beemer had managed to loop the split reins around the saddle horn. He spread his elbows far enough apart to clear his hatbrim and reached his arms back over his head, his fingers pawing inside his shirt-collar.

Urging his horse forward, Wyatt yelled, "What're you doing?"

"Got a bug down my back. You want to dig it out for me?"

"Not hardly." Wyatt eased back in his saddle while Beemer's fingers continued to scratch around inside his shirt-collar.

Wyatt realized his foolhardiness too late. Beemer's hands rose above his collar and sunlight flashed on metal. Again, he turned around in the saddle, his arms cocked near his chest. A bonehandled hunting knife was cupped between his palms. His arms kept moving and he flung the knife at Wyatt's chest.

Instinctively, Wyatt ducked and leaned forward across the buckskin's mane. He did not move quick enough.

The knife struck his upper arm with numbing force, tearing a three-inch slit in his checked shirt and sending a searing pain through his flesh. He dropped the reins and lost his balance in the saddle. He grabbed at the saddle horn, but the buckskin sensed something wrong and reared its front feet, throwing Wyatt to the ground.

He landed on his left side, but he had twisted his body in midair to cushion the fall. He was on his feet immediately, the pearl-handled Peacemaker jumping into his hand as he pushed himself erect. Ray Beemer tried to make a run for it. He jabbed his heels against the mustang's flanks the moment he threw the knife, but the horse had not yet settled into a lope when Wyatt's gun boomed and a bullet screamed across Ray Beemer's shoulders.

Beemer looked back and tried to draw his head and neck down in his collar as Wyatt raised the Colt for another shot. "The next one takes your head off," Wyatt shouted, and Ray Beemer brought the mustang to a skidding halt.

Blood painted a dark streak down Wyatt's left shirt-sleeve and he felt the dampness of it as it seeped down to his wrist. From the corner of his eye, he saw the knife lying in the short grass, its five-inch blade covered with dirt after bouncing across the ground. It was not a large weapon, but the heavy handle had carried enough force to drive the blade through flesh and carve a cut in Wyatt's upper arm. The knife had not found a vital vessel, but the burning pain from the wound caused goose pimples to pop out on the back of Wyatt's neck.

Keeping his gun aimed at Beemer, Wyatt walked over

and picked up the knife. He looked at it briefly, then threw it into the brush that lined the wagon road to town. Leading his horse with one hand and carrying his gun in the other, he walked angrily toward Ray Beemer.

He cursed himself for the oversight, which could have cost him his life. He had taken Beemer's guns, patted his chest, searched the uppers of his boots for a hidden weapon, and had felt confident the man had nothing left with which to fight. Wyatt had never encountered a knife-thrower, and it had not occurred to him to look for a neck sheath. It was a mistake he would not make again.

When he was five feet away from the mounted man, he ordered Beemer to dismount and step away from the horse. His shiny black eyes darting fearfully from Wyatt's face to the threatening Peacemaker, Beemer jumped to the ground.

"Take off your shirt," Wyatt ordered.

"What th—"

"Take it off!" Wyatt snapped.

"Hell, man, my hands are tied. I can't do nothing."

Wyatt eyed the man speculatively for a moment, then stepped closer and jammed the barrel of the Peacemaker against Beemer's belly. He shifted the gun to his left hand, feeling a stab of pain from the knife wound. Working with one hand, he removed the ropes, threw them aside, and stepped back.

"You can't stand kindness," said Wyatt. "I untied your legs hours ago because you said they were cramping. I tied your hands in front because you said it was the only way you could keep your balance. Now you've ruined all my faith in your good behavior. You know what I think?"

"I don't give a damn."

"I think I know how to make you behave without tying you up."

The blue eyes probed Beemer's face in an unwavering stare, and the skinny man began to fidget uncomfortably while he stared back and tried to read Wyatt's thoughts. Ray Beemer was six feet tall, but Wyatt Kirk was four inches taller, a man with powerful shoulders, flat hips, and an easy stride that allowed him to move about with the grace of a smaller man. Wyatt's anger was seldom heard in the volume of his voice, but the darkening of his skin from a golden bronze to a mahogany brown was a sure sign of the fury within him. His impulse was to hurt any man who threatened his life, and he had to curb a desire to pound his fists into Ray Beemer's face.

With a crafty squint, Wyatt leveled the six-gun at Beemer's chest and said, "Take off your clothes. Strip down bare naked. You can put your hat and boots back on, and that's all."

Beemer took a step backward, his eyes wide and dis-believing. He looked over his shoulder, then from side to side, as though he expected help from the silent prairie. He ran his tongue over his lips and extended placating hands.

"I'll take off my shirt so you can see I ain't hidin' nothin', but you can't make me ride into town with no clothes on. That's—that's—"

Wyatt shook his head, his thumb tight against the hammer of his Colt. "You got a choice, Beemer. You can

11

ride into Clayfield naked with your head up, or you can ride in naked with your butt up. If you don't get your clothes off, I'll knock you senseless with my gun butt, tie you facedown across your bronc, and take you in that way."

"I ain't goin' to do it. You got to leave a man some decency, no matter what—"

The explosion of Wyatt's Colt drowned out Beemer's protest. His voice rose in a fearful squall as the bullet kicked up dust next to his boots.

"All right, all right!" he cried, and began peeling off his clothes.

It was a sight unlike any the inhabitants of Clayfield had ever seen. Range-hardened horsemen halted their mounts in the middle of the street and stared in amazement. A group of children emerging from a footpath across a vacant lot clasped schoolbooks to their chest, whooping and giggling as they lined the boardwalk. An elderly lady in a gleaming buggy sawed the reins of her gray mare in such confusion that she steered the rig's wheels into a hitching rail and almost overturned before she regained control of her horse.

The naked man on the black mustang, clad only in a worn Stetson and stirrup-heeled boots, held his chin close to his chest. He kept his eyes lowered and appeared to be staring at the powder-white skin of his thin legs, which were strangers to sunlight. Riding close behind Ray Beemer, looking neither right nor left as they traveled along Main Street, Wyatt Kirk's face gave no indication that he saw anything unusual about their arrival.

Minor turmoil developed around them. Pedestrians stopped to stare and cluster in groups. The noise from boots clattering on the boardwalk mingled with the din of shocked voices. Wyatt heard a few of the comments despite the commotion. "Damndest thing I've ever seen," a man exclaimed nearby, and a woman shouted at the schoolchildren, "Run along, children! Shoo, now! I'll declare, I don't know what's going on, but this is not a decent sight."

Beemer sat his saddle like a man in a trance. As the crowd began to follow him, he made an effort to salvage a measure of modesty. He snatched his hat from his head and held it across his lap to cover his private parts. Humiliation had crushed the belligerence and defiance out of him, serving as a more effective restraint than ropes or the threat of a bullet.

Wyatt felt no sympathy for him. The flyer he carried in his saddlebags told him what kind of man Ray Beemer was. He was a killer and a coward, a back-shooter who had put a bullet between the shoulder blades of a gambler who had won twenty dollars from him in a poker game at one of the saloons in this pleasant little cowtown. Aside from a general description of the crime, there were few other details on the poster. Wyatt had learned enough, however, to know the man was deceptive and dangerous.

Rising in his stirrups to get a better view, Wyatt saw a flat-roofed adobe building midway along the street with a sign over the door that said COUNTY JAIL—JIM COLLEY, DEPUTY.

He opened his mouth to call out an order, but it was

13

not necessary. Ray Beemer also spotted the sign. He kicked his horse into a gallop toward the building. Wyatt chuckled to himself. It was the first time he had seen a wanted man who was eager to find refuge in a jail cell.

Scattering pedestrians and dodging the wagon traffic, Beemer did not slow his horse until he reached the hitching rail at the deputy's office. He flung the reins to the ground, leaped from the saddle, and dashed toward the doorway. The scraping of saddle leather against his bare skin had turned his inner thighs red and raw, but the rash did not slow his dash for privacy. He rushed inside and closed the door behind him.

Satisfied that Beemer was secure in the office, Wyatt took his time when he reached the jail. He tied the horses, then gathered up Beemer's clothes, which he had rolled into a bundle and tied atop the man's skimpy bedroll. The pain from the knife wound in his arm had settled into a throbbing ache. After forcing Beemer to undress on the prairie, he had no longer worried about him trying to escape. Keeping his gun within reach, he'd torn clean strips from one of the flour-sack towels in his saddlebags and bandaged the cut before they continued to town. As he tethered the horses at the jail, he was aware of crusted blood breaking loose beneath the bandage, but the injury was not a handicap to his movements.

Four or five men had followed him to the front of the jail. They stood in a semicircle behind him, exchanging murmurs among themselves. Tucking Beemer's clothes under his sore arm, Wyatt lifted his 12-gauge from the saddle boot with his other hand and turned to face the curious onlookers.

"The show's over, folks," he said, chuckling. "If you want to come around tomorrow, though, I plan to bring in a naked woman."

Realizing they were being teased, the men started to drift apart, cowed expressions on their faces. One man said, "Pshaw!" started to turn away, then looked back at Wyatt. "I know Ray Beemer. He's scum, but that's a pretty raw way to treat a man, no matter how bad he is. It ain't right."

Wyatt shrugged. "I figure a naked man ain't got time to think about much of anything except his nakedness. I feel safer that way, but you can go after the next killer who hits this town and bring him in any way you think best."

The man scowled, and went down the street with his friends. Wyatt stared at his back, feeling far less superior than he had sounded. He was not surprised by the man's parting comment. Texans despised the killers and thieves who preyed on the honest settlers who sought to tame this raw land, but their independent nature persuaded many to subscribe to a strange code of ethics. They believed it was the responsibility of legal authorities to bring outlaws to justice, and not a circumstance for anyone with a faster gun to profit from another's misdeeds.

It had not taken Wyatt long to learn that not everyone liked a bounty hunter. He had forced himself to ignore the insults that he heard whispered behind his back around livery barns and cowtown saloons. He was well aware that he would not become anyone's hero in this town. With a hard sigh he walked away from the horses and toward the deputy's office. He felt an odd sense of guilt because he was about to inquire about the two-hundred-dollar reward posted for the capture of Ray Beemer.

Until he stepped up on the boardwalk, Wyatt did not notice the lone man beside the jail entrance. He stood with his back braced against the front wall, his arms folded across a broad chest, and a half-smoked cigarette dangling from a corner of his mouth. Wyatt started to pass him by with a polite nod, but the man's voice stopped him.

"You keep pulling stunts like this and you'll end up like your old man." The words were softly spoken, but there was a challenge in the gritty tone and in the pale gray eyes that looked out from beneath the brim of a crisp black Stetson.

Wyatt stopped abruptly. "What do you know about my pa?"

"I know somebody slit his throat from ear to ear a few years back. That's about all I know about Aaron Kirk, but I know a lot about you."

Surprise held Wyatt speechless. He felt his pulse quicken and his throat was suddenly tight and dry. His first impression was that he was being confronted by a drifting hard-case, but the smooth-skinned face beneath the wide-brimmed hat belonged to a youngster who looked no older than sixteen or seventeen. Wyatt started to ask another question, but before he was sure of what he wanted to say, the gray-eyed youngster flipped his cigarette into the street and walked away.

TWO

For a moment Wyatt stood with his head down, his eyes fixed thoughtfully on his boots. He had not yet grown accustomed to being recognized by strangers. The gray-eyed man's remarks brought a flood of sad and bitter memories surging through his mind, and reminded him of a constant threat he tried not to think about. His reputation was becoming too well known, and such fame was accompanied by its own brand of danger.

Why had the man accosted him? There could be many reasons, or none of consequence, and Wyatt was annoyed that the brief exchange had made him nervous and apprehensive. The image of the man's face stayed in his mind. It was a young face, tanned and strong-boned, and the patches of beard on the chin and upper lip were soft and downy. His casual demeanor and hard-edged voice imitated the mannerisms of a seasoned brawler, but the stranger who had shaken Wyatt's nerves was too young to be convincing.

He carried the trappings of a man, however. Wyatt's quick appraisal of the youngster did not miss the cartridge-studded shell belt that held a double-action Colt .45 resting in a tooled leather holster on his right thigh.

Wyatt shook his head, dismissing the incident from his mind for the moment. He shifted the shotgun higher under his arm so he could open the door to the office. The door swung inward, and a big rawboned man with a star pinned to his hide vest stepped back to allow him to enter. Wyatt blinked his eyes to adjust his

17

vision to the gloom while Deputy Jim Colley closed the door behind him.

Ray Beemer stood in the center of the room, looking embarrassed. Jim Colley was paying little attention to the outlaw, but he kept his gun in his hand while he moved around.

Flicking his thumb toward the naked man, Wyatt said, "This feller's name is—"

"I know who he is," Colley cut in. "Who'n hell are you?"

Wyatt introduced himself and the deputy repeated the name, murmuring, "Kirk . . . Kirk . . . Wyatt Kirk. Yeah, I've heard of you. Gettin' yourself quite a rep. I see stuff in the papers about you every once in a while. Some say you've killed five men."

Wyatt's jaw tightened. "Some say seven," he said dryly. The numbers were wrong, but he had stopped trying to correct them long ago. During the past three years, he had killed three men, all in those frightening flashes of time when he had to shoot first or die from an outlaw's bullet. It was a subject he did not like to discuss, and the sarcasm in his voice discouraged any further comments from the lawman.

"Whatever," Colley grunted. "I should've knowed you. The papers always say you're not much more'n a boy, and that fits."

Deputy Jim Colley's remarks were meant as flattery, but they brought a frown to Wyatt's face. At twenty-three, his boyhood was far behind him. His softly rounded jaw, broad forehead, and full cheeks portrayed a youthful appearance, but there were hard edges in the

18

saddle-brown burn of his face, and the steady gaze of his china-blue eyes reflected a strong core of man-toughness.

"I'd like to get the business about the reward settled and move on," Wyatt said.

The deputy gave him a hard look, his short-cropped gray hair bristling across his round head. "Suits me. I don't hold much with bounty hunters. Law business ought to be handled by lawmen, not by any fast gun that comes down the road lookin' for quick money. Why'd you bring Beemer in bare-ass naked this way?"

"Just a whim, I guess. Seemed like a good way to quiet him down at the time."

"Uh-huh," Colley grunted. "I also read one paper that accused you of being the meanest man in Texas. I'm beginnin' to think you might be."

Frowning, Wyatt said, "You must've been reading that sorry little weekly called *The Prairie Scout* from over in Saddleback. There's some loco feller over there who writes what he wants to about me. It's mostly tales he makes up. Far as I know he's never seen me, nor me him. He started that 'meanest man' stuff."

"That ain't the kind of rep I'd want pinned on me."

Wyatt's chin lifted, and the deputy saw the impatience in his eyes. He said, "Sit a minute while I put this trash in a cage and we'll talk about your money."

A rolltop desk, its pigeon holes leaking papers that were jammed into every cubicle, sat against the office wall a few feet from the entrance to a hallway. Colley waved Wyatt to a seat in the cane-bottom chair beside the desk. "I'll be right back," he said, and marched Ray

Beemer down the hallway toward the cells.

Wyatt sat down, pushed his curl-brimmed Stetson back from his forehead, and rubbed his fingers through the thick brown hair that was matted with sweat. He propped his head against the plank wall and reached for the sack of Bull Durham in his shirt pocket, then changed his mind about smoking. He wanted to get his business settled and leave without becoming involved in a lengthy conversation with Jim Colley.

The clanging of an iron door echoed through the quiet building, and Wyatt heard the ratcheting sound of a lock being turned. Colley came back and sank into the low-backed chair at his desk, leaning back with his hands clasped behind his head. He stared briefly at the blood-stains on Wyatt's shirtsleeve, but did not inquire about the injury.

Wyatt studied the deputy from the corner of his eye. Jim Colley was annoyed that another man had done his job, and he resented Wyatt's presence. He wanted it known that he was a competent lawman, and not a man who shirked his responsibility. He was getting set to make those points clear, and Wyatt had a choice of hearing him out or offending him by walking away. He sat and listened.

"No matter what my feelin's are, I reckon you done this town a favor by bringin' Beemer in," Colley began. "I brung him in once, I'd have got him again in time. Five, six years ago I arrested him and his brother, Alvin, for rustlin', and the judge sent them to the Huntsville pen."

The deputy paused and lowered his eyelids while he

refreshed his memory. "Back then they was squattin' on a piece of Circle K range. Old Man Kegly left them alone when they said they was going to raise crops. What they was doin' was plantin' corn by day and rustlin' Circle K cows at night. They got out of the pen about a year ago. I don't know what happened to Alvin, but Ray showed up here one day last fall. He got into a poker game down at Goodloe's Bar, lost twenty dollars at Nick Roland's table, and left. Goodloe closed up about ten o'clock, and Roland was takin' a shortcut through the back alley to the hotel when he was shot. I—"

"That's printed on the reward poster," Wyatt said pointedly.

"Sometimes them posters get things wrong," Jim Colley said. "I figure Beemer was tryin' to get his twenty dollars back like any coward would do. He put a slug in Roland's back for no good reason. He didn't get nothin'. Nick always left his winnin's on deposit with Goodloe, who put them in his safe. A couple of waddies who was in the poker game heard the shot. They got into the alley in time to see Ray Beemer skeedaddlin' away on his horse. Roland lived about five minutes after they got to him, and he said Ray Beemer shot him. Beemer's probably headed for a life term or a hangnoose this time."

Wyatt offered no comment on Jim Colley's story, but the deputy seemed pleased that he had listened with interest. Wyatt understood Colley's desire to defend his office. Frontier lawmen pursued a thankless job. They were often overworked, poorly paid, and overwhelmed by the vast expanse of country they were expected to police. For most of them, respect was their greatest reward, and it was this that Deputy Jim Colley craved most.

Breathing a hard sigh, Colley said, "Well, I guess you want to get paid."

"Sure do," Wyatt replied. "When you get the paperwork done, have them send the money to my account at the Drovers Trust Bank in Rampart, Texas."

"That's up in caprock country, ain't it?"

"We're east of the scarp," Wyatt said. "It's fine cattle country—good grass and enough water. I move around a lot, so I keep an account in Rampart."

Jim Colley went to an iron safe in the corner of the room and took out a sheaf of bills from one of its cubicles. "Since the killin' happened here, the state left the reward on deposit with me," he explained, returning to the desk. "I can skip the paperwork and pay you off right now."

Wyatt held out his hand, then hesitated. "Tell you what, Colley. If it ain't too much to ask, give me fifty dollars for walking-around money and send the balance to my bank."

"No trouble," Colley said.

Wyatt shook hands with the deputy and thanked him for his time. He was turning to leave when Colley asked quietly, "They ever find out who killed your pa?"

"Damn!" Wyatt said through clenched teeth. "How does everybody know so much about my personal affairs? You're the second person to mention Pa."

Colley folded his arms and studied Wyatt's scowling face. "Is that what young Ken Holby was talkin' about?"

"I don't know his name, but some youngster was talking about the way Pa died."

"That was Ken," Colley said. "I saw him passin' the time with you before you came in. He's a fine youngster, like his daddy before him. We have a bronc-bustin' contest in Clayfield the second Tuesday of April. That's why we've got so many people in town today. I reckon John Holby brought Ken in for it. Ken usually wins it. He's the best at everything he tackles—target shootin', bronc ridin', arm wrestlin', or whatever. He just turned eighteen, but he can outdo most men."

Wyatt's eyes narrowed. "He's nosing into things that are none of his business. He'd better learn to keep his mouth shut if he wants to get much older. It beats me how people know so much about the Kirk family."

Colley looked out the window, avoiding Wyatt's eyes. "It probably galls you, but it ain't a big mystery to me. People talk about gunslingers, make heroes out of them. Drifters comin' through spread tales, stage drivers and freighters swap gossip, and lawmen talk to each other. Ken Holby goes farther than that. He gets a bundle of newspapers every time the stage runs and milks my brain about any killin' or shootin' I know about. He writes things down on a notepad so he can remember them. You're famous enough to keep tabs on."

"He's got little to do," Wyatt said sharply.

Colley had contributed to Ken Holby's store of information, and he felt compelled to admit it. He said, "I heard about how your pa died right after it happened. I took some prisoners over to Huntsville, and the sheriff from up your way was bringin' some in at the same time.

23

Aaron Kirk's murder come up when we was comparin' notes on what we was up against in our towns. I probably mentioned it to Ken Holby. Lester Mace got riled just talkin' about your pa. I figured he'd have the killer by now."

"I'm not sure he wanted to dig too deep into that mess," Wyatt said. "I'm not sure I do either."

A puzzled expression wrinkled Colley's face, and Wyatt decided to leave him that way. He headed for the door, calling over his shoulder, "I put Beemer's Colt on your desk. I'll leave his rifle in the saddle boot, and you can look after his horse when you get around to it."

"Strange," Jim Colley mused, picking up Ray Beemer's Colt.

"Something about the gun?"

"No. I was wonderin' why a bounty hunter like you keeps chasin' other outlaws instead of the one who killed your pa."

"Keep wondering," Wyatt said, and left. He was not sure he liked Jim Colley or the town of Clayfield. He had an uneasy feeling that the ease with which he had captured Ray Beemer and collected the reward was not an omen that his day would end well.

After slipping Ray Beemer's Winchester into the mustang's saddle boot, Wyatt backed against the hitching rail next to his buckskin and took his first good look at Clayfield's Main Street. It was a better community than many he had seen. The prosperity and permanence of such towns usually was measured by the number of saloons and churches within its limits. A sweeping glance showed Wyatt the steeples of three churches, and there were four saloons within sight of the jail. A hundred feet to his left he saw a sign jutting out over the boardwalk that identified Goodloe's Bar, and beyond that was the two-story structure of the Empire Hotel.

Wyatt changed his mind about hurrying away from Clayfield. He was hot, tired, and still somewhat shaken by the memories revived by the surprising encounter with Ken Holby and his conversation with Deputy Jim Colley. The buckskin was equally weary. It was bobbing its head, slobbering, and stamping its feet restlessly. Wyatt patted the horse's withers and glanced at the sky. An orange rim tinted the horizon over the rock hills, reflecting the glow in the shop windows along Main Street.

The day was slowly dying, and Wyatt did not relish the thought of more hours in the saddle. A leisurely drink at Goodloe's Bar and a night's rest in a soft bed at the Empire Hotel were far more appealing. He had no special place to go, no special plans, and tomorrow would be soon enough to follow a new trail. That trail should lead home, he told himself, if he could muster enough nerve to assert his rights and settle his differences with his brother. The same thought had passed through his mind every night for months, but he rose each day and went looking for another outlaw with a price on his head.

Shrugging aside concerns about his future, Wyatt moved to the buckskin's side, feeling the horse's body heat and breathing the earthy odor of animal sweat while he freed the reins. He raised his foot to the stirrup, then stepped back. Goodloe's Bar was the nearest place to get a drink, and it was only a short walk away. Staying close to the boardwalk to avoid passing riders, he walked toward the saloon, leading his horse behind him.

Most of those who had come to Clayfield for the bronc-riding show had departed during the time Wyatt spent talking with Deputy Jim Colley. There was little traffic on the street, and he saw only four or five people on the boardwalks. Three horses were tied in front of Goodloe's, but there was no activity around the batwing doors. Wyatt was relieved that the circumstances of his arrival had been forgotten, and he drew no special attention from the few pedestrians who were busy with their own interests.

Clayfield was ready to settle into the relative solitude that came to small towns at dusk. It was a time when men and women were busy with supper and household chores, and too early for the cowboys within riding distance of the town to scrub away the dust, sweat, and cattle smells, and change into clean Levi's for a brief spell of drinking and gambling. The quiet hours between the last sunlight and the first twinkling stars often filled Wyatt with nostalgia, a time when his thoughts drifted back to his childhood and youth at the Keyhole.

His had not always been a happy family, but he had been born to ranch life, and he longed for the days of purpose when he searched for new calves in the spring, branded steers, and rounded up strays for the fall roundup. The work was harder than bounty hunting, but the days began with a purpose and ended without misgivings. Texas cattle were vital to the nation's food supply, furnishing beef for eastern tables, remote mining

26

camps, and far-flung army posts. His father had taught him to take pride in the fact that the Keyhole Ranch and others like it benefited mankind around the world.

At times Wyatt admitted silently that a deep-seated resentment toward both his father and older brother had led him to the wrong decision when he left Justin behind to run the Keyhole to suit himself. If Justin pursued the course that Wyatt had opposed so adamantly, there might not be anything left of the ranch. The first year after he had ridden away in disgust, Wyatt had been so determined to live life his own way, he could savor his evening reveries without any feeling of homesickness. Lately, however, he'd been feeling restless and frustrated during these quiet hours, but it was still his favorite time of day.

Without warning or reason, Wyatt's expectations of a few minutes of solitude were shattered by sudden violence. He had paused in front of the Homesite General Store to admire a display of fancy saddles when it happened. While he was staring at the window, he dropped the buckskin's reins to the ground and lifted his hand toward his shirt pocket for tobacco and papers. Twenty feet to his left, at the mouth of a narrow passage that separated the Homesite General Store from Goodloe's Bar, he saw a slender figure leap out of the open space, and heard an excited voice yell, "I'm going to kill you, bounty hunter!"

There was no time to argue against a senseless gunfight. In the heartbeat of time that expired between the shouted threat and furious action, Wyatt recognized Ken Holby. His insides cringed. The youngster crossed the

27

boardwalk and jumped into the street with his feet braced and his hand grabbing instantly at the polished mahogany butt of his six-gun. While he watched the darting hand, Wyatt was aware that the youngster was good with a gun, but not good enough. Wyatt's skill was a natural talent, a gift of rapid reflexes and perfect coordination of mind and muscle. His hand seemed to act on its own command. It went swiftly down and up, and the Colt roared in Wyatt's fist. He felt the recoil run up his arm, heard the echo in his ears, and saw a puff of smoke float through the still air in front of him.

Ken Holby, who was the best at everything he did, expected to get off the first shot. His startled cry was a wail of pain as Wyatt's bullet drilled into his chest. The force of the slug whirled him around and drove him sprawling on his back. The barrel of Holby's weapon had cleared his holster, but Wyatt shot him before he had time to lift it higher. Holby fell hard. His gun slipped from a limp hand and kicked up dust as it bounced away.

Wyatt put his arm to his side, still holding the Peacemaker. He had been through this many times, but it remained an unsettling experience. Half-drunk cowboys and trail-town toughs looking for a reputation as a gunslinger usually tried to goad Wyatt into a showdown. They disparaged his ancestry, called him names, and dared him to offer them a fair fight. Many times Wyatt had walked away from such confrontations, agreeing with whatever insult was thrown at him. He left his adversaries bewildered by such remarks as, "You're too good for me, cowboy. I'm afraid of you and I ain't got the guts to draw on you."

Ken Holby was too young and inexperienced to know the ploy hard-cases employed to force a fight. He wanted to be sure he had a chance to match a famous gunman's speed, and his method was designed to accomplish his goal. He caught Wyatt off-guard, shouted a challenge and went for his gun at the same instant, knowing Wyatt had to draw against him or die in his tracks.

In the fleeting seconds before the echo of the gunshot faded, Wyatt's emotions shifted between anger and remorse. Before he could shake off the weakness that ran through him when he saw Ken Holby fall, he heard the sounds of people rushing toward him. He forced himself to move. He holstered his gun and walked to Ken Holby's side. He knelt over the silent form, his stomach roiling and his temples pounding. A dollar-sized spot of blood surrounded a round hole high on the chest of Ken Holby's blue shirt. The youthful face with its downy beard was pale and slack, and Holby was struggling to suck in air through his open mouth.

Booted feet thumped against the planked sidewalk, voices rose in the air as men called questions to each other, and long shadows fell around Wyatt as a crowd gathered. Behind him, the door of the Homesite General Store burst open and a stocky man in a fringed buckskin coat shouted, "Oh, my God! He's killed Kenny—he's killed my boy!"

THREE

The panic in his voice and the grim lines of the craggy face told Wyatt the man rushing from the store was John Holby. He pushed past Wyatt with such haste he almost bowled him over. The rancher dropped to his knees, lifted his son's head, and stroked the youngster's forehead. Ken Holby's eyelids fluttered, then opened wide. He stared vacantly for a moment, blinked, and moved his lips. His voice was a weak whisper as he looked up at the man who was cradling his head in the crook of his arm.

"Don't—don't be mad at me, Pa . . . I don't know why—why I thought I was a killer . . . I don't want to kill anybody. I just wanted to be famous . . . wanted to be the man who was better than Wyatt Kirk. I—I wanted you to be proud of me."

"It's all right, Son. All right." John Holby's deep voice choked in his throat and moisture glistened in his eyes. "I'm proud of you, always will be."

Ken Holby did not hear his father's reply. His body sagged and his eyes closed again. John Holby eased his son's head down, and looked around at the curious onlookers. "Somebody go get Doc Milford, for God's sake!"

"I'm here, John. I saw what happened from my window across the street."

A pudgy man in a white shirt, striped pants, and a derby hat pushed through the crowd and put his hand on John Holby's shoulder. He set a black bag on the

30

ground, flipped it open, and took out bottles and gauze. Squatting beside the fallen man, Doc Milford ordered John Holby to stand aside. He poured some liquid on a cloth and passed it under Ken Holby's nose, but the youngster did not move. The doctor dumped the bottle and gauze back into his bag and unbuttoned Ken Holby's shirt. He looked at the wound, grunted, and pushed the shirt loosely back in place.

He waved an arm at the crowd. "Couple of you men carry Ken over to my office. Go easy and don't shake him up too much."

As the rancher started to follow, the doctor held up a restraining hand. "You stay here, John, until I send for you. I don't want you fussing around while I'm working. Ken's not going to die, but he's going to hurt a lot. That'll be good for him. It'll teach him a lesson. Ken started the gunfight. I was passing my window when I saw him jump out and yell something, and go for his gun. This man with the buckskin had to draw to save his—"

"I know what happened," John Holby said. "I saw it from inside the store. You make sure you keep Kenny alive, Doc."

Doc Milford looked at Wyatt. "That was good shooting. Only a man as fast as you would have time to place a shot where it would miss the heart."

Wyatt nodded and said nothing. He had backed away after John Holby arrived, wanting to attract as little attention as possible. Despite criticism from those who had never been victimized by the lawless element of the frontier, Wyatt was not ashamed of his work. There were ranchers and shopkeepers, bankers and stage drivers in Texas whose lives and property would not be jeopardized by the outlaws he had sent to jail or to their graves. He had never killed a man who was not trying to kill him. Moments ago he had faced such danger again. He had to protect his life, but he had not honed his skill with a gun for use against youngsters like Ken Holby, whose worst crime was a misdirected craving for fame.

The doctor patted Wyatt's arm reassuringly and turned back to Ken Holby's father. He said, "Wait in the store, John," and hastened to overtake the men who were carrying Ken Holby.

Wyatt lingered at the scene, swallowing the lump in his throat that grew from a sense of guilt. He hoped Doc Milford's diagnosis was accurate. He wanted to say something to John Holby, but could not find the appropriate words.

Fortunately, he was given more time to think about it. He had not noticed Jim Colley's arrival, but as the crowd broke apart he saw the lawman standing at John Holby's side. Colley turned his back toward Wyatt and began talking to the rancher. They spoke quietly, nodding their heads in unison several times. Finally, they walked over to face Wyatt Kirk.

John Holby cleared his throat and coughed. He held out his hand and said, "Colley tells me you're a professional gunfighter. I figured as much when I saw how easy you beat Kenny to the draw. I want to thank you for what you did."

"For shooting your son?" Wyatt asked, surprised.

"For not killing him. I know you could have done that."

The rancher turned and went back to the general store.

Wyatt felt Jim Colley's eyes on him. The deputy was looking him over as though it were the first time he had seen him. He said, "John's a fair man. There won't be no charges against you."

"I didn't expect any," Wyatt said coolly.

Colley spat into the dirt. "Funny thing about Texan men," he mused. "They all want to be tough—Texas tough. Most can't stand the notion of somebody being better with a gun, better at ridin' a mean bronc, or better with a woman than they are. It makes them want to test a man's reputation."

Wyatt gave Colley a hard look. "I hate that kind of foolishness. It gets people killed."

"Well, it's something a man in your line of work has to face whether he likes it or not." The deputy tugged at his hat and chewed at his lip. After a pause he said, "Maybe I was a mite testy with you at the office. I've got some flyers you might want to look at. Some right fair rewards hangin' on two or three—"

"Appreciate it," Wyatt cut in, "but I'm not interested."

"Are you on somebody else's trail?"

Wyatt shook his head. The decision he had wrestled with for months was made the moment he saw Ken Holby fall into the dust of Clayfield's Main Street.

"My bounty-hunting days are over," he said quietly. "I'm going home."

Wyatt did not spend the night in Clayfield. He stayed

in town only long enough to let his horse drink from the watering trough in front of Goodloe's Bar. Afterward, he mounted and headed toward home—riding with the sun and stars to guide him, riding with a knot in his belly because he was not sure what kind of reception he would receive when he returned to the Keyhole Ranch.

During his years of hunting outlaws Wyatt had covered a wide expanse of Texas, carrying reward posters in his saddlebags and going wherever the warmest trail led him. He was a long way from home and he had no maps or signposts to guide him. His destination was almost due north. He knew some of the landmarks he would have to pass on the way, and he would have to keep an eye out for them to be sure he was on the right course.

Eagerness replaced the reluctance and dread that had kept him away from the Keyhole for so long. Once he was on his way, he felt an urge to ride as fast as he could. His plan was to travel cross-country as the crow flies, tracing a straight line between Clayfield and the Rampart range, but the Texas terrain would not allow such convenience. Clayfield lay in high, rough country. Craggy flat-topped hills, rocky draws, and arroyos rimmed by stands of cedar, mesquite, and thick brush slowed his progress. He was driven by a compulsion to get far away from the town of Clayfield.

It was a foolish effort, but he admitted to himself that he was trying to distance himself from the memory of his shoot-out with young Ken Holby. In the fearful seconds while he stared at the youngster lying silent on the ground, the image of his brother's face had flashed through his mind. There was a time when Justin Kirk might have looked the same—a crumpled, bleeding heap gasping for life. Long ago, Wyatt's quick temper and fast gun had brought him perilously close to killing his own brother.

The trouble with Justin had started less than an hour after Aaron Kirk's funeral. Although he and his father did not enjoy a close relationship during the final years of his life, Wyatt's love for him was deep and sentimental. It was ingrained from his childhood days when his father was a frequent companion, teaching him to ride, rope, handle a gun, make a night camp, and live off the land. Those were good days and good times, all events that had occurred before Wyatt's mother packed up and left home. Those memories were on his mind as he and Justin and Wilma drove their rig away from the cemetery two miles outside the town of Rampart.

Justin took the reins and Wyatt assumed they would turn east along the wagon road toward the Keyhole when they reached the bottom of the slope. His brother took the horses toward Rampart's business section instead.

"We're through here," Wyatt said. "Where are you going?"

Wilma answered for her husband, as she frequently did. She adjusted her broad-brimmed straw hat, straightened the collar of the flowered dress that hugged her breasts too tightly, and said, "We want to settle things while we're here."

Wyatt frowned. "What things?"

Justin replied in the oratorical, authoritative tones that grated on Wyatt's nerves. "We need to talk with Lawyer

Will Barclay. He's got Pa's will. We need to know what's in it."

"My God!" Wyatt said angrily. "Can't we wait until his body gets cold before we start picking over his leavings? Let's go home, act like decent folks, and come back in a few days. We know the ranch will go to you and me, so why rush things?"

Justin Kirk gave his wife a quick glance, nodded as though she had prompted him for his next words, and Wyatt knew they had made their plans sometime during the night before the funeral. Justin had long assumed that his standing at the Keyhole was a step above Wyatt, and constantly sought to assert his position as Aaron Kirk's second-in-command. With Wilma to prod him, he could become overbearing in enforcing rules of his own making.

"Before we go home I want to know how Pa made the division of property—whether it's fifty-fifty or if one of us will be in charge," Justin declared. "It'll keep down arguments if we know where we stand."

From his seat in the rear of the buggy, Wyatt stared at his brother's back until Justin looked over his shoulder to see how his remarks were being accepted. Their eyes locked and held for a moment, and color crept slowly over Justin's face. He was three years older than Wyatt, but he looked younger. He was slightly less than six feet tall, a compact, slow-moving man whose hazel eyes seemed always clouded with serious thoughts. His skin was barely tanned, indicating he spent most of his time indoors. He was well-built, but his body lacked the hard muscles so common among working cowhands. He wore his Stetson cocked at a rakish angle, but it was an affectation and foreign to his personality.

"I see you don't favor the idea," Justin said as Wyatt continued to glare at him.

Wyatt shrugged. "All we do is raise cattle and sell beef. What else is there to be in charge of? If we're going to hang around town, we ought to be talking to Sheriff Lester Mace and find out if he's doing anything about finding Pa's killer."

"It—it's a disgraceful mess," Justin snorted, facing forward again. "We're better off to leave things alone and not stir up a lot of talk. Pa's been lying to us about his weekly trips to town. Lester Mace has already told us enough to make me ashamed to be seen in public. I can't bring Pa back, and I can't help the sheriff. My concern now is how we're going to run the Keyhole. There's more to it than counting cows. Somebody has to make the business decisions—about hiring the right crew, when to market our cattle, and how we can start investing our profits to make the money grow. Pa depended on me for such things, and I have to know if he expected me to do the same after he's gone."

He pulled on the reins and edged the rig alongside the boardwalk in front of the brick structure midway along Front Street that housed the Drovers Trust Bank. A doorway at the corner of the building opened to a stairway that led to the second floor and to Will Barclay's office.

Pushing at the strands of ash-blond hair that had slipped from her hatband, Wilma Kirk twisted in her seat and gave Wyatt a frozen smile. She said, "I certainly hope we can get along now that Aaron is gone. We're all family."

"Not all of us," Wyatt said.

Ignoring their exchange, Justin walked around the buggy to help Wilma disembark. He took one step, then hesitated as Wyatt remained seated. He said, "If you don't want to go with us to see the lawyer, you don't have to. It's up to you."

Wyatt folded his arms and looked aside, watching those who had ridden their horses to the cemetery begin to return and tie up at the hitching rails, their destinations divided between the Family Emporium, Ranchman's Outfitters, and the Wildfire Saloon. A few buggies carrying family groups went on through town, taking trails that led to outlying ranches. Wyatt had wanted to get a second look at the friends and acquaintances who had attended Aaron Burke's final rites. He had not seen Dr. Evan Halsey or his wife, Bertetta, at the cemetery, and he wanted to be sure he had not overlooked them. It was soon clear that they had not been among the mourners, and Wyatt was pretty sure he knew why they had avoided the gathering.

"What about it?" Justin asked impatiently.

Wyatt drew a deep breath and stepped to the ground. "I'll go with you and see if the death fairy was good to you."

Apparently, Will Barclay had entered through a rear entrance and had arrived only moments before they reached his office. He was in the process of draping his blue suit coat on the back of his chair when Justin Kirk pushed open the door and went inside with

Wilma and Wyatt close behind him.

"I just got back from the burying," he said, brushing sweat from the folds of fat that formed his cheeks and chin. He chewed on the stub of a cigar, working it to a corner of his mouth. "I didn't expect you folks so soon, but I know why you're here. I looked over Aaron's will this morning. I can tell you what's in it in a few words, or I can read you the whole blamed thing."

"The main points will do until we—" Wyatt began, but Justin cut him short.

"I think it would be appropriate to read everything Pa set down." Justin insisted.

The lawyer sat down and read the will. Aaron Kirk had devoted considerable thought to his last testament. Aside from the legal provisions, the rancher left behind several nonbinding suggestions and instructions for his sons. Among them was an explanation as to why he did not leave Wyatt and Justin equal shares in the Keyhole Ranch.

Fifty-five percent of the ranch was to be owned by Justin and forty-five percent by Wyatt. It was not a matter of favoritism, Aaron Kirk had written, but an expression of his belief that equal ownership in a business enterprise led to bickering, stalemates, and indecision. "A ship can't run without a captain, and a ranch can't run without a boss," Aaron stated. He went on to explain that he had selected Justin for this role because he was the older of the two, and because he was more educated in the principles of accounting and finance.

"I've got no objections to that," Wyatt said when the lawyer finished. "Justin's half afraid of horses and throws a rope like a woman. He's spent half his life with papers and books, and it's all right with me if he goes on with it."

Rising stiffly, Justin drew his chin close to his stiff collar and gave Wyatt a solemn look. "I'll be doing a little of everything—riding with you some, supervising our crew, and handling the Keyhole's money. I'm the boss. Remember that."

"Don't get uppity with me," Wyatt snapped. "You can be the boss, but you don't own the whole spread. You'd better talk things over with me before you make any big moves."

Justin relaxed and forced a smile. He had lived with Wyatt long enough to spot his anger when it began to smolder, and he wanted to quench it before it exploded. "I didn't mean to sound so arbitrary. I'll be fair. You know that."

"Good enough," said Wyatt. "You've spent so much time trying to get book-smart, you've forgot how to raise cattle. If you want to help me and the Keyhole crew, it'll be appreciated. You ain't the worst cowhand I ever saw, but you come close."

Wyatt chuckled to ease the tension that had hovered over them in the lawyer's office. Justin was relieved. With unusual enthusiasm he grasped Wyatt's hand as they left the office and said, "How Pa divided the ranch doesn't really matter. We're still brothers and we'll keep the Keyhole going the way he wanted us to. I hope you're not mad over the way he set things up."

"Suits me," Wyatt said. "If we have any profits to split, there won't be that much difference."

"Everything is working out real well," Wilma said happily.

Despite the sorrow that hovered over his thoughts, Wyatt left Will Barclay's office in a pleasant mood. Wilma walked between Wyatt and her husband, holding to their arms, and Wyatt almost forgot his earlier displeasure over the way she had dressed for the funeral. When he saw her that morning in her sky-blue dress with its design of giant white and yellow flowers, he had disapproved of her taste. It reminded him of one of the costumes she had worn while she was appearing with the traveling theater group that had been left stranded and broke in Rampart when Justin first met her.

Wyatt did not realize it at the time, but their visit to the lawyer's office was the beginning of hard feelings between the brothers. As time went on, their relationship became more strained and antagonistic. Finally, in a heated argument one night over the use of the Keyhole's funds, Justin became so angry he shoved Wyatt hard enough to send him tumbling over a chair.

As Wyatt fell, he rolled on his side and came up on one knee with his gun in his hand and his finger twitching on the trigger. Just in time, he controlled his fury and lowered the gun. He rose with a shiver of fear running along his spine. He glared silently at Justin for a minute, then made his decision.

"I'm pulling out in the morning and leaving you to run the Keyhole any way you please," he said grimly. "You pay yourself a fair wage, pay our crew and our debts every year, and deposit my share of the profits in the Drovers Trust. I'm going to take a horse as far as Ram-

part and catch a stage somewhere. You can have somebody pick up the horse at the livery barn. I'll need some
traveling money. I'll take a hundred dollars from the
Keyhole account at the bank, and that's all."

He turned his back on Justin Kirk and spoke a final
warning over his shoulder. "If you keep listening to
Wilma, we're going to lose everything, so you'd better
wake up. If the Keyhole goes broke, I'll come back and
tear your head off."

Afterward, Wyatt was not sure whether he left the
Keyhole because of anger or fear—anger over Wilma's
grandiose ideas of using the Keyhole profits to expand
into new and unknown businesses, or fear that Justin
would push him so far that he would end up killing him.
Before the first leg of his stage ride was over, an unexpected event led Wyatt into the bounty-hunting trade,
and he had tried to stay too busy to think about his
brother and the Keyhole Ranch.

He thought about both now. As he spurred his buckskin along unfamiliar trails beyond Clayfield, his face
was lined with worry and his nerves were taut with
apprehension. He wondered how many stories had been
told about his father since he left Rampart, and if Sheriff
Lester Mace had remained as reluctant to search for
Aaron Kirk's killer as he was when Wyatt last saw him.
Had the Keyhole remained profitable enough to pay its
debts, or had Justin squandered the ranch's money on
the ideas that his ambitious wife had put into his head?

The answers to these questions lay at the Keyhole, and
Wyatt could hardly wait to get there.

FOUR

By the time Wyatt left the plateau surrounding Clayfield and dropped down into rolling country, dusk was coloring the sky and casting a blue haze over the sage and grass around him. He kept his buckskin at a steady canter, peering into the gloom to pick out passable trails that would lead him northward.

Worries that he had pushed to the back of his mind pressed at him, and he did not want to stop riding until he knew all that had happened since he left the Keyhole. For two hours, he maintained the ground-eating pace. Finally, when his horse faltered as he skirted the edge of a canyon and started across the level plain that flared away from it, Wyatt realized he had to be logical and patient. He was more than three hundred miles from home, and he could not push his horse too hard if he expected the buckskin to get him there.

As soon as he was away from the brush and boulders that sheltered the mouth of the canyon, Wyatt drew rein and stepped to the ground, only now feeling the fatigue and numbness in his limbs that too many hours in the saddle had put there. He patted the buckskin apologetically, brushing at the lathery sweat and cursing himself for being unkind to the animal. Twenty or thirty miles a day was all a man should ask of a horse, and Wyatt was sure he had covered almost forty since sunup.

"Sorry, old boy," he murmured as he checked the bits and rubbed the horse's ears. It had been dark for almost an hour, but a half moon hung low in the eastern sky, lighting the prairie with a metallic sheen.

While the horse rested, Wyatt walked around to loosen his muscles. He surveyed the land ahead of him. A mile or two away he saw trees limned against the sky, forming a continuous line typical of growth along a waterway. He glanced at the sky, spotted the North Star, then looked again toward the trees. He knew where he was now, and he was satisfied with his progress. He stepped into the saddle and headed for the river, where he would have water for a bath, for coffee to go with a quick meal, and enough grass to feed his horse through the night.

He camped on the bank of the South Llano, but his weariness did not put him to sleep as quickly as he thought it would. Lying on his blankets, listening to the gurgling water of the river and the snip-snip of his hobbled horse's muzzle against the grass, Wyatt could not force his mind to grow idle and let him rest.

Misgivings invaded his thoughts, and he wondered if he was doing the right thing. Perhaps Justin was operating the ranch efficiently, depositing some of the profits from the Keyhole to Wyatt's account, and would be better off left alone. Deep inside, Wyatt dreaded the ordeal of trying to work with his brother again unless Justin's domineering attitude had changed. He tossed restlessly for half an hour before he dispelled the doubts. He went to sleep at last with a firm conviction that life at the Keyhole could not be worse than facing the life-long prospect of using his gun against men with whom he had no quarrel.

At dawn he was on his way again, no longer riding

with the reckless haste that had punished his horse the day before. He chose his route more carefully, measuring in his mind the miles he would cover between night camps. Even though he rode through regions he had never seen, he had no fear of losing his way. In his wanderings in search of wanted men, he had ridden many strange trails, and had learned that the rivers of Texas were a good guide for a rider on a long journey. At one time or another he had seen a branch of most of them, and they had become the milestones that told him how far he had come and how far he had to go.

Across the North Llano he went, then on to the San Saba, and days later he forded a broad shallow sweep of the Colorado. He traversed an ever-changing landscape. Sometimes he felt he was the only form of life in an ocean of grass that stretched from horizon to horizon on treeless plains. There were days when he spent hours riding along switchback trails over craggy hills or between the sandstone walls of canyons where cougars prowled through the brush and rattlesnakes slithered through the rocks.

Until he made his second stop to replenish his food supply, Wyatt thought he had left his bounty-hunting reputation behind him forever. He should have known better. The reporter who worked for *The Prairie Scout* was obviously fascinated by violence, and he devoted much of his writing to Wyatt's career. From town marshals and deputies, Texas Rangers and county sheriffs who had processed reward payments for him, the newsman had gathered details of Wyatt's manner and appearance. He had his own vision of a man he had never seen. He portrayed Wyatt as a boyish gunman with the face of a choirboy, a dark and nerveless man who seldom spoke more than the one word, "Draw!" when he confronted an outlaw.

The writer called himself Mark Wright, and Wyatt suspected the name was as fictitious as many of his reports. He pretended to relate eyewitness accounts of gunfights and arrests. The stories contained a few facts and a host of exaggerations. Although *The Prairie Scout* was a small newspaper, it found readers far from its south Texas home. Stagecoach patrons, long-haul freighters, and drifting cowboys carried it from town to town, and other editors lifted reports from its pages and reprinted them.

On his ninth day out of Clayfield, Wyatt crossed another river and saw the morning sunlight shining against the notched crest of a mountain on the western horizon. He recognized the landmark from tales he had heard in the past, and it was a pleasant sight. He was at the Double Mountain Fork of the Brazos River. The town of Rampart, the Keyhole Ranch, and home were only a day's ride away.

Before he broke camp that morning he cleaned out his saddlebags and disposed of the last symbols of his recent profession—a half-dozen wanted posters, that he had regarded as prospects for future rewards. He threw them on his campfire, watching hazy photographs curl into black embers. His breakfast exhausted most of his food supply, leaving him with two cans of beans and a few shriveled potatoes.

Wyatt was slightly off his course. He needed to bear

eastward from Double Mountain to reach Rampart, and he looked for a trail that would take him in that direction. Shortly after noon he crossed a brushy ridge, rode down to a narrow valley, and struck a wagon road that showed frequent use. As he followed the road eastward, Wyatt saw bunches of longhorn cattle grazing in the lush grasslands on either side of him, and far off to his left the silhouette of a hip-roofed barn was visible against the sky. He was pleased by the first signs of civilization he had seen in days. Now that his destination was near, Wyatt was more relaxed, no longer the captive of a nagging urge to push himself and his horse to the limit of endurance.

The long ride had taken its toll on both man and horse. The buckskin was becoming gaunt, and Wyatt's mind was so dulled by fatigue that most of his actions were guided by instinct and reflex—saddle and ride each day, find a creek or a spring for a night camp, eat, sleep, and ride again. The sight of cattle and barns made him feel less lonely. A mile along the wagon road he came to a signpost that spelled out the name of a nearby town: BUCKHEAD 2 MI.—POP. 382.

Wyatt smiled, and spoke aloud to his horse. "You're in for a treat, old boy. I'll leave you at a livery where they'll feed you a bucket of grain while I buy some grub and get myself a couple of drinks. We'll rest our bones in Buckhead for three or four hours, then move on. What do you think of that?"

A few minutes later the buckskin's hoofs rattled the planks of a bridge that spanned the creek at the edge of town, and Wyatt's sweeping glance quickly settled on the two or three places he needed to visit. The stooped, toothless liveryman appeared to be only half listening as Wyatt gave him instructions for the care of his horse. The man studied him boldly, his glance holding to Wyatt's face at length before finally settling on the glistening pearl of the Peacemaker's butt plates. Wyatt found the scrutiny discomforting. The liveryman thought he should know the dark-faced stranger. He was searching his mind for a clue to his customer's identity, and Wyatt wanted to leave before he found it.

Wyatt paid in advance for a bucket of grain and walked down the stony path that led from the barn to the street. He had no trouble finding his way. Buckhead's main street was barely a hundred yards long, bordered on each side by sun-grayed buildings. Wood awnings jutted out over the boardwalks at intervals, and signs of varying designs identified the shops and saloons. On his way to the livery, Wyatt had spotted two saloons, Buck Wrenn's Ranch Store, and a two-story clapboarded hotel at the far end of the street.

Wyatt headed for Buck Wrenn's Ranch Store, planning to make his food purchases before he sampled the liquor at one of the saloons. He passed three or four men on the street, and saw a pretty auburn-haired young woman inspecting the merchandise inside the New York Dress Shop, next door to Buck's. He slowed his steps as he passed in front of the shop's windows, enjoying the sight of a shapely figure.

For a fleeting moment he thought of Laurie Custer, the blond, brown-eyed girl who had filled him with desire each time he touched her hand or slipped his arm around her waist when they were lovesick youths during their school days. He had abandoned Laurie, just as he had abandoned his interest in the Keyhole Ranch, and he was not sure either of them would welcome him back.

Pushing aside the nostalgic memories of Laurie, he entered the Ranch Store. The air was permeated with the interlaced odors of leather goods, cured meat, coffee beans, and the new denim of ranch clothing. It was the kind of place that would tempt a man to linger and rummage around, an excuse to escape the glare of the sun and the stifling heat radiating from the boardwalks. He had only a few minutes to enjoy the pleasant atmosphere of the store before it was spoiled by a threat that Wyatt always dreaded.

There were two men inside the store. Wyatt assumed the round-bellied bald man behind the counter was the proprietor, Buck Wrenn. His customer was in his late twenties, a narrow-waisted man in range clothes and work-scarred boots. He was leaning across the counter with the brim of his Stetson close to Buck Wrenn's face, and they appeared to be reviewing the items on a sheet of paper that was spread out so both could read from it.

As Wyatt approached them, Buck Wrenn looked up, nodded, and returned his attention to the customer's supply list. The younger man glanced over his shoulder at Wyatt, then faced the counter, asking about a price on something.

Wyatt walked ten feet to the left and stopped with his back against the counter to await his turn with the storekeeper. Buck Wrenn trudged through the doorway to his storeroom, saying he needed to check his supply of some of the items the man had requested, and Wyatt was left alone with the other customer. The man straightened slowly and backed toward the center of the store. There was a wary, frightened look in his nervous gray eyes.

Wyatt's spine tingled with anticipation as he got a good look at the man's face. The customer stood now with feet spread apart. He hooked his right thumb in his belt with his fingers a few inches above the walnut butt of a Smith & Wesson .45. Their eyes met and held for a second, and Wyatt was the first to look away. He knew what was about to happen, and he wanted to avoid it by indicating a lack of interest, but it was not that easy.

"Don't I know you?" the man asked quietly.

"Maybe. I think I know you, too."

Wyatt's reply was an understatement. He knew that face. He had last seen its likeness when he burned the reward posters he had carried in his saddlebags. The man's name was Purvis Boothe, but Wyatt recalled that the information on the flyer regarding Boothe's crime was vague. It was a trifling matter concerning theft, and he was wanted for questioning. The reward was only fifty dollars, a sum not worth Wyatt's time unless he stumbled upon him by chance.

Color drained from Purvis Boothe's face. His gun hand dropped away from his waistband to hang closer to his holster. Wyatt knew the man had recognized him. Boothe did not believe their meeting was accidental. He thought Wyatt Kirk—the bounty hunter he had read about in *The Prairie Scout*—was here to take him to jail.

"You're Wyatt Kirk, right?" Boothe asked.

"That's right."

Boothe's eyes held the defiant gleam of an animal preparing to fight its way out of a trap.

He said, "You need to know that saddle I was accused of stealing when I was working over San Marcos way was mine. The skinflint I was riding for tried to keep it to make up for a steer that got crippled when we was trying to pull it out of a bog. He had his rope on it, too, and he was the one who got in too big a hurry. He was holding on to my saddle and cussing me out when I knocked him down and took it. I pulled out then and there and I ain't going back—no way, no time."

Wyatt put the man's mind at ease. He said, "I ain't either. I'm going to buy a few vittles and head out."

Boothe did not grasp the significance of Wyatt's reply immediately. A quizzical expression passed over his face, but his body remained poised in the stance of a man ready for a gunfight.

The door opened and the young woman Wyatt had seen at the dress shop stepped inside. "You about ready to go home, honey?" she asked Purvis Boothe.

Wyatt was grateful for the interruption. It was taking the man a long time to realize that Wyatt had no interest in him. Finally, when Wyatt tipped his hat to the woman and turned his back toward them, Purvis Boothe answered her. "It'll be a little while," he said.

Buck Wrenn came out of the back room and spoke to her. "Hello, Phoebe! You here to help your old man haul this stuff out to the Bar Ten?"

She gave the storekeeper a flippant answer, and they began to joke with each other. Purvis Boothe joined them, but he seemed disinterested and restless. He kept shifting his glance toward Wyatt, who was standing aside and staring idly through the windows at the street traffic. Boothe was not going to be completely comfortable until Wyatt was gone.

Interrupting the storekeeper's chatter he said, "I'm not in a big hurry, Buck, and this other feller might have a short list. You can take care of him first if he's—"

"Matter of fact, I am pushed for time," Wyatt cut in, and added a comment for Boothe's benefit. "I've got a ranch near Rampart that I've been away from a long time. I want to get back to it as soon as I can. All I need is a pound of coffee and a slab of salt bacon to keep me going."

Wyatt thanked Boothe for his courtesy, made his purchases, and left the store without looking again at the young couple.

Outside, he paused on the boardwalk and gazed tentatively at the Blue Moon Saloon. He had looked forward to a drink and a few hours of relaxation, but the incident at the store caused him to debate the wisdom of staying longer in Buckhead.

He made his decision in favor of caution. Among the assortment of candy jars, coils of rope, and boxes of cartridges scattered along the counter in Buck Wrenn's Ranch Store he had seen an old copy of *The Prairie Scout*. He had no way of knowing if it contained any news about him, but Purvis Boothe had recognized him, and Wyatt knew of no other place the man could have found a detailed description of him. If there was a copy of the newspaper at Buck's, there might be another at the Blue Moon Saloon, and it was a chance he did not want to take.

Shaking his head, cursing the reporter named Mark Wright under his breath, Wyatt returned to the livery stable. He picked up his buckskin, ignored the liveryman's curiosity about his brief stay, and headed again into open country. His visit at the store had allowed time for his horse to have a bucket of grain, but little rest. Wyatt meant to remedy that situation. He rode only far enough to put the town out of his sight. Five miles from Buckhead, he cut away from the wagon road and stopped beneath a grove of white oaks that grew beside a sparkling creek.

As he prepared to rest through the afternoon and night, Wyatt was in a dour mood. His confrontation with Purvis Boothe was fresh in his mind, and he feared it was not the last of such incidents. A reporter's incessant attention had turned him into a marked man, publicizing him so extensively that he was recognized when he least expected it. The notoriety deprived him of such small pleasures as having a drink in a strange town or enjoying a few minutes of camaraderie with other men.

The afternoon seemed to drag on forever, and Wyatt was glad to see dusk creep over the land. He ate an early supper, moved the buckskin's hobbles to a fresh patch of grass, and turned in early. Sometime tomorrow he would be home, back among people who had known him for a lifetime. He was not sure what lay ahead of him, and he went to sleep wondering how long it would be before he lived down his reputation as a bounty hunter and was free to move about without the fear of being challenged to kill or be killed.

An even greater fear touched his thoughts briefly and sent a shudder along his spine. He had not forgotten the time when his fiery temper had brought him close to using his gun against his brother, and he hoped Justin had done nothing in his absence that would bring him to that point again.

FIVE

At three o'clock in the morning Rampart was as barren and still as a ghost town. The false-fronted buildings along Front Street rose against an overcast sky like gravestones. It was a silent, motionless place undisturbed by any of the familiar night sounds of the rangeland. Wyatt Kirk felt like an intruder in a forbidden land as he slow-walked his buckskin through town.

It was a town in deep sleep, without a lamp or candle showing anywhere in the blanket of darkness. Even the stone-faced jail was dark. Either it held no prisoners, or Hap Gilley, the night jailer, had turned down the lamps and gone to bed in the back room. The stillness was unreal, and Wyatt looked farther away for signs of life, but he could barely see the black shapes of the houses in the residential area that bordered the curve of Jimpson Creek south of Front Street. Most of the homes belonged to townspeople, shopkeepers, and professional men who were not the type to be carousing through the night.

He was not surprised that he was the only person astir at this hour, but the atmosphere seemed charged with unknown threats. The fine hairs on the back of his neck crinkled with a premonition that his homecoming would not bring him the satisfaction and contentment he had hoped to find.

He tried to shrug the feeling aside, blaming his uneasiness on the second thoughts he was having about his decision to return to the Keyhole. Within minutes, he realized the sixth sense that had warned him of something amiss was not false. For the first hundred feet of his ride down Front Street, Wyatt stared straight ahead, paying no attention to individual storefronts. He had walked these streets since childhood, and he assumed the town would be much the same as it was when he left it. He was wrong.

For as long as Wyatt could remember, there had been a weed-grown lot between Sampson's Saddlery and the Rampart Opera House. The gap between the buildings no longer existed, and it was enough of a change to arouse his interest. Where weeds and brambles had grown before, a new clapboarded structure with wide windows had been added to the shops on Front Street.

Curiosity drew Wyatt closer to that side of the thoroughfare. The building was vacant. The windows were dirty and devoid of displays. He squinted to read the sign that spanned the arched doorway. A surge of angry blood darkened his face. The paint was cracked and peeling, but there was enough left for him to read the words: KIRK'S FINE CLOTHING.

He lowered his gaze and studied the hand-lettered placard in one window that said Out Of Business—Interested Parties Inquire at Drovers Trust Bank.

He went back along the street for a look at areas he

had mistakenly believed were too familiar to notice. He found two more vacant buildings, both reflecting failures of the former owner.

The rough pine exterior of the shop formerly occupied by the Oriental Laundry had been improved with painted clapboards and new windows. Fancy gilt letters identified it as WILMA'S GOLD MINE, and smaller type below the name advertised Tasteful Trinkets, Rings & Solid Gold Chains. A soiled poster on the door of the store stated that it was Closed Until Further Notice, and there was no merchandise visible inside.

"Damn that Justin!" Wyatt whispered grimly.

His hunch that there was more to see proved correct. At the western edge of town, where the prairie ended and Front Street began, Wyatt spotted another unfamiliar structure. It was set back two hundred feet from the street, accessible through the alley that ran behind the business section or by crossing the stretch of open land between the street and the alley.

Wyatt guided his horse through the weeds and tall grass of the vacant lot and dismounted on the packed earth in front of the building. It was of rough construction. The glass was gone from one window and another was badly cracked.

He set his hands on his hips and gazed at the abandoned building. The sign on the false front said KIRK BROTHERS FEED & SEED. The cardboard placard on the door offered the building for sale or rent and invited prospective tenants to call at the Drovers Trust Bank.

"Kirk brothers," Wyatt muttered. "Now he's dealt me a hand in his pipe dreams."

Wyatt's stomach churned. His head ached and he realized his teeth were clenched so tightly the pressure hurt his jaws. He picked up the buckskin's reins and blew out his breath in an attempt to calm the angry tremors that shook his body.

His journey should end here and now, he thought ruefully. He should get in the saddle and turn the buckskin southward, go back to the manhunt trails where he was his own man and his chief worry was staying alive. He had no idea how much money his brother had spent, or whether the bank had seized the Keyhole Ranch as payment for debts, but Justin should be left to stew in his own juice.

It was a passing thought, and Wyatt would not pursue it. Bounty hunting had become more of a habit than a job, and he took no pride in it. He had come too far to turn back, and he never again wanted to be forced into another gunfight by some wild-eyed kid such as Kenny Holby.

If there was anything left of the Keyhole Ranch, Wyatt meant to salvage it. Despite the weaknesses that he had grown to despise in Aaron Kirk, his father had been a good cattleman. His ranch had been successful and growing. He had lived through droughts and blizzards, good times and bad, and like all who matched their strength and wits against the wildness and desolation of the frontier, he wanted to leave his mark on the land he had conquered—a heritage that would live on in his name. Wyatt wanted as much, and more.

He wanted to make sure Aaron Kirk's life had not been lived in vain; he wanted a comfortable home, a place to bring a wife and raise children someday—children who would be proud of their forebears and do their part in feeding a growing nation and in bringing civilization and prosperity to Texas. The Keyhole Ranch was his only chance to have these things, and Wyatt would not leave it again without trying to hold on to his part of it.

Determination, amplified by anger, gleamed in the china-blue eyes as Wyatt stepped into the buckskin's saddle and rode down the alley road behind Rampart's business district. At the edge of another vacant field he passed Charlie Blake's livery stable and breathed a sigh of relief when he saw that the name on the barn was still the same.

Purchase of the livery stable was to have been the first step in Justin Kirk's plan to expand the Keyhole's interests. Wyatt had opposed the idea, calling Justin big-headed and stupid, and accusing him of becoming a puppet that Wilma manipulated to satisfy her lust for wealth and prestige.

Justin was generally mild-mannered and less vocal than Wyatt, but he was not a weakling. He had his boiling point, and he had reached it while they argued that night at the kitchen table in the main house. He had interpreted Wyatt's remarks as an insult to his wife, and had stormed toward his brother, cursing his lack of ambition and reminding him of the terms of their father's will. Justin Kirk would chart the course of the Keyhole, he'd declared, and he would not tolerate any more defiance. He was tired of Wyatt's interference, and he let him know it by giving him a hard shove toward the door.

Caught off guard, Wyatt had lost his balance and stumbled across a chair, then to the floor. Blind fury took control of his senses. His gun came into his hand, but before he squeezed the trigger he realized his target was Justin. It had been a scary moment. Afraid it might be repeated, he had left the ranch. At the time he had no plans, but he had known that he had to get away before another tragedy struck the Kirk family . . .

Wyatt turned back to the street to pick up the trail out of town after giving the barn a second look, holding to the memory of the role it had played in his relationship with Justin. He fixed his eyes on the eastern horizon, that had been his only interest when he came into town. Fifteen miles away, past the rolling hills that were like a rumpled black quilt against the dark sky, lay the Keyhole Ranch. It was a three-hour ride, and when Wyatt got there it was sure to be the scene of a tumultuous showdown.

Darkness and dawn were vying for possession of the earth when Wyatt stopped his horse atop a bald hill a mile west of the Keyhole headquarters. A frosty rim of diffused light pushed the night away from a brushy ridge on the eastern horizon, but a layer of sooty clouds lowered the heavens and daylight came slowly.

Below him, the prairie stretched away in alternate expanses of flatland and gentle swales, broken by ridges dotted with hackberry bushes and winding creeks banked between rows of cottonwoods and willows. Squinting through the dim light, Wyatt sorted out the distant gray shapes of two large barns, a scattering of corrals, the outbuildings, and the gabled roof of the main house at the Keyhole Ranch.

He felt no sense of joy or excitement as he looked down at the place of his birth, at the home where he had listened to the squabbling and raging of his mother and father through countless evenings during his childhood. The quarrels were disconcerting mysteries until he was about twelve, and by then he recognized the meaning of the words that were used between them. At last, he understood why housekeepers and cooks for the Kirk household came and went at regular intervals. Aaron Kirk did the hiring, selecting the daughter of some hard-pressed rancher or a young woman who worked in one of Rampart's establishments. Their employment usually lasted from a week to a few months before Liza Kirk sent them packing.

He wondered if his life might have been different if Maggie Gregg had stayed longer at the Keyhole. She was the only hired help Liza Kirk had been permitted to choose, a plump apple-cheeked woman in her mid-forties who brought peace and cheerfulness to the ranch for a while.

Maggie baked delicious cobblers, sang hymns while she cooked and cleaned, and ordered Wyatt and Justin around as though they were her own. She stayed for two months before she was offered a similar job at the Sunset Hotel, that was a short walk across the alley from her little house in Rampart. The day after she left, Aaron Kirk hired a pretty young waitress from one of the cafes in town to take her place, and the arguments between

Wyatt's mother and father began anew.

The heated exchanges from his parents' bedroom filtered through the walls of Wyatt's room and made him feel lonely and scared. At times he would tiptoe down the dark hallway to Justin's room, seeking comfort in companionship, but his brother seemed indifferent to the dissension in the house. He usually found Justin lying on his bed, his head buried in a book. Justin pretended not to hear the arguments, but Wyatt listened and worried about his mother's unhappiness.

He remembered her tearful voice—and many of the phrases he overheard when she was berating her husband . . . "Yes, I fired her, Aaron . . . You've been sneaking out of bed for nights, and I knew where you were going . . . How can you tell me nothing happened after I caught both of you naked on her cot . . . You're such a bad liar, telling me you're going to brand yearlings today, and then I find you and Betty going at it in the hayloft . . . You keep begging my forgiveness, and promising you'll change, but you won't. One day I'm going to kill you—or leave you . . ."

Liza Kirk kept her word. She left the Keyhole when Wyatt was fourteen. Despite her inability to live with Aaron Kirk's infidelity, she loved him too much to harm him. She did not kill him, but someone else did.

The memories that flooded Wyatt's mind while he rested his horse were forebodings of worse things to come. He dreaded facing Justin, and he needed time to prepare himself for it.

Dropping the buckskin's reins to the ground so it could nip at the grass, he hooked his leg over the saddle horn, shifted to a more comfortable position, and took the sack of Bull Durham from his pocket. He smoked a cigarette slowly, staring into the murky dawn and trying to spot some sign of activity. Unless they were already camped somewhere for the spring calf roundup, the Keyhole crew should be moving out for their day's work. He saw no one near the ranch house. As the sky grew lighter, his eyes searched for cattle, looking in areas where they should be grazing in bunches, but there was none in sight.

A worried look pinched Wyatt's face. Squaring his shoulders in the manner of a man preparing for battle, he lifted the buckskin's reins and left the hill. By the time he rode into the ranch yard, birds were skipping through the branches of the two post oak trees, that shaded each end of the gallery porch, and he heard a horse nicker somewhere near one of the barns. The smell of fresh coffee was in the air, and a window on one side of the L-shaped house showed the yellow glow of lamplight.

Wyatt tethered his horse at the rail near one end of the porch and stood in the yard a moment. His legs were stiff and slightly unsteady, but he was not painfully tired. He had expected to arrive at the Keyhole in the evening, but he had misjudged the distance. It had been difficult to find a good trail in strange country after he left his camp on the outskirts of Buckhead, and he had been delayed by several wrong turns. Night was upon him when he had finally picked up the stage road into Rampart and stayed on it, knowing the shortest route to the Keyhole went straight through town.

He was here at last, filled with a mixture of dread and anticipation as he stepped up on the porch. Although it had been his home for most of his life, he had not lived long in the house after his father died, and he was reluctant to intrude on a married couple's privacy. He knocked and listened for the sound of movement inside. Shadows were beginning to creep across the porch as the sun broke through the thin clouds and brightened the day.

While he waited, he glanced past the end of the porch toward the long, slant-roofed bunkhouse, that was a hundred feet west of the house. He did not expect to see anyone there unless Newt Hardy, the Keyhole foreman, had stayed close today to work around the corrals and outbuildings, but the deserted look of the place gave him the uneasy feeling that the ranch was unattended.

The Keyhole seemed to be as lifeless as the town had been. The only indication of habitation was the coffee odor in the air. When his second knock drew no response, Wyatt pushed the door latch and went inside. He stood in the oblong foyer and studied the framed needlework his mother had hung on the walls years ago.

Moving to his left, he peered into the parlor and saw that it was not the room he had known in his youth. The leather-covered settee and chairs were gone, replaced by an overstuffed couch and chairs that were upholstered in heavy wine-colored velvet. An oval mirror in a carved frame hung over the stone fireplace where Aaron Kirk's gun rack had been, and the oil lamps on the tables at each end of the couch were decorated with embossed flowers.

Frowning, he yanked off his Stetson and slapped it against his thigh. He crossed the foyer and stuck his head through the doorway to the hall that led to the bedrooms. The silence of the house was beginning to get on his nerves, and evidence that more of the Keyhole's funds had been spent for new furniture heightened the anger aroused by the sights he had seen in Rampart.

"Justin!" Wyatt yelled, his voice echoing through the narrow passageway. "Justin, get your butt out here!"

"What . . . Who in the world? Mercy! Is that you, Wyatt?"

The startled voice calling from the bedroom that once had been occupied by Wyatt's parents belonged to Wilma Kirk. A door cracked open and a splinter of sunlight fell across the floor. Wyatt got a glimpse of Wilma's blond head as she peeped out.

"My goodness, it is you, Wyatt!" Wilma sounded breathless. "Give me a minute, but don't you move until I get there!"

Wyatt put his hat on the wooden bench beside the front door, and rested his back against the wall. He folded his arms and waited. Wilma took her time, but she finally came through the doorway in a rush and threw her arms around him.

The warmth of her greeting surprised him. For a few seconds he remained motionless, not sure of what to do with his hands, then he put them lightly around her shoulders. Wilma clung to him, pressing her body against his and nestling her head on his chest. Her blond hair was just below his chin and he could feel the bulge of her breasts through his shirt. Her closeness warmed his blood with desire. He thought of drawing her closer and allowing his hands to explore the curves of her body, but the impulse died as it dawned on him that he was holding his brother's wife.

He pushed her gently away. "I—I didn't figure you'd be this glad to see me. You keep this up and Justin might get the wrong idea. Where is he?"

Wilma Kirk studied Wyatt's face with a dreamy, half-lidded look in her almond eyes. While her coffee was brewing in the kitchen, she had taken time in her bedroom to color her lips and rouge her cheeks as had always been her custom. Wyatt had never felt close to her, but he was always conscious of her beauty.

Apparently his arrival had interrupted her routine before she was dressed. She was wearing a pink cotton wrapper that was closed by a belt looped around her waist. In her haste, she had not drawn the overlapping edges of the robe close around her, and it fell loosely away from her shoulders to reveal an expanse of white skin and the upper mounds of her breasts. She hesitated before answering Wyatt's question, and she appeared to be weighing a decision.

Presently she said, "We'll talk about Justin in a minute, but right now I'll bet you're ready for some coffee and a good breakfast. Caleb Frye went out with the range hands today and he's not here to help. I'm not much of a cook, but I can do fairly well with bacon and eggs. Did you sleep at your cabin, or were you on the trail all night? If you'd like to rest later, I—"

"I had some rest," Wyatt cut in. She was talking too fast and giving him too much attention. Wilma was

65

stalling for time, and Wyatt wondered about her reasons. He said sharply, "I rode a long way to see my brother. He can't dodge me all day, so you might as well go get him."

Wilma's eyes met his in a searching stare. Her lips parted and she moistened them with the tip of her tongue. Her small chin trembled, and Wyatt was not sure if the expression on her face was born of passion or fear. She said huskily, "Justin's not here."

"Where is he?"

"He's in town. He's being held in the Rampart jail on a rustling charge."

SIX

Silence hung between them while Wilma watched Wyatt's face. Pale spots appeared on the point of his cheeks. She raised a hand toward him, then hesitated, unsure of herself. She waited to see if he was going to explode with anger or offer his sympathy.

Wyatt found the room suddenly too stuffy to permit a deep breath. The air was heavy with the intermingling scent of boiling coffee and Wilma's lilac perfume. His face was hot and sweaty.

He clenched and unclenched his fists. From the moment he looked down from the hills at the Keyhole, Wyatt had sensed that it was a ranch in trouble—a ranch with too little activity and too few cattle. The barns, corrals, outbuildings, and main house were well-kept, but the Keyhole was clouded by an atmosphere of stagnation and neglect. He thought he was prepared for the

66

worst, but Wilma's news about Justin stunned him.

He stared at the blond-haired woman in disbelief. "Somebody must be loco. Nobody who knows us would believe bookwormish old Justin would steal another man's stock."

"Sheriff Lester Mace seems to believe it," Wilma said. "I told him I'd try to dig up bond money if he would let Justin come home, but he said he couldn't set the bail for a crime as serious as rustling. He says the only person who can do that is Judge Haywood. Justin's been in jail for ten days, and the sheriff says the judge won't be in Rampart for another two weeks."

Wyatt shook his head. "There's something bad wrong. Lester Mace has been a friend of the family for a long time, and he knows Justin's not a thief."

"He's not saying Justin is the actual thief. He's saying whoever rustled the Lazy L calves was acting as—as what he calls an agent for the Keyhole. Since the stolen animals were found on Keyhole range, he says Justin has to take the responsibility."

"Lazy L? We've been driving Matt Latham's strays back to him for years. I can't believe he'd think we're rustlers."

"It's not Matt Latham. He sold his ranch and moved to a place on the Leon River. A man named Herbert Naylor bought him out, but Naylor kept the Lazy L brand. Some of his men found the calves over on Castle Creek near our—your—cabin. Naylor swore out the warrant for Justin's arrest, and Sheriff Mace says he had no choice but to serve it."

"Damn!" Wyatt ran his fingers through his hair and

looked around for a place to sit. He backed toward the bench next to the door where he had left his hat, stopping as Wilma reached out and grasped his arm.

"Let's go where it's more comfortable, and we'll talk," she said. "I—I'm so glad you're here, Wyatt. We've had a hard time."

"I guessed that when I rode through town," Wyatt said flatly.

"Oh?" She knew he had seen the failed business ventures in Rampart, and the word fell from her lips like a nervous sigh. "I guess you're pretty mad about what we've done."

"I sure as hell am, but we'll get to that later. Right now I'm more concerned about this rustling business."

Wilma held to his hand and guided him into the parlor. "I know you can help Justin. Folks around here will be afraid to cross you, Wyatt. We've been hearing about your—your work, and I think Mr. Naylor will stop fussing about five calves when he runs up against a fast gunman like—"

"I'm not here to kill anybody," Wyatt interrupted coldly. He sat down on the velvet sofa and surveyed the room, feeling that he was in a stranger's home. The sun had overcome the clouds and attained its usual searing brilliance, casting lacy shadows from the pin oaks across the windows. Wilma sat on the cushion next to him, turned so that her knees rested against his thigh. She continued to study him with eyes that hinted of secret thoughts.

"You won't hurt Justin, will you?"

Wyatt frowned. "Hurt him? What do you mean?"

She put her hand on his arm again. "Beat him up, or shoot him, or run him off the Keyhole . . . you know, because of all the money we've lost."

He made no attempt to conceal his displeasure. "I warned Justin not to use Keyhole money on foolish notions. I don't know what I'll do with him. Right now I want to find out more about this charge against him. Real rustlers don't fool with calves much. They want good fat steers they can turn into fast money."

"According to Sheriff Mace, the Lazy L people claim that's part of Justin's clever doing," Wilma explained. "I don't understand it all, but the sheriff can tell you about it. They found five calves wearing the Keyhole brand running with Lazy L cows. Naylor claims they were hidden out until the calves were weaned, then we'd drive the cows back and keep the calves until they were full-grown."

Wyatt shifted his position to move away from the warm touch of Wilma's legs. "A man would have to be desperate to try to build a herd that way. Mace knows the Keyhole ain't that hard up."

Avoiding Wyatt's eyes, Wilma said, "But we are. Justin has sold off a lot of the herd to pay our debts. We still owe the bank a lot, but I don't know exactly how much. The sheriff says our situation makes things look worse for Justin."

Wyatt pushed to his feet. He set his hands on his hips and gave Wilma a hard stare. "Justin's a damn fool! I'll ride on over to Castle Creek and clean up a bit, get a little rest, then go into Rampart and see if I can get Justin out of jail. If he's been there for ten days, a few more

69

hours won't make any difference."

Uncurling her legs from the sofa, Wilma rose slowly and backed two steps away from him. Her eyes were wide and her bosom rose and fell with quick, short breaths. She toyed with the belt that held her pink robe in place and said, "Would you like to go to bed here?"

"No. I might as well go ahead and get my place in shape."

"I meant with me."

Wyatt's chin lifted and he stared at her in disbelief. She was Wyatt's age, but she looked like a frightened schoolgirl contemplating her first intimate experience with a man. A flood of conflicting emotions erupted in his mind. He hesitated before he spoke, not sure if Wilma was serious or trying to lighten his mood with a clumsy joke.

He managed a chuckle and said, "I don't think we'd like ourselves if that ever happened."

He started toward the foyer, but Wilma moved first. With a flip of her fingers, she loosened her belt and let one side of her robe fall open far enough to reveal a shapely thigh.

Cocking her head coyly, she asked, "Are you sure, Wyatt?"

He felt a brief surge of desire, followed immediately by anger and revulsion. He turned his head away and replied without looking at her. "Cover yourself and act decent, Wilma! I've always known you're a pushy, scatterbrained filly, and here to get what you can out of Justin, but I didn't know you were a whore!"

Her reaction was swift and violent. She fastened her

70

belt quickly and lunged at him, a plaintive cry sounding in her throat. Before he could defend himself, he felt the sting of her hand on his cheek as she slapped him fiercely. She lifted her hand to strike him again, eager to scratch and claw at him. Wyatt caught her wrist in mid-flight. He grabbed her other arm as it darted upward, and held her at bay.

"Don't you dare call me ugly names!" she shouted, squirming to free herself. "I'm not a whore! You're nothing to brag about yourself. You—you're a gun-slinger and a killer for pay. I've read all about you—the meanest man in Texas, they say. You—you're—"

The accusations drowned in a sob. Her shoulders slumped and she stopped struggling. Tears welled in her eyes and she looked up at him with her chin quivering. Words of apology and explanation tumbled from her lips. "I—I'm sorry, Wyatt. I—I'm sorry. I don't think I could have gone through with it, but I'm so scared I don't know what I might do. I'm afraid of you—afraid of what you'll do to us. I don't want to be unfaithful to Justin. I love him! I—I thought if I got you in my debt, or made you feel like you'd done Justin wrong, you wouldn't be so hard on us. God, how could I be such a fool?"

"Seems to come pretty easy to you," Wyatt said. "Get out of my sight and stay out of it."

She looked at him through teary eyes, opened her mouth as if to plead with him, then ran through the foyer and on toward the bedrooms. Shaking his head, feeling like he had been in a brawl, Wyatt walked to the entryway and picked up his hat. He heard Wilma's footsteps and turned around. She came to the hallway door, clutching her arms around her. "You won't tell Justin I—you won't tell him what happened, will you?"

"On one condition," said Wyatt. "You get out of this house before morning, and I won't tell him. You can leave Justin a note—tell him you're going to join another show troupe, or a medicine show, or whatever. I want you off the Keyhole."

She started to turn away, then whirled around to face him again. She stood erect, her eyes fiery with determination. "Maybe you think it would be good for Justin if I left, but I don't. To begin with, I don't have any place to go. I don't have any family, or any friends around here. I'm a good singer, a good dancer, and I could be a performer if that's what I wanted. I want to be Justin's wife and I'm going to be. I won't leave! We've made a lot of mistakes, and Justin's got a lot of trouble on his hands. He needs me more than ever. If you think you can run me off, you're wrong! I—I'll tell Justin myself. He'll be hurt but he'll understand my—my confusion."

"Suit yourself," Wyatt said.

Wilma went back down the hall. Wyatt jammed his hat on his head, shifted the pearl-handled Peacemaker to a more comfortable angle, and reached for the door handle. He pulled his hand away and stood still, listening to the firm echo of Wilma's footsteps. He thought about the expression he had seen in her eyes when he first arrived, the brightness that could have been fear or passion. It was not passion, although she later pretended it was.

He stepped to the center of the foyer and called Wilma's name. She came hesitantly into the room, clutching her robe around her, and waited for him to speak.

"I've—changed my mind," Wyatt said. "I reckon I never thought about how much I scare people. I'll give you credit for being honest with me, and for going as far as you did to help Justin."

He forced a weak grin. "Forget about what I said and stay on. Nothing happened here worth talking about. There's no need for us to mention it to Justin. He's got enough worries. We'll live as friends and see if we can hold onto this place long enough to turn it into a ranch again. I've got a feeling Justin hasn't told you how bad things are, but he'll tell me. I need to talk with the sheriff real bad, and maybe I'll visit Herbert Naylor."

Wilma breathed a deep sigh and some of the sadness left her face. She moved toward him, but this time she did not come so close. She shook his hand. "Thank you, Wyatt. I'd never hurt Justin unless I could help him at the same time. I know some of our troubles are my fault, and I'll do my best to make up for it. I—I've been a good wife to Justin."

"I believe you," Wyatt said.

Mutual understanding eased the strain between them and they felt more at ease with each other. At Wilma's insistence, Wyatt agreed to let her fix his breakfast. While she worked in the kitchen, he went to the well pump at the rear of the house and washed the dust from his hands and face. Afterward, he sat at the round table in the kitchen and ate alone.

Telling him she wanted to get dressed before preparing her own breakfast, Wilma excused herself and went to her bedroom. Wyatt suspected she was staying busy to avoid answering questions about the vacated businesses he had seen in town, but that was a matter to be settled with his brother. He wanted to hear more about the rustling evidence against Justin, but Wilma had professed to know only what she had told him. She was counting on Wyatt to persuade Sheriff Lester Mace to release her husband.

Although she had married Justin and moved to the ranch two years before Wyatt left, Wilma did not know enough about the customs of the West to grasp the full implications of the charge against her husband. Wyatt understood them. In this country, ranchers who found their cattle in another man's possession often administered their own brand of justice. They hanged the rustler from the nearest tree. Wyatt had once seen an example of the custom in south Texas—the shrunken shape of a week-old corpse dangling on a rope, with clothing shredded and bones exposed by the beaks and talons of buzzards that had ripped the flesh away.

Justin was lucky to be in jail, and he probably owed his safety to Lester Mace's reputation for strict and honest law enforcement. The veteran sheriff would not tolerate a lynching in his jurisdiction without tracking down those who had usurped his authority, and his ire was not a force to be taken lightly.

The sheriff had virtually ignored his duty three years ago, however, when he made only a token effort to find Aaron Kirk's killer. Wyatt knew the reason for Lester

74

Mace's attitude and blamed himself for not insisting that the lawman do his duty. He also blamed his brother.

Justin felt that their father had died in disgrace, leaving his sons to live with a name sullied by his womanizing. Rather than become the subject of the rangeland gossip that would result from a continuing investigation, Justin preferred to let Aaron Kirk's death remain a mystery. Finally, despite his brother's objections, Wyatt had given Lester Mace information that pointed to a definite suspect in the killing. He had spoken too late, but he was sure the subject would arise again when he visited Lester Mace to discuss Justin Kirk's arrest.

It was good to sit in a comfortable chair, with walls around him and a roof overhead, and Wyatt took his time eating the eggs, potatoes, and lean bacon Wilma had prepared for him. Outside, the day was bright and he could hear birds singing in the trees, but the house was so still he believed Wilma had no intention of joining him before he left.

He drank a second cup of coffee, smoked a cigarette, and was annoyed with himself for using up so much time. As he was leaving, Wilma came to the foyer to tell him good bye. Her hair was pulled back from her face and wound into a bun at the back of her neck. She had swapped the pink wrapper for a gray riding skirt and a loose cotton shirt.

"Even though we pushed you out, I want you to know this is still your home, Wyatt," she said. "I guess I thought I was marrying rich, and wanted to act rich, but

I've learned a lot in these last years. All I want now is to be a ranch wife. I'm sorry about the way I behaved after Aaron died, and if you'd like to move back we'll make room for you."

Wyatt shrugged and shook his head, silently amused by an invitation he had never expected to hear. He said, "Don't worry about it. Castle Creek grows on you, and I think I'll stay there. I'll see you before dark if I can get Justin out of jail."

"Let me know something, whatever it is."

"I'll do that."

She followed Wyatt to the porch, drawn to him by worry and fear. "You won't get in trouble, will you?" she asked in a small voice. "You won't kill somebody in a gunfight and end up in jail, will you? With things piling up the way they are, this place is too much for me. I don't know what our riders are doing, or anything about the cattle, or what to do about our debts. I need you here until Justin is cleared. Please don't be reckless with your gun."

Hard lights danced in his eyes as Wyatt glared at Wilma. "Why does everybody think I'm a killer? You've been reading too many lies about me." As he strode toward his horse he called, "I'm not the meanest man in Texas. I don't shoot anybody unless they're trying to shoot me."

The buckskin had been standing for more than an hour, but the horse appeared content in the shade of the tree near the tie-rail. Wyatt stepped into the saddle and waved farewell to Wilma. He skirted the corner of the house, riding slowly while he swung his gaze about to refresh his familiarity with the ranch layout. Midway between the back door of the house and the bunkhouse was the cookshack. It was located so food could be carried in either direction, where housekeepers in years past had prepared meals for both the family and the Keyhole crew.

The house had its own kitchen, but Liza Kirk had detested cooking, and Wyatt judged that Wilma also disliked the chore. After Aaron Kirk's death Justin had assigned the cooking duties to Caleb Frye, whose advancing age was pushing him toward retirement. The cookshack was deserted. Wilma had told him that Caleb was again riding with the Keyhole crew, another indication, Wyatt thought, that the ranch was suffering hard times.

He went to the corral next to the nearest barn, looking over the three horses that were munching hay inside the pole fence. Among them was the line-backed dun that had been Wyatt's favorite cutting horse, three years older now, but still strong and frisky. The buckskin had covered a long trail and deserved a rest. Wyatt put the buckskin in the corral, roped the dun, and reloaded his gear. He left the ranch yard with his eyes on the hills three miles to the east that lay between the Keyhole headquarters and the cabin on Castle Creek.

He rode with his teeth clenched and his hands locked tightly on the reins—a tense, worried man who had returned home to seek a better life than a bounty hunter would ever know, but had found instead a ranch on the brink of ruin and his brother in jail.

There was much Wyatt needed to know, and Wilma

had pleaded ignorance regarding the details of the Keyhole's affairs. He had known from the beginning that he would have to talk again with Sheriff Lester Mace, visit Banker Lloyd Rocker, and hear from Justin an explanation of the events that had led to his arrest. Apprehension and a feeling of hopelessness strained Wyatt's nerves as he considered the possibility that what they had to say might spell doom for the Keyhole, for Justin, and for himself.

SEVEN

Half an hour after he left the corral, Wyatt reached the crest of one of the flat-topped hills. Before he started down the other side, his attention was drawn to a horseman who was coming around the toe of the ridge on the prairie to the south. Halting the dun, he watched the rider until the man came closer to the base of the slope where he could get a better view of him. The horseman was not a stranger. The stooped shoulders, thin profile, and the floppy black hat were familiar enough for Wyatt to recognize Caleb Frye, heading toward the Keyhole headquarters.

Wyatt turned back the way he had come, taking an angle that would intercept Caleb near a stand of mesquite. He was within fifty yards of him before the cook saw him coming. Caleb Frye stopped his horse and waited.

"That you, Caleb?" Wyatt called.

"Damn right it's me," the cook shouted, his drawling voice crackling with surprise. "You're either a ghost or

Wyatt Kirk, and I hope, by God, you ain't a ghost."

Caleb stepped to the ground with a grunt. His grin was distinguished by glistening gums where two of his lower front teeth were missing. Wyatt drew rein and dismounted beside him. They shook hands, grinning and slapping shoulders.

Caleb Frye had not changed much since Wyatt had last seen him. He still smiled quickly, swore often, and his leathery face showed few additional wrinkles. He did not move as spryly as he once did, but Caleb was not a man who would use his age or the pains of rheumatism as an excuse to avoid work.

"Wilma told me you're working the range again," Wyatt said. "Newt Hardy takes what he can get when he's behind in his work."

Caleb nodded. "Yeah, I do what I can, 'cause we ain't got much of a crew left. Just the four of us, counting me, and I wear down easy. Newt Hardy ain't bossing me these days, though. Sam Hopson's giving the orders."

"Who's Sam Hopson?"

"Sort of a strange bird, a loner who keeps to himself pretty much except when he's working, but a good cowhand. He come out of New Mexico Territory after you left, and Justin took him on."

Wyatt frowned. "What happened to Newt? He's been the Keyhole ramrod for ten years and I didn't figure he'd ever leave. Did he get a place of his own?"

Caleb shook his head and spat into the grass. "No. It got to the point where him and Justin argued all the time about the way things are being done here. About three months ago Justin upped and fired him. Newt said that

79

suited him fine. He told Justin the Keyhole is going to hell in a hand-basket and he didn't want no part of it nohow."

"I'm going to break Justin's neck," Wyatt muttered.

"You'll have to get him out of jail first. You hear about that?"

"Yeah," said Wyatt. "Wilma told me, but she didn't say anything about Newt Hardy. Where'd he go?"

The former Keyhole foreman had moved first to the nearest ranch, Caleb told him, which was Herbert Naylor's Lazy L. Apparently, he was not content there. After two months he moved on to Paul Sipe's Arrowhead south of town. Caleb had not seen him since he left, but another of the Keyhole's riders had run into Newt in Rampart and learned of his new post.

"I need help I can count on," Wyatt said. "Do you think I could hire Newt back?"

"Maybe," Caleb replied. "He won't work for Justin again, but he might work for you. Newt don't think Justin has sense enough to run a spread like this, but we've got all the trouble we need around here. If you go second-guessing and hire Newt back, you and Justin'll be going at each other's throat again."

"Not any more," Wyatt said flatly. "If they don't hang him, Justin is going to get his pants back in the saddle and go to work like the rest of us. From now on I'm running the Keyhole."

"You've got a big job on your hands. That claim against Justin don't hold water. He ain't the kind to do any branding by himself, and none us would steal cows if he asked us to. One thing after another's beating us

80

down. The Keyhole is just about a goner. You don't know how bad things are."

"Tell me about it," Wyatt urged.

They led their horses into the shade of the nearby mesquite trees to talk. Caleb did not want to leave the impression that he was meddling in ranch affairs, but he wanted Wyatt to know Justin's actions had affected the life of everyone at the Keyhole.

"I reckon Justin got himself in a money bind when his stores closed up," Caleb speculated. "For two years after you left we sent our usual eight hundred head to market, but here lately we've sold cattle two or three times when we couldn't spare them. We didn't get much of anything for them either. Naylor's Lazy L ruined the prices for us."

Caleb curled his lips like he had a bad taste in his mouth and spat again. "The last time we got ready for a sale Naylor got wind of it. He put a herd together and offered them to the broker for ten dollars less than we was asking. We had to meet his price or drive them back home."

"I'm getting a bellyful of this Naylor feller real quick," Wyatt said. "What's he up to?"

"Beats me. I've never seen the bastard. I hear he's so rich he ain't even trying to make money out of the Lazy L. Looks like he gets his enjoys out of beating people down with his pocketbook. It's like he's playing a game. That might be why Newt Hardy left the Lazy L so soon."

"I need to talk with Newt," Wyatt said earnestly. "Naylor can't be that much of a fool. Something's going on at the Lazy L that's coming to roost with us. Maybe Newt knows what it is."

Caleb Frye squinted thoughtfully. "Maybe Newt signed on over there to see what he could learn about Naylor. He was mad enough to kill the son of a bitch when he ruined our cattle sale. Newt was just as mad at Justin, though. He was raising hell with Justin about too many roundups. He said we was selling off too many yearlings and too many young heifers, and we couldn't get enough calves to keep the herd built up."

"He's right. It's a lousy way to run a ranch." Wyatt shook his head and took a deep breath. "How many head do we have left?"

"Hard to tell. We don't have enough hands to get a good tally. I'd guess six, seven hundred—maybe eight, with calves."

"Damn!" Wyatt said softly. "Pa usually ran about twenty-five hundred, sold eight hundred or so each fall, and the herd was growing fast. He was aiming at building up to about five thousand. He used to say we'd live rich when we got that big. He had that in mind when he bought that last twenty thousand acres of graze— something we was paying for right along, but I'd bet my hat we're behind at the bank on the note now. We've got sixty thousand acres of land and six hundred cows. I thought Pa left us well-off, but Justin's sure made us poor."

Rubbing sweat from his face with his shirtsleeve, Caleb related another incident that had displeased the Keyhole crew. When Justin opened his feed store in Rampart, he had called in six farmers to plow up an area known as Eagle Flats. He planted it in corn, believing he could net large profits by selling grain at the new store. Unfortunately, it was a year of drought. The corn failed to sprout, the winds that swept through the valleys blew away the topsoil, and Eagle Flats was still bare and dusty.

"He ruined some good graze," Wyatt growled. "I was afraid Justin would get carried away with his book-learning. He used to preach to Pa about diversifying and growing on leverage—that's using a little bit of your money and a whole lot of what you can borrow to buy into things. Pa liked to listen to Justin's big talk, but he always ended up by saying we'd better stick to what we know. When I got out of his way, Justin had to try to prove he's smarter than anybody else, but he's—"

"I got to be going," Caleb interrupted. He was watching Wyatt's face, and the fury in the hard eyes made him uncomfortable. "I helped the boys look for strays for a while early on. We wasn't finding much, and Sam Hopson figured I'd do more good at the ranch. I need to get in wood and scrape up something for supper. Sam will want some hot grub when he brings the hands in tonight, and Miss Wilma will want me to fix something special for her. I could say more, but I purely do need to go."

"Appreciate your time," Wyatt said.

Caleb mounted his horse and showed Wyatt his gap-toothed smile again. "Everybody's going to be glad you're back home. We're cow people, not store people, and we like to work for a man who knows what he's doing. You're like your pa and . . . that is, you're like him when it comes to talking straight and . . . that is, you're like him in most ways, but I didn't mean—"

Wyatt grinned wryly. His father's reputation for womanizing was not much of a secret on the Rampart range. He said, "I know what you mean, Caleb."

Afterward, Wyatt rode across the hills with his head down and his nerves taut. He had more to think about than his mind could handle. There were too many problems ahead of him to be solved in a day, but he had to start somewhere—and soon. First, he wanted to see his cabin again, to feel the ties to home that he had hoped to experience on his arrival at the Keyhole. He needed a bath, a change of clothes, and time to regain a sense of belonging here so he could believe the Keyhole was again the center of his ambitions and worth the effort it would require to make it profitable again.

He came down into the bottle-shaped basin where he had lived in the honeymoon cabin formerly occupied by Wilma and his brother. It was a two-mile stretch of rolling land, sheltered on the west and north by hills and on the east by terraced stone bluffs. Southward, the hills and bluffs curved toward each other, sloping down to leave a hundred-yard gap where the creek that ran through the center of the basin flowed through the opening and snaked its way across the prairie.

Wyatt had once viewed the basin as a place of involuntary exile, mainly because his first few days here were clouded by a surly mood and a feeling that he was a victim of the high-handed attitude of Justin and Wilma. At breakfast one morning, three days after Aaron Kirk's funeral, Justin proposed a new housing arrangement for the family. Before the discussion ended, it was clear to Wyatt that Wilma had done the planning.

"Now that Pa's gone," Justin began tentatively, "I've been thinking how things might look to people. This has always been the owner's house—headquarters for the boss. Now that I'm in charge, I was thinking I ought to live here. Wilma and I were talking about it, and we think it might be a good idea if we moved in here and you took over our cabin on Castle Creek. What do you think?"

Wyatt gave his brother a cynical smile, thinking that Justin's preoccupation with appearances was comical. He said, "There's room in the house for everybody. You and Wilma can take Pa's room. Yours will be vacant, and I can stay where I am."

Justin and Wilma exchanged glances, and Justin fiddled with his coffee cup before continuing. "Wilma wants to get that old oak desk and my clutter of books out of the parlor and set up an office in your room. She thinks we'll be having overnight company now and then, and she wants to turn my room into a guest room."

"We going to turn this place into a social club?"

"Oh, pshaw!" Wilma chuckled, and brushed her hand across the back of Justin's neck. "We're not trying to act fancy, but it seems that we should be the master and mistress of the main house. We can't make you move, but it would be a favor to us. We're still practically on our honeymoon, you know, and we'd like . . . well, you know, our privacy."

"You've been married two years," Wyatt said. "I reckon privacy is as good an excuse as any to get me out."

His voice was brittle with resentment, but he knew the subject would come up again. He did not want to argue about it. He packed his belongings, took a final look around the room that had been his since childhood, and moved out at noon.

Aaron Kirk and the Keyhole crew built the cabin on Castle Creek as a wedding gift for Justin and Wilma. Care was taken to assure that it was more attractive than the spartan shacks that became the first home of many young couples. The chinking was whitewashed, window and door casings were painted a rustic brown to blend with the logs, and a stone porch extended halfway along the front wall.

It contained only four rooms, but they were spacious and airy, and the house was built for easy expansion when the time came for Wilma and Justin to start a family. Wyatt helped with the work, but he had no reason to suspect that he would become the cabin's sole occupant someday.

In time he grew fond of his new surroundings despite a lingering grudge over being forced from his own home. The rhythmic murmur of the stream swishing against its banks a hundred feet from the front door was a lullaby that helped him sleep soundly at night. He learned to admire the picturesque beauty of the basin when sunset transformed the bluffs into a flaming red backdrop for the greenery in front of them.

The best trail to the cabin lay parallel to the creek.

Wyatt let the dun pick its way through the undergrowth at the base of the hills and headed for the road, which had been packed hard over the years by wagons and hoofs. Ahead of him, something moved in the brush and he jerked erect in the saddle. He saw the white flash of a deer's tail as it bounded away from a clump of hackberry and disappeared among the willows and cottonwoods that marked the course of the waterway. Wyatt slowed his horse and scanned the land around him, wondering if the doe had heard the dun's hoofs, or if he was being watched by another rider.

He picked up the trail, glancing often over his shoulder, but he saw nothing to support his suspicion. Crows cawed in the cottonwoods and far off a coyote howled. Except for nature's sounds, the basin was quiet and peaceful. He muttered to himself. The only pressures on the Keyhole, aside from Justin's troubles with the law, were financial. Wyatt had no reason to feel that his life was in jeopardy, but he did.

Blaming the effects of his bounty-hunting days for his uneasiness, Wyatt shrugged off his apprehensions and rode on. When he came within sight of his cabin, his suspicions were renewed. He had expected to find the place deserted, weed-grown and unkempt from neglect. Instead, he saw flowers blooming in beds beside the step that led to the stone porch, sunlight gleaming on clean windows, and two horses in the pole corral beyond the house.

Wyatt went ahead cautiously. He stopped the dun fifty feet from the porch and stepped down on the short grass. He lifted his 12-gauge from the saddle boot and strode toward the cabin. When he was ten feet from the porch, the door swung slowly inward. He raised the shotgun to his shoulder and aimed it at the opening.

A young woman stepped into view and Wyatt lowered the shotgun, his mouth agape. He stood dumbfounded while his eyes drank in the beauty of Laurie Custer—the blond, brown-eyed girl who had flitted through his dreams often during many lonely night camps. She was even prettier than he remembered, more mature and womanly than the girl of nineteen he had held in his arms the night before he left the Keyhole. Her close-fitting Levi's and yellow blouse revealed that her slender, compact figure had grown fuller and shapelier.

"Laurie!" Wyatt shouted, and hurried toward her. He paused to prop the shotgun against the porch railing, and opened his arms to draw her close to him.

The look in her eyes stopped him. Her first glance at him brought a brief flicker of joy to her face, but it was quickly gone. Slowly, awkwardly, he dropped his hands to his sides. Laurie's smile was almost a sneer, and he could see she would not accept his embrace. Instead, she extended her arm to keep him at a distance and offered him a limp handshake.

"This is quite a surprise," Laurie said evenly. "I—I didn't know you were back home."

His arrival stirred her emotions more than Laurie wanted to reveal. Her words came out on the tail of short breaths and her hands were trembling, but the hickory-brown eyes remained cold.

Before Wyatt could speak she added, "Of course, I had no idea whether you were alive or dead, either. It's been three years, Wyatt . . . three years and not even a letter from you. I—"

"We'll talk about that," said Wyatt. "I had my reasons for not writing."

In his own mind his reasons were sensible and logical, but this was not the time for explanations. He had become a bounty hunter, a profession that put his life at risk every day, and he thought it would be unfair to Laurie to continue a relationship that might bring her nothing but grief. His feelings for her were as strong as ever, but his lack of attention had left her feeling rejected and abandoned, and he feared she had found someone else who meant more to her.

Her behavior killed the excitement he felt at seeing her, and he suddenly remembered the horses in the corral that had caused him to approach the cabin with a gun in his hand.

Wyatt's eyes narrowed and his voice matched the coolness of hers. "I've been home only a couple of hours, Laurie, and so far nothing has gone right—including the way you're acting. What are you doing here, anyway?"

She made a nervous movement with her hands and forced another thin smile. "I wanted a quiet place to work in my spare time, and I remembered that your cabin wasn't being used. I asked Wilma about it, and she gave me a key. I've been coming out here on week-ends and whenever I have time off from my job."

"Your job? What kind of job? I thought you were still helping out at your pa's spread."

"Well, I'm not," Laurie said. "The world didn't stand

still while you were gone. I went away to college for two years, and now I'm the teacher at the Rampart school."

She kept a room in town, she told him, but when school was not in session she visited her parents at the Anchor Ranch, or came to Wyatt's cabin. While she was in college she had become interested in writing, and was hoping to become a published poet. She found the serenity of the basin inspiring.

"During the week I keep a journal, then come here to organize my thoughts into something others will understand." Laurie became more animated as she spoke of her ambition, but Wyatt's cold stare curbed her enthusiasm. In a weaker voice she said, "I've taken care of the place like it was my own."

Wyatt tried to sound encouraging. "I hope your poetry works out. You've become a real professional lady. I reckon school is out for the calving season so the kids can help out at home, and you've got some extra time on your hands. You're welcome to stay as long as you want. Did you bring a girl friend with you?"

Her hands were nervous again. "Oh, you saw the horses in the corral. I didn't bring a girl friend. The pinto is mine, and the sorrel belongs to Ward Chesser. He works for Herbert Naylor's Lazy L. Sometimes he stops in for a visit when he knows I'm here. Ward knows a lot about literature, and he's been a big help to me. Come on in and meet him."

Color flooded Wyatt's face, and his response was dictated by a surge of temper. Herbert Naylor was the man who had accused his brother of rustling, and Wilma had told him the calves in question were found in the basin. Wyatt had heard enough about the Lazy L.

"I don't mind you using my cabin," Wyatt said, "but I don't aim to have it turned into your private love nest! I want you to leave, and I don't want to meet anybody named Ward Chesser."

"You got no choice, mister!"

The deep voice belonged to a muscular, sandy-haired man who appeared in the doorway and spoke before Laurie Custer could react to Wyatt's accusation.

"You owe Laurie an apology," Ward Chesser declared. "I'm going to see that she gets it."

Wyatt stared at the hatless man. He was about thirty, with gray eyes that had a look of daring in them. His clothes were better than most cowhands could afford— sharply creased tan trousers tucked into tooled leather boots, a fine woolen shirt, and an oak-handled Colt resting in a holster on his right thigh.

Ward Chesser's ultimatum started Wyatt's heartbeat thumping in his ears. He had no proof that the man was Laurie's lover, but he had made up his mind that he did not like anyone who rode for Herbert Naylor. Wyatt was frustrated and angry, afraid the future he had counted on at the Keyhole was a lost cause. He was in no mood to bandy words with the man in the doorway.

Bracing his legs, the china-blue eyes bright and threatening, Wyatt asked softly, "How do you aim to do that, mister?"

If Ward Chesser knew anything of Wyatt's reputation, he was not impressed by it. He put a hand on his hip, his fingers on the shell belt a few inches above his holster.

His reply was grim and confident. "Either I'm going to shoot holes in your feet until you start talking or beat an apology out of you with my fists."

Wyatt's chuckle sounded ugly. It was time to find out if Ward Chesser was Texas tough, or a man who tried to bluff his way through life. Wyatt stepped off the porch and walked into the yard, moving at an angle that would allow him to see the man without Laurie standing between them. When he was fifteen feet away, he turned to face Chesser again.

"Come down in the yard, mister," he said crisply. "I don't want to get blood all over my front porch."

Wyatt's shoulders were erect, like a coiled spring waiting to unwind, and his gun hand was relaxed and ready to do his bidding. He said, "Some say I'm the meanest man in Texas, and today I'm ready to prove they're right. If that hand on your hip moves one inch I'll kill you."

EIGHT

Moments such as this were not new to Wyatt Kirk, but they were rarely initiated by him. He had faced a score of reckless men who had tried to shoot their way to freedom rather than face prison or a hangnoose. His quickness had left some wounded and others dead. The speed of his hand was a natural gift, flowing from fluid muscles and perfect coordination. He had never abused his talent by killing to settle a personal affront, but he was on the verge of doing it now, driven by jealousy and a fiery temper that ran out of control.

He watched Ward Chesser's face, looking for signs of doubt, and waited to see if the man would fight or back down. Chesser's eyes, as flat and gray as a mountain rock, told him nothing. Wyatt had seen eyes like that before—the eyes of a gunfighter.

Breathless seconds ticked away while Chesser hesitated. He glanced furtively at Laurie Custer, and then back at Wyatt. The thumb of his right hand remained hooked in his belt as he stepped warily into the yard, and his expression slowly changed. Wyatt saw a sheen of sweat spread across the man's forehead, saw his nostrils flare, and he knew Chesser's stomach was full of hard, hurting knots. Wyatt knew this because they were in his own, born of the realization that somebody might die in the next few minutes, and neither man knew who it would be.

Wyatt felt his fingers tingle expectantly. He fought down an impulse to grab for his Peacemaker and force Ward Chesser to make an attempt to beat him to the draw. He was looking at the man who had stolen his girl, and his fury urged him to make the first move. A voice of conscience held him motionless, telling him he had allowed the incident to go too far. He should have talked Chesser out of a life-or-death showdown, as he had done with other men when minor incidents mushroomed beyond their importance. He was not sure he had a choice now.

Laurie Custer stood on the porch a pace behind Chesser, paralyzed by shock and fear as the two men stood fifteen feet apart in the morning sunlight and measured each other's nerve. She regained her senses and leaped from the porch, crying, "No! No!"

She grabbed Ward Chesser's arm and tried to pull him toward the doorway. "Don't try to fight him, Ward! You're talking to Wyatt Kirk! He's a professional gunfighter and he'll kill you."

She darted in front of Chesser, blocking his gun hand with her back. The creamy tan of her face had faded to the color of parchment and her eyes were dilated with fear.

"I know who he is," Chesser said tightly. "I heard you call his name. You've told me about him, but I'm not afraid of him. He thinks he can come back here and throw his weight around, but he's wrong. If I can't beat him, I know people who can."

"Don't be a fool," Laurie pleaded. "Wyatt has killed a dozen men, and one more won't bother him."

"Some say twenty," Wyatt snapped sarcastically, unable to ignore Laurie's disapproving tone. The repetition of lies and rumors had branded him with a history he did not deserve, and the girl he once thought he loved was calling him a killer.

"It doesn't matter," said Laurie. "I won't watch a man die."

She turned and pushed her hands against Ward Chesser's chest. "Go inside. We're not going to have any shooting here."

Chesser elbowed her aside. "He talked to you like you're a slut, Laurie, and he can't get away with it. I don't believe half the stuff I've read about him and I'm going to prove that Wyatt Kirk's not the fastest gun in Texas. He refuses to say he's sorry for what he said, and

I'm going to back up what I promised. I'm going to put a bullet in him!"

"Hard thing for a dead man to do," Wyatt said flatly.

Before Chesser's last words were out of his mouth, Wyatt's shoulder dipped slightly. His hand and wrist were blurred by movement, and the Peacemaker's muzzle was aimed at the man's head.

"Oh!" Laurie screeched. She clapped her hands over her ears and ducked, bracing herself for the thunder of gunfire.

"I'm not going to kill him," Wyatt said. "I'm going to save his life. He's afraid you won't think he's much of a man if he turns tail now. He's talked too big. He's got to fight me, but I won't let him do it with a gun. He'll have to use his fists."

Chesser's face was as pale as Laurie's. He swallowed hard and stared at the gun that had seemed to materialize from the air. He mumbled under his breath, moved his hand away from his belt for the first time, and studied Wyatt warily.

Gesturing with his Colt, Wyatt said, "Put your gun on the porch and I'll put mine down. I drew first because I know I won't shoot a man while his back's turned. I don't know that about you."

Chesser yanked his weapon from the holster and laid it at Laurie's feet. He came back to stand in front of Wyatt with his fists knotted. "You're going to regret this the rest of your life," he said.

Wyatt did not want to be handicapped by extra weight. He returned his gun to the holster. He removed his gunbelt and buckled it so he could loop it over his saddle horn. Just as he reached his waiting horse, he heard the crunch of a footstep and realized Ward Chesser was tiptoeing up behind him. He tossed the belt over the horn and tried to whirl around. He moved too late.

Ward Chesser's fist slammed into the back of his neck. It was a powerful, jolting blow that landed with such force that Wyatt's hat flew off his head. Waves of pain ran down his spine and he felt like he had been hit by a thunderbolt. He staggered forward and fell against the dun's shoulder. The horse sidestepped, and Wyatt went to the ground on his belly.

He tried to push himself up with his hands, but his arms were limp, his muscles numb. Before he could regain his strength, Ward Chester landed on his back, knees first. The impact drove the air out of his lungs. The world turned black except for the red and yellow lights flashing in his brain. His head rocked again and he bit his tongue as the sandy-haired man sat astride him and hammered his fists against the bones behind Wyatt's ears.

The biting pain was a stimulant to Wyatt's senses and his vision cleared. He gasped for breath, bowed his back, and heaved himself upward like a bucking horse. Chesser slid off his back, and Wyatt managed to get to his feet. With both of them unarmed Wyatt had expected a fair fight, but Ward Chesser had taken no chance that Wyatt would land the first blow. He'd struck quickly and unexpectedly while Wyatt's back was turned, hoping to beat him senseless before he had a chance to defend himself.

In shadowy saloons of lawless towns, Wyatt had seen brawlers rip flesh with spurs, gouge out eyeballs, bite off fingers and ears, and blind opponents with streams of tobacco juice. He knew such tactics, and Chesser had invited him to use them.

In the time Chesser spent scrambling to his feet, Wyatt caught his breath and could think straight. As the man started toward him, Wyatt cocked his fist to draw his attention, then lashed out with a sharp-toed boot and kicked Chesser's right kneecap. Chesser cried out in pain, and the leg collapsed beneath him. He fell on his side, his face contorted in pain. Wyatt leaped to his side and stomped a foot in his face.

Chesser's cry was muffled this time, but his injuries were not bad enough to take the fight out of him. He grabbed Wyatt's leg, wrenched at it to slow him down, and rolled away. Blood stained his fingers as he stood up with his hands covering his bruised nose and mouth. He backed away a few steps, hurt and dazed. Sprigs of dead grass clung to the front of his shirt and he was covered with dust. He surveyed Wyatt speculatively, considering the best way to get at him.

It was only a momentary pause. Chesser ducked his head and charged forward, aiming his body like a battering ram at Wyatt's midsection. He might have bowled over a man with slower reflexes, but Wyatt was an elusive target. Stepping aside, he stuck out one leg, braced his heel against the ground, and felt his bones rattle as Ward Chesser tripped and sprawled forward on his face.

Wyatt dashed to Chesser's side. He grabbed the man's

shirtcollar, yanked him a foot off the ground, and flipped him over. He straddled Chesser's waist and hit him in the face. Chesser's hands reached for him, scratching and clawing, but the efforts were feeble and Wyatt ignored them. He hit the man again and again, seeing red lumps and raw skin appear where his fists landed. Laurie Custer screamed at him, but he did not look at her. He was seeking a release for all the worry that had piled up in his mind, and it felt good to strike out at anyone. A vicious streak he did not know as a part of his nature controlled him, and he wanted to keep punishing the man who had threatened to shoot him.

Above the roar in his head, Wyatt heard Laurie scream at him, but he did not look at her. Ward Chesser's body writhed beneath him. Suddenly, the man summoned enough strength to turn abruptly and topple Wyatt on his side. His breath hissing in and out like a maddened bull, Wyatt regained his balance and cocked his arm to deliver another blow. He was unable to land it. Two slender hands grasped his hair and pulled so hard his scalp burned with pain. Laurie Custer's face appeared above him and she kept tugging at him until he fell on his back.

"You're going to beat him to death!" she yelled in Wyatt's ear. "Stop it!"

Wyatt lay still, his chest heaving. He pushed Laurie's hands away and sat up. Ward Chesser was far from dead, but he was thoroughly beaten. He raised up on one elbow, shook his head, and got slowly to his feet.

Wyatt also stood. He looked at Chesser's battered face, unable to believe he had done far more damage than was necessary to win the fight. The throbbing ache in his head kept him from feeling any regrets.

Laurie left Wyatt and went to Chesser's side. She put her hand on one arm while the Lazy L man used the other hand to wipe blood off his face with the tip of his yellow neckerchief. Chesser glared at Wyatt through pain-filled eyes, but he had nothing to say. They started toward the house, and Laurie's anger was evident by the flush of her cheeks.

She glanced over her shoulder and said, "You showed how mean you've become, Wyatt, but you didn't fight fairly."

"I fought his way," Wyatt snapped. "At least he's alive. If he'd pulled a gun on me he wouldn't be."

Wyatt's next words were directed at Ward Chesser. He said, "Get your hat and leave my place. Go out the back way, get your horse, and don't ever come on my land again."

"I'll go with him," Laurie said, flashing her eyes at Wyatt. "I won't be back either."

"Figures," Wyatt said.

He turned his back to the pair, retrieved his own hat, and walked away to stand beside his horse. He picked up the reins to calm the still-skittish dun and watched as Laurie and Ward Chesser entered the cabin. He stared stonily at the closed door with Laurie's sharp words still ringing in his mind.

He had hoped the exaggerated tales that originated in *The Prairie Scout* had not reached the Rampart range, but it was obvious that they had. Friends and foes alike were going to view him as a notorious gunman, and he wondered if he could ever live down the reputation. As long as it existed, there would always be those whose egos would push them to prove they were better with a gun than Wyatt Kirk. It was a shallow ambition, but pride had made fools of many men, and Wyatt had not met the last of them. Unless he could bury his past, he would meet a man someday whose hand was quicker. It was not the way Wyatt wanted to die.

While he waited beside his horse, the weariness in his arms and legs subsided, but his anger at finding Laurie Custer in his cabin with another man would take a long time to cool. Either Ward Chesser had spent the night here, or he had risen early for a rendezvous with the girl. The boundary line between the Keyhole Ranch and the Lazy L was only a few hundred yards past the sandstone bluffs, but Herbert Naylor's headquarters was six miles away, and it was not an easy ride.

The layered cliffs, that rose twenty feet above the apron of grassland on the far side of Castle Creek, were split in places by erosion and rockslides. Finding a path to the higher ground atop the bluffs was not as difficult as riding away from them. From the green of the basin the land changed to brown brush and gray sand. Arroyos and dry washes—steep-walled ravines deep enough to hide the horizon—scarred the earth for three miles before the badlands ended at the banks of a creek on the Lazy L. There were better, but longer, trails to Naylor's ranch, and Wyatt surmised that Ward Chesser had chosen one of them. The handsome, sandy-haired man was not dressed for riding the badlands. His finely-woven pants and wool shirt were not suited for range work, and Wyatt was curious about Chesser's duties at the Lazy L.

Laurie and Chesser were inside the cabin for half an hour, and Wyatt was growing restless and impatient before he saw them come from the rear of the house and go toward the corral. Chesser looked refreshed, and Wyatt assumed he had stopped at the well pump near the back door to wash the blood from his face.

Laurie held a small backpack atop her shoulder with one hand and carried a bundle of books in the other. Walking beside her, Ward Chesser appeared to be talking rapidly and earnestly. He held out his hand as though offering to carry part of her belongings, but Laurie shied away and spoke from the side of her mouth. Her manner indicated they were engaged in an argument.

He thought about going inside and ignoring them while they saddled their horses, but he could not take his eyes off Laurie. Disappointment tugged at his heart, but he was still fascinated by the golden hair, the lithe figure, and the feisty way she bobbed her head when she talked. Still angry, uncomfortable with the thought of Laurie in another man's arms, Wyatt kicked idly at tufts of grass and waited for them to leave so he could care for his own horse.

Finally they rode out of the yard, passing within twenty feet of him. Wyatt tightened his hold on the dun's reins and started toward the corral. Saddle leather squeaked, a bridle bit rattled, and he knew one of the riders had stopped. He glanced over his shoulder and saw that it was Laurie. She turned her horse and looked directly at him.

"Maybe we can talk the first time you come to town," she called. Her voice was barely loud enough for him to hear. "I keep a room at the Sunset Hotel when I'm teaching."

"You'll see me again, too!" Ward Chesser shouted.

A ridge of muscle rose along the edge of Wyatt's jaw. He remembered Chesser's threat when the man said, "If I can't beat you, I know people who can." Wyatt had made an enemy who would carry a grudge for a long time. Regardless of whether she shared his feelings, Chesser was in love with Laurie Custer. He would not rest easy as long as Wyatt was alive to compete for her affection.

Wyatt declined to reply to either of them. He squared his shoulders stubbornly and took the dun to the corral. Watching covertly while he unsaddled the horse, he saw them follow the beaten trail beside Castle Creek. Ward Chesser did not intend to ride home across the badlands. He would choose an easier route to the Lazy L at the mouth of the basin, or go on with Laurie. Surely, Wyatt thought hopefully, Chesser's duties at the Lazy L would prevent him from spending the day with her.

There was firewood beside the iron stove in the kitchen, canned goods in the cupboards, oil in all the lamps, clean blankets on his bed, and extra shirts and Levi's still in the dresser drawers where he had left them three years ago. Crocheted doilies were draped over the backs of the mohair couch and chairs in the parlor of the cabin, and the planked floor appeared to have been scrubbed recently. Wyatt spent a few minutes walking through the house, pausing in each room to observe the cleanliness and care of a woman's touch.

Afterward, he sat on the edge of his bed with his bedroll spread out on the floor while he sorted through it, arranging its contents in piles according to where they were to be stored in the house. His mind was not on what he was doing, and he worked slowly. He could not get Laurie out of his mind, and his sorrow at the thought of losing her made him listless.

She had not denied she was having a love affair with Ward Chesser, but perhaps that was Wyatt's fault. He had ordered her to leave without giving her a chance to enlarge upon her explanation that Chesser's visits to the cabin were motivated by their mutual interest in poetry. She was aware of Wyatt's quick temper, and her fear of a violent confrontation might have been responsible for her nervous gestures and suspicious behavior. He recalled her sad face and muted voice as she suggested they meet in town, but he was not sure he could face her again without saying things he would regret.

Tossing a dusty pair of Levi's into the stack of dirty clothes, Wyatt swore to himself and got up from the bed. He could not waste time feeling sorry for himself. His brother's life was in danger, and the future of the Keyhole Ranch was in jeopardy.

At the peak of his fury over Justin's abortive efforts to become a business tycoon, he had told Wilma he was in no hurry to get his brother out of jail, but his sense of loyalty had overpowered his anger again within moments. Despite their differences, Wyatt loved his brother, and he had to free him from the Rampart jail before Justin faced the uncertainty of a judge's verdict.

Wyatt admitted to himself that he was using time on a menial chore as an excuse to delay his trip to town. He was trying to put it off as long as possible because he feared a meeting with Sheriff Lester Mace would open doors to the past that were sure to add to his misery.

The day was still young, but it seemed that Wyatt had experienced a lifetime of unexpected encounters in a few hours. His brother's wife had hinted she might seduce him. Caleb Frye had filled his mind with concerns over the loss of the Keyhole's longtime foreman and Herbert Naylor's deliberate ploy to drive down the price of cattle. And the final blow to his hopes of enjoying his homecoming had come when he found the girl he loved with another man in what appeared to be intimate circumstances.

Aside from skinned knuckles, he had no visible injuries as a result of his fight with Ward Chesser, but long days on the trail and the emotional upheavals of the morning had sapped his energy. The fight had added to his weariness, but his conscience would not allow him to take the nap he had promised himself. Instead, he took clean clothes from the dresser and went to the creek for a bath. Half an hour later, shortly before ten o'clock, he saddled the dun and rode toward town.

NINE

Unlike the graveyard stillness he had found when he passed this way before dawn, Rampart was alive with activity when Wyatt came off the prairie and started down Front Street. A haze of red dust floated above the street as wagons and horsemen moved about. Men in curl-brimmed Stetsons and women in colorful bonnets strode from shop to shop, and the tinny notes from a player piano floated across the batwing doors of the Wildfire Saloon.

Wyatt rode with his hatbrim pulled low and his eyes focused straight ahead. He hoped to pass without attracting any undue attention before he reached the jail. From the corner of his eyes, he saw several people stop and stare at him. There was no indication that anyone recognized him until he passed in front of the Sunset Hotel, which was one of Rampart's favorite loitering places. Three men were sitting on one of the benches beside the entrance, whittling on cedar sticks and spitting tobacco juice. One of them looked directly at him, turned to the others, and spoke loud enough for his words to reach the street.

Nudging his nearest companion, the man said, "By God, that's Wyatt Kirk! If he knows about his brother, there's likely to be hell to pay in town before the day's over."

Wyatt pretended that he did not hear the remark, but every time he passed the Sunset Hotel he thought about his father's death, and his suspicions regarding the motive behind it.

Three hours after sunup on a Thursday morning, Lester Mace's jailer and unofficial deputy Hap Gilley had brought the news to the Keyhole Ranch. First he talked with Justin, who was busy with his bookkeeping at the house, then they rode to the south range where Wyatt and the Keyhole crew were castrating calves.

Wyatt knew something was wrong when he saw them coming. He rode away from the other men to meet them. There was moisture in Justin's eyes. He folded his hands on the saddle horn and started to speak, but his voice choked. He said, "You tell him, Hap."

Hap Gilley's sunken jaws appeared to shrink closer to his teeth and he rocked in his saddle a minute before he spoke. "Your pa's dead. Somebody killed him in his room at the Sunset Hotel last night. The sheriff sent me to fetch you."

The jailer waited for the shock to leave Wyatt's face, then related the details as he knew them. Aaron Kirk's death had come silently and swiftly, causing no disturbance among the other guests. George Chaney, owner of the Sunset, had discovered the body while making his early-morning rounds through the hotel. He spotted a trail of bloodstains leading away from Aaron Kirk's room and down the stairway that led to the rear entrance on the ground floor. When he entered the room, he found the rancher lying naked on his back, his mouth open and his pillow soaked with blood.

"After George Chaney sent for us, we looked over your pa's room and followed them blood spots down the stairs. We lost the trail in the alley."

Hap Gilley lowered his head, and his high-pitched drawl was softer than usual. "It's a puzzlement. Chaney thinks your pa wounded the killer and that's why there was blood in the hallway. The sheriff don't think so. Lester figures Aaron was killed in his sleep. It warn't an ugly cutting—just a little slit under each ear, but there was a lot of blood. The sheriff said one cut got the big vein. Aaron's throat was cut with something keener than any razor—slicker'n a whistle and no torn skin."

"Like a doctor's scalpel, maybe," Wyatt said grimly.

His mind had flashed back to a scene he had witnessed in Rampart a month earlier. Bill Bartlett, one of the Keyhole riders, had been thrown into a rock pile when his horse was spooked by a rattlesnake. His left leg was broken by the fall. When Wyatt saw the injury, he knew the rider would require better medical care than the usual ranch-style doctoring.

Newt Hardy helped him load Bartlett atop a pad in a wagon bed, and Wyatt raced to Rampart to let Dr. Evan Halsey treat him.

It was his first visit to the office above the Family Emporium, and one he would not forget. He was not familiar with the building's layout, and there was no one in sight when he burst into the small outer room that served as a waiting area. A few feet away he saw a closed door marked Private. Wyatt was too concerned about Bill Bartlett's suffering to care about intruding while the doctor was with a patient.

He shoved the second door open and stopped in shock. His father was seated on a stool near the center of the room, his forearms resting on the edge of an examining table. Standing behind him, her starched white uniform unbuttoned to the waist, was Dr. Evan Halsey's wife. As Wyatt entered the room Bertetta Halsey was in the process of massaging Aaron Kirk's bare back, sliding her hands upward across his shoulders and leaning forward to press her naked breasts against his skin.

She whirled, her tawny skin flushed, her dark eyes flashing with anger and embarrassment. Aaron Kirk looked swiftly over his shoulder. He slid one hand toward his holstered Colt. His relief was apparent when he saw that the visitor was his son.

"Can't you read, cowboy?" Bertetta Halsey screamed at Wyatt. "The sign on the door says Private, and that's what it means."

Her fingers flew over the upper buttons of her smock. In her haste, she missed the first buttonhole. While she fumbled to find it, her dress gaped open and Wyatt caught a second glimpse of her round white breasts. She turned away, fastened the buttons, then looked back at Wyatt. Still flustered by his abrupt entrance, Bertetta Halsey sought to defend her indiscretion with anger.

"If you'd been half raised, you wouldn't be barging in on people without knocking! I'm sure you know that what goes on in a doctor's office is highly confidential, and you're not to talk—"

"Let it go, Bertetta." Aaron swung around on the stool, picked up his shirt from the examining table, and slipped it on as he walked over to stand beside her. "He's been raised pretty good. This is my son. He knows I've got a bad back, and that all you were doing was trying to work out the kinks."

Aaron was forty-two, ten years older than Bertetta Halsey, but he had the smooth skin and firm jaw of a man much younger. Sun and wind had been kind to him, toning his face to the shade of old gold and complementing the few strands of gray that showed in the raven-black hair at his temples. He moved with the grace and ease of a dancer, a handsome square-jawed man whose easy grin could settle an argument, avoid a fight, or persuade a woman to take him in her arms. He smiled at his son now, his white teeth gleaming against his bronzed skin.

The smile was meant to reassure the woman, but Wyatt saw the alarm in his father's eyes. "You must need me real bad, Wyatt, to come looking for me here."

"I wasn't looking for you," Wyatt said. "I was looking for the doctor. Bill Bartlett's down in the wagon. He's got a busted leg and he's hurting real bad."

The rancher glanced at Bertetta Halsey, then back at Wyatt. "Doc Halsey's not here. He's seeing patients over in Spurlock today, and won't be back until tomorrow. What happened?"

"That's not important at the moment." Bertetta Halsey was calm now, and her voice was its normal throaty tone. "We need to see if we can help the poor man."

She surveyed the room, pushing her long black hair away from her face, then took a leather satchel from a shelf and began loading it with gauze and vials. "I suppose the best thing to do is to take him to the hotel overnight," she said. "We don't have a bed for patients here, but he needs to lie still."

She glanced at Wyatt, lowering her long lashes to hide the shame that lingered in her face. "I'm not a doctor, but I'm a trained nurse. I'll try to make him comfortable until my husband gets here. If you and Aaron will take him on to the Sunset, I'll search around for some splints and be along in a few minutes."

They did as she suggested, and Bertetta Halsey soon

109

joined them at the hotel. She gave Bill Bartlett a dose of laudanum to deaden the pain, bound his broken leg between slats of wood, and promised to check on him again before nightfall.

"You can go on home, Son," Aaron said after the woman left. "I'll stay in town with Bill until Doc Halsey sets his leg and gets him fixed up right. Get my horse from the livery stable and leave the wagon."

Two days passed before Aaron brought Bill Bartlett back to the Keyhole. Wyatt wondered if his father had spent most of his time with the injured rider or with Bertetta Halsey.

After Hap Gilley expressed his sympathy and headed back to town that day, Wyatt told his brother for the first time about the scene he had witnessed in Evan Halsey's office. "So that's what you meant when you told Hap Pa's wound was like an incision a doctor might make," Justin said. "You think he was with Bertetta and that Doc Halsey killed him."

"It crossed my mind," Wyatt said. "I'll have to talk to the sheriff about it."

"I don't want it mentioned," Justin declared. "There's no use in ruining a woman's name. Pa's destroyed everybody's respect for our family, and that's enough. Accusing innocent people of something we're not sure about will make things worse. Keep your mouth shut about what you saw."

Sheriff Lester Mace had moved Aaron Kirk's body to Baker's Mortuary by the time Wyatt and Justin arrived in town. He walked with them to the undertaker's establishment at the end of the street, talking quietly as they went. The sheriff was shaken and saddened by the death of his old friend, and he was reluctant to discuss what action he might take. In response to questions from Justin and Wyatt, Lester Mace reviewed the events of the morning. Mace told them he had interviewed the hotel owner and the four other guests who had spent the night at the Sunset Hotel, but had learned nothing that offered a clue to the rancher's killer.

"I'm pretty sure there was a woman in that bed with Aaron," Lester Mace had said, "and she might have got hurt, too. There was blood on both pillows, and one of them smelled like a woman's perfume. I asked George Chaney about that, but he shut his mouth like a damned tortoise and swore Aaron came in alone. He'd lie about that, most likely, because he don't want his hotel to get the name as a house of fornication. If there's a woman involved, I've got to go slow in pryin' too deep."

Wyatt and Justin exchanged glances, and Justin said to the sheriff, "I don't want people running Pa's name down—or ours. We'll never know who killed Pa, so let's close the book on it."

"I'm sort of bound to leave it be," Mace had said.

The sheriff's remark stuck in Wyatt's mind. It was unlike Lester Mace to ignore any crime committed in his jurisdiction, much less one that resulted in the death of a friend. In the musty, morbid atmosphere of the funeral parlor, Wyatt could not get a grip on his own feelings. He wanted his father's killer punished, but he knew the pious element of Rampart would be inclined to brand the sons with the stigma of an immoral father.

Wyatt believed it was more important to bring the

killer to justice than it was to conceal the circumstances surrounding their father's death. His name was his own, and he expected to be judged by his personal behavior rather than by that of Aaron Kirk. His conscience told him to demand that Mace do his job, but he remained silent. Justin was adamant about protecting the family name, and this was not the time or place to start an argument.

Following the funeral, and the reading of Aaron Kirk's will, Wyatt went back to the Keyhole without speaking again with Sheriff Lester Mace. After moving to the cabin on Castle Creek, he saw little of his brother. He tried to deal with his grief through hard work, riding out each morning with the Keyhole crew and returning at dusk. Justin secluded himself with his books and papers inside the ranch house.

Hard days in the saddle and the condolences of the Keyhole crew were not enough to bring peace to Wyatt's mind. Alone in his cabin at night he was nagged by guilt, feeling that he had betrayed his father. He had difficulty sleeping, rising frequently to smoke cigarettes, pace the floor, and gaze idly into space. During those restless nights he cursed Lester Mace for his indifference to the rancher's death, and remained puzzled by the frustration he saw in Mace's face when the sheriff had mumbled, "I'm sort of bound to leave it be."

Just as often he cursed himself. He had withheld information from Lester Mace, and he was wrong to let Justin influence his decisions. Ten days after Aaron Kirk's funeral, he rode back to Rampart and told Sheriff Lester Mace about seeing his father and Bertetta Halsey together in the doctor's office.

Wyatt had been suspicious of his father's activities, but Aaron Kirk was not a man who tolerated interference in his personal affairs. Three or four months before his death, the rancher developed a mysterious back ailment. On most days, Aaron was as active as usual, riding the range, checking the work of his crew and issuing orders, but he claimed an old injury had become agitated and needed regular medical attention. Every Wednesday morning he left the Keyhole for a visit to the doctor's office, spent the night in Rampart, and returned the next day.

Justin and Wyatt had been puzzled by their father's recurring pain, but the mystery ended when Wyatt discovered the kind of treatment Aaron was receiving from Bertetta Halsey.

"Aaron was a schemin' old devil," Lester Mace had said after listening to Wyatt's story. "Doc Halsey's not in his office on Wednesdays, so it figures that Aaron picked that day to see Bertetta. Doc rides over to Spurlock every Wednesday and don't come back until Thursday."

The only doctor in Spurlock had moved away, Mace explained, and Evan Halsey had agreed to make calls in the town until the residents could find a replacement.

"Doc was supposed to be twenty miles away the night Aaron was killed," Mace said. "He could have doubled back if he was suspicious of his wife. I ain't exactly been sittin' on my hands. I sent Hap Gilley over to Spurlock to ask around. Nobody saw Doc Halsey over there that day. Maybe that means something, maybe not. It don't matter much now. Halsey's gone, and nobody's seen Bertetta since the day before Aaron was killed. At least, nobody will say they have."

Mace told Wyatt about other events that had transpired in Rampart after Aaron Kirk's death. When the sheriff went back to his office after the funeral that day, Dr. Evan Halsey was waiting for him. The doctor reported that his wife was missing. He feared she had met with harm, and wanted Mace to help him find her.

He had returned from Spurlock about noon, the doctor said, stopping first at the house the couple rented two miles out on the stage road, then at his office. Bertetta was not at either place. The sheriff could find no clue to her disappearance, and two days later Dr. Evan Halsey left town. Sometime in the middle of the night the doctor had cleaned out his offices, removed his belongings from the furnished house, and pulled out of Rampart.

His landlord was Bob Erskine, who owned the Family Emporium and several other properties around town. Erskine had awoken one morning to find a month's rent wrapped around a note that had been slipped under his door during the night. Evan Halsey explained that he was too distraught over the loss of his wife to continue his practice, and was leaving Rampart to search for her.

"You and Justin got out of town too fast after the buryin' for me to tell you about my talk with Halsey," Lester Mace said. "I've sent telegraphs to lawmen all over Texas, but nobody's seen the Halseys. That's all I can do. I'm goin' to give it up."

Wyatt's temper exploded. He swore at Mace and said,

"I used to think you were a hell of a good lawman, but I was wrong. You're as bad as Justin. You're going to let Pa's killing go because you think you're keeping his name clean. You ought to turn in your badge."

The sheriff spread his hands and sighed. "I've got a hard nut to crack here. There's plenty of signs pointin' to Doc Halsey and Bertetta, but I can't prove anything on 'em. Aaron was always chasin' after some other man's wife, and it could've been anybody who done him in. That's one thing. Another is, I promised him five years before he died that if he ever got killed over a woman I wouldn't dig into it and embarrass innocent people. We was drinkin' and I thought it was whisky talk, but Aaron had a hunch he might end up like he did. I was fool enough to tell him I'd do what he wanted. Drunk or sober I've always kept my word, and I feel squeezed two ways on this thing."

The hard set of Lester Mace's jaw told Wyatt there was no point in talking further, and he had left the office in disgust. When he returned to the Keyhole, he told Justin of his visit to the sheriff's office, and it resulted in another of the heated arguments that seemed to develop between them on any subject they discussed.

Perhaps, Wyatt thought as he rode into Rampart this day on another mission, it was the combination of grief and guilt over not pursuing their father's killer that had shortened tempers and eventually led to the flare-up that sent Wyatt riding away from the Keyhole. His leaving was a mistake. He should have stood his ground with Justin and insisted on operating the ranch as his father had done. From now on it would be that way, and he meant to reach an understanding with Justin before he left the jail today.

In the burning sunlight of early afternoon, Wyatt stood beside his horse at the hitching rail at the sheriff's office and looked up and down the street. Rampart had changed more than he thought. The names were different on many of the signs above the shops on Front Street. His glance passed quickly over the empty windows of Justin's jewelry store and the men's shop. He noticed two other vacant buildings where businesses had not survived, and scowled as he read the names on the windows. One had been the Paris Jewelers and the other the Texas Haberdashery. Justin was not the only businessman who had found that the residents of Rampart had little interest in fancy merchandise.

The vacant buildings were a painful reminder of the money Justin had wasted. Wyatt's chest began to swell with anger. He wanted to be calm when he talked with his brother, and he lingered at the tie-rail. On his way to town he had promised himself he would not belabor Justin's mistakes. He could not change the past, and Wyatt was sure Justin was as worried as he was about the Keyhole's decline. The threat to their future was Justin's fault, however, and it was hard for Wyatt to accept that truth quietly.

He smoked a cigarette while he waited for his rapid pulse to subside and the blood in his flushed face to cool. It did not take long. He felt guilty about killing time. His brother was a few feet away, locked in a cell at the rear of the sheriff's office. Undoubtedly, Justin was lonely, fearful of an uncertain fate, and wondering if he had a friend in the world.

Wyatt was ready to face him at last. He threw his cigarette away and took a deep breath. He walked to the door of the sheriff's office and stepped firmly inside.

TEN

Sheriff Lester Mace was expecting him. He was standing five feet from the front window of his office with his hands on his hips, wearing the expression of a man who had just heard bad news. He held out his hand and said, "Saw you passin' the time with a smoke out there. Justin's wife send for you?"

"I came on my own," Wyatt said, shaking the sheriff's hand. "Nobody knew where to find me right off. I came home to take up ranching again, but I see I've got other things to do first."

"Uh-huh," Mace grunted. He moved away and leaned his hips against a cluttered desk. The floor squeaked under his two hundred pounds of big bones and hard muscle. His years of riding through hot summers and cold winters had not slowed his stride or affected his ramrod posture. His disheveled black hair, showing a scattering of gray, bristled like a lion's mane when he bowed his head to stare thoughtfully at the curled-up toes of his boots.

He looked at Wyatt through steel-gray eyes that gave no hint of the thoughts behind them. He said, "I hope you ain't goin' to raise a ruckus over this difficulty Justin's got himself in. You let things run their course, and it'll be better for everybody. I won't stand for anybody tryin' to run roughshod against the law."

"What're you getting at, Lester?"

"Just this: I been wearin' a badge here for seventeen years—since I was twenty-eight—and we ain't had more'n four, five serious shootin's in Rampart in all that time. We ain't had 'em because I don't allow known gunmen to take up residence for more'n a day before I run 'em out. Now and then a couple of drunks act up and somebody gets winged with a bullet, but that blows over when they sober up. You ain't a drunk cowboy. You've heard by now that Herbert Naylor put out the warrant on Justin, and that's within his rights. He's got evidence and it's goin' to be looked at by Judge Haywood. There ain't goin' to be—"

"Whoa, Lester!" Wyatt grinned innocently. "Don't go putting your spurs in me before I catch my breath. Do you think I'm a kill-crazy gunslinger?"

The sheriff rubbed a callused palm across his chin. "I used to know what you were, but I don't know what you are now. People change. Folks in Rampart are mighty interested in them that come from these parts, and they try to keep up with 'em. They read stuff in the newspapers, carry tales, and some make up lies. I hope you ain't gone bad, but I hear you've killed three men."

Wyatt shrugged. "Three's the right number. They were killers, and I wanted them in jail. They didn't want to give up. When it came to a showdown, I went with the notion that I'd rather see them dead than me. I'm glad you don't think I've killed a dozen."

The expression on Lester Mace's craggy face became less stern. He flipped through a stack of papers on his desk. Wyatt saw the bold WANTED caption printed on some of the sheets and got a glimpse of blurred photographs.

"I been keepin' up, too," Mace said. "I've seen the flyers on the riffraff you've been chasin'. When one's nailed, somebody notifies me. I got notices about half a dozen hard-cases you captured, and three that you killed. I stick to what I know and don't pay much attention to idle talk. I got nothin' against bounty hunters, but you ain't followin' that trade in Justin's case. His troubles ain't goin' to be settled with a gun."

"We'll see," said Wyatt.

Lester Mace drew his shoulders erect and ran his hands through his unruly hair. "No, we won't see!"

The sheriff's mellow drawl became harsh and commanding. "One thing I didn't mention about them gunslingers who've tried to set up here over the years. Some of 'em didn't want to leave when I told 'em to go. They're buried in the town cemetery. Aaron Kirk was my best friend, and I'd hate to shoot one of his sons. I'll do it if it means seein' justice done. Don't push me into drawin' on you. Chances are I can beat you."

Wyatt doubted that Lester Mace could match his gunspeed, but the conversation had drifted in a direction he wanted to avoid. He had known Mace for as long as he could remember, and the sheriff had taken many Sunday dinners at the Keyhole Ranch. Mace and Aaron Kirk were the same age, and had arrived in the Rampart area at about the same time. Wyatt's father had come to buy a few acres of land and establish a ranch, and Lester Mace was a young Texas Ranger whose duties brought him this way occasionally.

They had become friends in those days over drinks at the Wildfire Saloon. Aaron Kirk's herds grew, he acquired more land, and eventually Lester Mace resigned from the Rangers and became the Keyhole's first foreman. His popularity among the ranchers, and his experience as a lawman, made him an ideal candidate for public office. Aaron Kirk talked Mace into seeking the sheriff's job. He won his first election by a landslide, and had remained in office ever since.

Despite family relationships, Wyatt knew it would be a mistake to offend Lester Mace. He was as tough as he looked, and he would not back away from a fight if it came to that. Wyatt did not like the sheriff's harsh manner, but he kept his voice calm. "You seem a mite more set on upholding the law in Justin's case than you were when I talked to you about Pa's killer."

"I knew you'd bring that up," Mace said. "You rawhided me pretty good about that situation and you was more right than me. It was hard to go back on what I promised Aaron, but it was harder to live with myself if I didn't do my job. I've kept diggin' around for somethin' that would lead me to the killer. It's been a dry run and I've lost the man you had pegged for it."

The sheriff captured Wyatt's full attention. "Are you talking about Evan Halsey?"

"The same," Mace replied. "Doc Halsey's dead. I got a letter from a U.S. marshal about ten, eleven months ago. Doc was found laying dead in his buggy on a brushy trail five miles outside of Rumford. Somebody put a rifle bullet in his back."

"I'll be damned!" Wyatt murmured. "He didn't drift too far. Rumford's only a hundred miles east. You know who killed him?"

Mace shook his head. "Findin' a bushwhacker in country as big as this is a hopeless proposition. I corresponded some with the lawmen down that way, but they didn't catch anybody. They think some hard-case figured Doc was carryin' a wad of cash on him, and killed him to get it. Nobody's seen Bertetta to this day, but I can't get the Halseys out of my mind. Somethin' in my gut keeps tellin' me it's more than a happenstance that Aaron got killed, Bertetta disappeared, and Doc Halsey was wiped out by a bushwhacker. Somethin's missin'. It aggravates me that I can't pin it down, but I can't talk to dead people."

"Maybe you can," Wyatt said dryly. "Maybe we'll run into their ghosts some day."

The sheriff scowled, and hitched at his gunbelt. "That might not be as funny as you think. Way back in my Ranger days I spent two years trackin' a hombre who'd killed his wife and two kids with an ax, then blew out the brains of the sheriff who tried to arrest him. I gave it up for a while after a notice was sent out that somebody had blasted him to hell with a sawed-off shotgun. Shot him square in the face. That kind of fire turns a man's face into somethin' like a calf's liver. There ain't much left you can recognize. He was identified by the stuff that was on him. About six months later I came face to face with his ghost in a bar on Galveston Island. He—"

"You must've been drunk, Lester," Wyatt cut in. "I didn't ride all this way to listen to tall tales."

"I ain't tellin' tall tales," the sheriff said. "He wasn't a ghost. He was real. Everything was cleared up after I arrested him. He'd found a man of his size and hair color, tore up the man's face when he killed him, swapped clothes with him, and figured he had set up a way to get the law off his back. He'd grown a beard and shaved his head, but I recognized him by a scar over his left eye which he couldn't do nothin' about. He's dead now. The judge ordered him hanged."

Wyatt guessed what was in the sheriff's mind. "You're trying to tell me Doc Halsey might still be alive and that he's out to get his revenge on Pa's family."

"Could be," Mace said. "Evan Halsey hadn't been in Rumford long enough to be well known. The marshal found a wallet and some papers on the corpse with Evan Halsey's name on them. That's all he had to go on. Doc could have killed somebody and set up his death just like my ghost killer did."

Mace had spent considerable time thinking about the possibilities of chicanery. Despite the hint of ridicule he saw in Wyatt's face, he was determined to share his speculation.

"If Doc killed Aaron because he was sleepin' with Bertetta, that might not be enough to satisfy him," Mace said. "He could've framed your brother. He may be behind the sniper fire that Justin says has been keepin' people on edge at the Keyhole. Some men go loco when they learn their wife's been unfaithful. They never give up tryin' to get even."

Wyatt's response was a bitter laugh. "You ought to be looking for the reason Herbert Naylor wants Justin in

122

jail. You're reaching into the spirit world to make excuses for him. I won't swallow your ghost stories and I won't swallow this rustling charge. I'm here to get Justin out of jail. Naylor's men found the calves and Naylor swore out the warrant. The frame-up was planned at the Lazy L and I'm surprised you went along with it. You know Justin's not a thief."

"I know your pa didn't raise him that way." Mace's tight lips reflected his stubborn will. "Aaron was so honest he'd try to pay you back if he borrowed a match. Ordinarily I'd bet on Justin bein' as square, but the evidence I've got makes him out a thief."

"Yeah, so I've heard," Wyatt said coldly. "I want to check out that evidence for myself."

"You got a right," Mace said. He opened the desk drawer and took out a wire ring with three keys on it. "Give me your gun and I'll give you the keys. They're numbered, and you'll find Justin in cell number one. He's the only one back there."

Wyatt pushed his hat up on his forehead. "Are you afraid I'll shoot up the place and pull a jailbreak?"

"Not a'tall. I know you're nervy, and you're hard to figure. Things pop into your head that nobody else would think about, but you ain't stupid. You'd have to pass me to get out, and I don't think you'd make it."

"I wouldn't bet on that," Wyatt said, smiling to let Mace know it was not a serious possibility.

"I ain't worried about you. I worry about Justin."

Mace hastened to explain his remark. Justin was behaving strangely, and the sheriff feared he was so irrational he might grab any convenient gun and destroy himself. He paced his cell constantly and mumbled disjointed phrases for hours. His business failures were on his mind, and he kept telling an imaginary listener he had tried to make the family name so important that others would forget the way his father had sullied it. Sometimes he thought he was talking to Wyatt, cursing him for not preventing Aaron Kirk's murder. He could have avoided all his troubles, Justin reasoned, if Wyatt had acted sensibly.

"I hear him when I pass by, but I don't know what he's talkin' about most of the time," Mace concluded.

"You know," Wyatt said bluntly. "He thinks I should have talked to Evan Halsey about his wife and put a stop to what was going on between her and Pa. Justin thinks what we think. He believes Pa was sleeping with Bertetta Halsey when he was killed, and that Doc Halsey did the killing."

Lester Mace drew in his chin, and impatience rumbled in his throat. "I don't know what happened at the Sunset Hotel that night. I know if Doc Halsey caught Aaron in bed with his wife he'd likely kill both of them, and maybe he did. I've run out the string on the Halseys and I'm tired of plowin' old ground."

"We waited too long," Wyatt said. "I was wrong when I held back on telling you about Pa and Bertetta because Justin thought it was a disgrace to the family. Now he's living with his own disgrace. He's innocent and I want him out of here."

The sheriff's steel-gray eyes were as hard and unyielding as his voice. "Two ways you can do that. You can get Naylor to drop his charge, or you can convince Judge Haywood there ain't enough proof to bring Justin to trial. I know there's something bad wrong about this deal, but my hands are tied. Talk about a killin' dies down in a few days. Stealin' cows is somethin' else. They hold a man's hopes and dreams. Every critter is a piece of his life. The ranchers would have my hide if they thought there's a rustler runnin' loose and I didn't do nothin' about it."

The sheriff repeated his assertion that it was his duty to hold Justin until a judge determined the value of the evidence. Mace had impounded the five calves with Keyhole brands. At the sheriff's request, Naylor's cowhands drove them from Castle Creek to Charlie Blake's feedlot behind the livery stable.

"If you're too hardheaded to spot a frame-up when you see it, I reckon I'll have to persuade Naylor to withdraw his warrant," Wyatt said solemnly.

"I hope you ain't thinkin' of persuadin' him with a gun. That'll get you a cell next to your brother."

"We'll see."

Wyatt handed his Peacemaker to the sheriff and took the keys. As he went toward the hallway that led to the cells, the sheriff cautioned him against creating a disturbance. His night jailer was asleep in the back room, Mace told him, adding that a man Hap Gilley's age needed all the rest he could get.

A narrow passage separated the jail cells from the rear walls of the sheriff's office. Brackets held an oil lamp beside each barred door, but they were seldom used. The only light came from a slitted window high in the back wall of each cell. The hallway was gloomy and hot. The air was stale, heavy with the smell of old tobacco smoke and sweaty blankets.

Wyatt stopped in front of cell number one. He blinked to adjust his vision and looked at his brother for the first time in three years. Justin was lying on a wooden bunk with his face turned toward the wall. His legs were drawn up close to his stomach and his hands were locked between his knees. He looked like a frightened child rolled up in a ball to hide from the dark.

He remained as he was, ignoring the sound of booted feet until Wyatt turned the lock and swung the door open. He rolled over slowly, appearing bewildered. His eyes had a hollow look, his cheeks were sallow and unshaven, and he had lost weight.

It took Justin a few seconds to get his bearings. He moved his lips silently, brushed his hands across his eyes, then swung his feet to the floor and stood up. Surprise flickered in his eyes, but he did not greet Wyatt with elation. He extended his arm hesitantly to shake hands as Wyatt stopped in front of him.

Justin's voice sounded rushed by fear. "I—I didn't expect—I was hoping—" He took a deep breath to calm his stammering. "Wyatt, you're going to kill me when you see what I've done to the Keyhole! I was trying to do good for both of us, but it went wrong. Now there's a new owner at the Lazy L who's accusing me of rustling. I—I—"

Justin fumbled for Wyatt's hand, stretching to keep an arm's length between them. He shrank back quickly, as though he was afraid Wyatt might strike him. A lump rose in Wyatt's throat. He pushed Justin's hand aside and put his arms around his brother's shoulders and hugged him. It was a quick, impulsive gesture. When they stepped apart, there was a film of moisture in Justin's eyes.

He smiled wanly. "I thought if I ever saw you again, the first thing you'd do would be to bust me in the nose. I told Wilma not to try to find you after Lester put me in jail, but I guess she didn't listen."

"I came home because that's where I belong," Wyatt said. "I took up bounty hunting to keep me going until I landed something better, and I stayed at it too long."

Justin sat down on the bunk and Wyatt took a seat beside him. There was an awkwardness between them for a while and they sat staring blankly across the room, each waiting for the other to speak.

Finally, Justin broke the silence. "I've read about you and I was afraid for you. How'd you fall into such a risky business?"

"I'll tell you about it sometime," Wyatt said. He told Justin what he had learned from Caleb Frye and Wilma. "I'd rather talk about what's going on between you and Herbert Naylor. Is he trying to squeeze us out and take over the Keyhole?"

A forlorn expression settled across Justin Kirk's face. His reply was so meek it was barely audible, but the longer he talked about the Lazy L owner the more animated he became. He voiced conflicting opinions about Herbert Naylor, however, and Wyatt listened with a growing belief that his brother's mind was too confused for clear thinking. Justin should have been boiling mad, but he appeared to regard Naylor with more wonder than anger.

Wyatt had gained an understanding of Justin's predicament and the struggles of the Keyhole from Wilma Kirk and Caleb Frye, but they had spoken in general terms. They had omitted the details they thought he should hear directly from his brother.

Herbert Naylor had moved to the Lazy L eleven months ago, surprising neighboring ranchers that he had been able to persuade Matt Latham to sell to him. At that time Justin was just beginning to get his Rampart stores in full operation. Business started off well, Justin recalled, but shortly afterward his daily receipts dwindled to a paltry figure.

The wealthy Missourian opened competing stores— the Paris Jewelers and Texas Haberdashery. His managers—suave, educated men from the East—sold merchandise at prices far below those offered by Justin. A price war began that Justin could not win. Every time he reduced his prices, Naylor's people went still lower until both were selling suits and jewelry below cost. Justin tried to hang on too long. He piled up debts until the bank moved in and forced him to close his stores, foreclosing on the buildings and staging a distress sale to recoup some of the money Justin had borrowed.

While the merchandise war was going on in town, the Keyhole was experiencing other troubles. Two water holes were poisoned with strychnine. Twelve steers died at one and eight at the other before Newt Hardy and his crew could fence them off and clean them up. For no reason that anyone could fathom, the Keyhole became the target of a hidden rifleman. A sniper's bullets, coming from the hills or clumps of underbrush, whistled over the riders' heads in daylight and pelted the earth around the ranch house and bunkhouse in the middle of the night. They were random shots, intended to rattle nerves and create unrest rather than kill or wound.

Even as he tried to defend his actions, Justin's voice was a mournful cry of the suffering and disappointments he had endured in past months. "It wasn't my stupidity that ruined me. It was Naylor's money. I can't call him a crook just because he's rich enough to lose me out of business. There's no proof he poisoned our water or that his men are shooting at us. Somebody framed me for rustling, and I can't even swear it was Naylor's people. He doesn't seem to be the type."

"Men with axes to grind come in all types," Wyatt said.

Justin shook his head. "I don't know. Naylor's got a way of handling himself. When my stores were going downhill, I ran into him one day at the Wildfire Saloon and asked him why he undercut our cattle prices and forced me out of business. He looked real serious and told me it was nothing personal. He claimed it was his way of establishing his name and getting to be known in Rampart "

"That's hogwash!" Wyatt said, exasperated. "Stop looking up to him and backing off because he's rich. Nobody bothered the Keyhole before Naylor took over the Lazy L. You had cattle dying, you lost half your crew because they were tired of being shot at, and you wasted time and money trying to be a big shot in the business world. I ought to hit you for that!"

Justin raised his head, his eyes weak and bloodshot. "I wasn't trying to cheat you, Wyatt. I was using Keyhole money, but I meant to bank half the profits in your name."

"You can't bank what's not there," Wyatt said. "I left because I was tired of arguing with you and Wilma, but I thought it was clear between us that you'd stick to raising cattle. You've read too many books about people making fortunes without learning any lessons from the people who didn't."

Justin bowed his head and scrubbed his hands over his stubbled face. "What are we going to do? The bank's after me, we might lose the ranch, and folks think I'm a rustler. I can't make any sense out of it."

"Naylor's trying to drive you crazy or break the Keyhole," Wyatt snapped, annoyed that Justin was unable to comprehend the obvious. "It looks like he's about done both."

A choking sound rattled in Justin's throat. He slid deeper into his bunk and slumped listlessly against the wall. "I know what they do with rustlers. What if they hang me?"

"In that case you'll be dead."

His curt, indifferent reply to his brother's question was meant to stiffen his resolve and arouse his fighting instinct, but Wyatt was not sure it had the desired effect. They spent another ten minutes together. Justin wanted to know what was going on at the ranch, and Wyatt sought to find out the total amount of the Keyhole's notes at the bank. Wyatt's remarks were brief, and Justin was so vague about his financial dealings with the bank that Wyatt gave up hope of learning the truth about them.

He rose abruptly from the bunk, indicating the visit was at an end. He was reaching for the barred door when Justin leaped from the bunk and rushed toward him, asking plaintively, "You're not going to leave me here, are you?"

Wyatt turned and put his hands on Justin's shoulders, rocking him gently. "Lester Mace is so stubborn I can't do much today, but what I've heard about rustling and price-cutting has been an education. Maybe I can use enough of it to get you out of here in a day or two."

Justin appeared encouraged. "Are you going to talk with Herbert Naylor?"

"I'm going to do more than talk," said Wyatt. "I don't know how tough he is when he's backed into a corner, but I'm going to find out real soon."

ELEVEN

Bloodshot eyes, clammy hands, a hollow-eyed face, and a mind overwhelmed by fear and failure was the image of Justin Kirk that Wyatt carried with him when he left his brother alone in the gloomy cell. He had spent an hour with Justin, feeling his anger fade as sympathy for his brother grew, but the meeting was not a satisfactory one.

During the final minutes of their conversation, Justin expressed his concern for Wilma. He wanted to know if she was well, and if she was disappointed in him.

Remembering those startling moments when Wilma had hinted at seducing him, Wyatt found himself stammering with embarrassment as he assured Justin that his wife was well, but worried about him. He wondered if his brother noticed his discomfort and the blush he felt burning his face. Justin barely acknowledged Wyatt's comments. He sat staring at the floor, his mind too preoccupied to notice Wyatt's reaction.

When Wyatt had inquired about the Keyhole's debts, Justin's answers became vague and rambling. He was either uninformed or evasive, saying he was not sure of the exact amount he owed. As security for his borrowings, Justin had pledged his share of the ranch, but he was confident the bank would give him plenty of time to repay the debt. Wyatt could hardly believe his ears.

"You could take my word about the evidence, but I'll be glad to walk over to Charlie Blake's place with you," Mace drawled when Wyatt returned to the office and handed him the cell keys. The sheriff lifted his sweat-stained black Stetson from the peg above the desk and added, "I reckon seein' is believin'."

"Maybe, maybe not," Wyatt said.

At the corner a few doors beyond the jail, the sheriff stepped off the boardwalk to cut toward the alley that led to Charlie Blake's livery stable. Wyatt took hold of his arm. "I need to stop by Del Avery's blacksmith shop."

"Only a few steps out of the way," Mace said. "You break something?"

"No. Del's always made the Keyhole branding irons

and he keeps the master pattern at his shop. I want to borrow it."

The lawman glanced at Wyatt and frowned. They were in the busy part of town, nearing the Sunset Hotel and the Family Emporium, and matching strides with other pedestrians. "You're goin' along like a sneakin' coyote—hat down, chin low, and dodgin' everybody's eyes," Mace said from the side of his mouth. "You know these people and they know you. If you got nothin' to hide and nothin' to be ashamed of, you ought to look 'em in the face."

"I'm not feeling too kindly about the way you're hounding Justin," Wyatt said. "Don't make it worse by bossing me around."

"Just a thought," Lester Mace murmured. A dozen steps later, the sheriff looked away and grinned when he noticed that Wyatt had pushed his hat back, raised his chin, and was speaking to some of the people who passed them.

They crossed the street and went between two buildings to reach the wagon-rutted field where Del Avery's blacksmith shop stood in the shadow of a single pin oak. The double doors of the planked building were open and there was no fire in the forge. Wyatt saw Del Avery and another man perched on stools on opposite sides of an upturned crate beneath the tree. They were hunched forward on their elbows, both staring at the checkerboard that was spread out before them.

Wyatt and the sheriff were within an arm's length of the men before Del Avery took his eyes off the board and looked over his shoulder. Rising slowly, he said to his companion, "I've got you beat, Jesse, so don't bother the board while I'm busy."

Jesse chuckled, and fumbled in his shirt pocket for tobacco and papers. "You're about as close to beating me as I am being elected governor of Texas. I got no reason to cheat."

Del Avery did not look like a blacksmith. He was Lester Mace's age, a man of average height, slender and wiry, with shaggy brown hair and an easygoing nature. His eyes widened momentarily at the sight of Wyatt, then he acted as though he had seen him only the day before. He nodded and said, "Afternoon, Sheriff. Afternoon, Wyatt. Something I can do for you?"

Wyatt told the blacksmith the purpose of his visit, and Del Avery went into his shop to get his pattern of the Keyhole branding iron. He returned with it in his hand, wiping it with a burlap cloth before he handed it to Wyatt.

"I keep my patterns locked in a cabinet and oiled to keep the rust off," he explained. "If you think you'll ever need any more irons, you'll have to bring it back to me."

"I'll do that," Wyatt said.

Before Wyatt walked away with Lester Mace, Del Avery introduced him to his companion. "Shake hands with Jesse Estep. He's riding for the Lazy L, but if he's as dumb about cows as he is about checkers, that ain't likely to last much longer."

As Jesse Estep stood up, his long legs rocked the packing crate and scattered checkers in all directions.

"Damn you!" Del Avery shouted. "You did that on purpose."

Jesse Estep looked down at the board, rubbed his chin, and grinned sheepishly. "You know I wouldn't pull a trick like that, Del." He held his hand out to Wyatt. "I've heard of you."

The mention of the Lazy L aroused Wyatt's interest in the man. Estep appeared to be in his late thirties, with the firm hands and muscular shoulders of a working cowhand. The hard glint in his eyes and his habit of toying with the butt of the holstered six-gun on his thigh seemed to contradict the friendly grin on his clean-shaven brown face.

"You know anything about the misbranded calves Charlie Blake's holding at his place?"

The hard edge in Wyatt's voice erased the grin from Estep's face. He shook his head. "Nothing except what they tell me at the Lazy L. Them calves were found by Naylor's manager, and he sends me into town every day to keep an eye on them. It's a waste of—"

"Manager?" Wyatt asked, not sure he had understood the man.

"Ward Chesser," Estep replied. "Naylor was a big businessman in Saint Jo, Missouri, before he moved out here. He likes business titles. He don't know about ram-rods, segundos, and such, so we've got a ranch manager. Ward Chesser's rode for a lot of brands, and he knows better. You'd have to meet him to know how proud Ward is to be called a manager."

"I've met him," Wyatt said coolly. He signaled to Lester Mace that he was ready to leave, and the two of them walked toward the grazing lot at the rear of Charlie Blake's livery stable.

Their path took them a hundred yards to the rear of the hip-roofed barn, and Wyatt was relieved that he would not have to consume time chatting with Charlie Blake. A zigzagging rail fence enclosed a ten-acre plot of grass that the liveryman utilized to supplement the grain he fed his animals. At the far side of the enclosure half a dozen horses were grazing contentedly, but the five Lazy L longhorns and their calves were near the fence where Wyatt and the sheriff stopped.

They rested their arms on the rails and stared at the cattle for a few minutes. Wyatt looked at the Keyhole brands on the calves, then at the branding iron in his hand.

"I know what you're up to," Lester Mace said quietly. "Let's get at it." He set his boot on the lower rail and began climbing over the fence. "I'll keep the mothers off your butt while you see if that iron matches the brands on the calves."

"They won't. I can see that from here."

"Prove it to me."

Wyatt did just that. While Lester Mace waved his hat and whooped at the cows until they trotted farther into the field, Wyatt moved quickly to the side of one of the calves. He dropped the branding iron, grabbed the ear of a calf, twisted its head with both hands, and flipped the bawling animal to the ground.

"Get the branding iron and give me a hand," Wyatt yelled.

Mace hurried to his side and pressed the iron over the brand on the squirming calf. The keyhole shape on the calf's flank was completely covered at the edges, but it extended half an inch above the top of the branding iron.

"Don't match," the sheriff said. "This brand's not as wide as Avery's pattern, and it's longer."

Wyatt freed the calf and both men leaped aside as it thrashed its legs, bounced to its feet, and ran toward its mother. Wyatt sleeved sweat from his face. "That calf was branded with a running iron—a rustler's iron. I've heard that a man who's good at it can do it with a cinch ring, a hot poker, or the handle of an iron skillet. Somebody at the Lazy L branded their own calves with our brand to frame Justin."

They crossed back over the fence and caught their breath. Wyatt said, "You're right about one thing, Lester. Seeing is believing, and you've seen that the brands are fake."

"If all your brands match that pattern," Mace countered.

"They're all the same. Pa looked ahead just in case something like this ever came up. He insisted on Del Avery keeping the pattern, and when we break an iron or warp one, Del makes sure the new one is an exact copy."

Mace tugged at his hatbrim and looked into the distance, his eyes suddenly sad. "Aaron was a smart cattleman. I miss that big smile and go-to-hell laugh of his." He hitched at his belt and added, "I believe what I saw and I'm glad it turned out this way."

"Fine," Wyatt said. "Let's go get Justin out of jail."

The sheriff shook his head. "I can't do that. I can testify about evidence, but I can't decide on it. That's up to

Judge Haywood. We'll have to wait until he gets here. I've still got Naylor's warrant, and it ain't in my power to dismiss it."

"To hell with you," Wyatt exploded. "You're doing better by that badge than you did a few years ago. Go on back and guard your dangerous prisoner. I've got better things to do than waste time with a fair-weather friend like you."

If Wyatt's angry outburst bothered Lester Mace, he did not show it. He set his steel-gray eyes on Wyatt's face and asked suspiciously, "What kind of better things?"

Without slowing his pace as he strode toward the blacksmith shop, Wyatt said, "You're getting too nosy to suit me. You mind your business and I'll mind mine."

"I get paid to be nosy. I'd rather keep a man out of trouble than arrest him for gettin' into it. You worry me. You was always the rowdy one of Aaron's boys, but you was just hurryin' to grow up. Aaron told me you was layin' up with some of the schoolgirls when you was fourteen, and I know you was talkin' older men into sneakin' drinks out to you in the alley behind the Wildfire Saloon by the time you was sixteen. That was just devilment, but you've changed. You've got hard and mean, and I don't know what you might do before I get a handle on this case."

Mace was thinking again about the stories he had read of a relentless, quick-shooting bounty hunter, and it was not the image Wyatt wanted to perpetuate. The sheriff's words reflected genuine concern. Wyatt had nothing to gain by adding a new burden to the sheriff's thankless job, and Mace would not relent in his determination to adhere to the letter of the law.

Wyatt slowed his steps. "You start bringing up my sinful boyhood and you'll ruin my reputation, Lester." He chuckled at the irony of his remark. "Stop worrying. I don't settle all my complaints with a gun. Sometimes I try to outsmart people, and maybe that's what I need to think about now."

Aaron Kirk had kept few secrets from his friend, and Wyatt decided it might be wise if he was just as frank with Lester Mace. He said, "I couldn't get much sense out of Justin. I need to talk to Lloyd Rocker about the Keyhole's debts. I know the bank's closed on Saturday, but I thought I'd try to track him down. Does he still have his ranch?"

Mace nodded. "Yeah, he still runs a few head on that little spread next to Paul Sipe's Arrowhead. He don't go out to check on his crew except on Sundays. His wife died a year or so ago, but Lloyd kept his house in town. He's got no family, nothing much to do except work, and he'll be at the bank. The doors will be locked and the shades drawn, but he might as well stay open. His desk is in sight of the side window. Folks who have business with him go down between the bank and Opera House and peck on the window. If Lloyd knows 'em, he opens the back door and lets 'em in. I think he enjoys the company."

"I doubt that he'll enjoy mine."

"Lloyd's a fair man."

"I don't need a fair man." Wyatt shook his head worriedly. "I need a generous man. I think Justin played dumb with me because he didn't want to admit we're in a hell of a mess."

Mace agreed. "That's the gossip around the range, all right. Except for the fact that he should have stuck to his knittin' instead of goin' into business, nobody figures how Justin got himself in the shape he's in. There's bad things goin' against the Keyhole, and Herbert Naylor's name keeps comin' up. I got no proof against him, but the stunts he's pulled makes him look like a crazy man. Did you know Justin made a deal to sell eight hundred cows to a broker out of Caprock Junction for twenty-five dollars a head, and Naylor headed the man off and offered him the same number for fifteen dollars a head?"

"I heard about It. Justin met the price because he was pressed for money. That was dumb." Wyatt's next words were like a whispered curse. "I aim to break Naylor of his bad habits."

Lester Mace cringed. "Don't jump the traces on me, Wyatt. When I show Judge Haywood that the brands on the calves don't match the Keyhole's iron, he'll know Justin was framed, and he'll let him go. That won't prove Naylor did it, but I'll be watchin' the Lazy L like a hawk from now on. I want you to stay away from Naylor's place and let me handle things."

While the sheriff talked, Wyatt was thinking about ways to even the score with Herbert Naylor and free his brother from jail at the same time. The fragments of a plan had occurred to him while he was visiting Justin in his cell, and the more he thought about it, the more determined he became to put it into effect.

He said, "The bank may run us off the Keyhole for Justin's debts, but I won't let Herbert Naylor do it. I'm going to pay him a visit in a day or two. You won't have to worry. I'm not going alone. I'm taking you with me."

The sun was bearing down on them from a cloudless sky, and its heat seemed more punishing while they were standing still. Mace used his neckerchief to rub the sweat from his neck, falling in step as Wyatt went on toward Del Avery's shop.

"You keep talkin' me in circles," Mace said wearily. "I'd like to know why you want me to go with you to the Lazy L, and I've got a hunch you ain't going to tell me until you're ready."

Wyatt grinned secretively. "If I told you any more, you'd want to put me in jail."

Mace gave him a searching look, and walked on in silence. They parted before they reached the blacksmith shop. Mace left Wyatt to return the branding iron to Del Avery and chose a shortcut that would take him to the street near his office.

The checkerboard still lay on the packing crate, but the stools were vacant. Wyatt heard the clanging of iron and saw Del Avery moving around inside the shop, rearranging stacks of bars and sheets of metal. The blacksmith saw him and came outside, peeling off his leather apron and wiping his face.

Wyatt handed him the branding iron. "I see you've lost your playing partner."

"Yeah, he went back to the street for a while. Jesse don't like this kind of duty. He walks up there and looks at them calves once in a while, then comes back.

It's boring and the day gets long for him. He ain't much of a drinker, don't gamble, and he can't find much to do except play checkers when I'm not busy. Jesse ain't happy at the Lazy L. He'll be drifting before long."

"Looks like he's got it pretty easy," Wyatt said.

Del Avery laughed. "Too easy. You know how cowboys are—they gripe if they have to work hard, and gripe more when they don't have nothing to do. Jesse says nobody does much at the Lazy L. Naylor don't associate with the crew, Ward Chesser spends his time in an office Naylor built for him, and the Lazy L riders just sort of roam around. Naylor don't know whether his cattle are trapped in bogs, sick with the hollow horn, strayed miles away, or whatever. Nobody seems to care one way or the other. Jesse says Naylor don't have any interest in cows, and he can't figure out why he's here. If I was a cowhand, I believe I'd stay away from a spread like that."

"Likewise," Wyatt said. "It sounds like a badman's hideout."

Glancing across the alley at the rear of the buildings along Front Street, Del Avery said, "Maybe you could find Jesse Estep and have a drink with him if you've got the time. He's your kind of cowhand. I think you'd like him."

"I'd have a hard time liking anybody from the Lazy L."

The blacksmith blinked and looked away. Like everyone else in Rampart, Del Avery had heard of the charge against Justin Kirk, and he had spoken without thinking about it. "I reckon that was a dumb thing to say," he murmured.

"Not between friends. I'm getting testy these days, and I need to watch myself." Wyatt shook hands with Del Avery again. "Much obliged for the loan of the branding iron."

"Any time. I guess I'll be seeing you again." It was more of a question than a statement, and it was as close as Del Avery would come to prying into Wyatt's past or his future plans.

"For the rest of my life," Wyatt replied, and headed back toward the street to see if he could find Banker Lloyd Rocker.

He wanted to assure Del Avery that he had returned home to stay, but he was not sure he was telling the truth until he heard what Lloyd Rocker had to say about the bank's plans for settling the Keyhole's debts. He might have to leave Rampart to look for a job as a ranch hand, or take up bounty hunting again, but he would not go without showing Herbert Naylor how tough Texans could be when they were pushed too far and had to fight fire with fire.

TWELVE

On his second trip along Front Street, Wyatt felt more at home and more at ease. He nodded to those who recognized him, but he had no desire to stop and talk until Ben Dorsey waylaid him.

He was a block away from the Drovers Trust Bank when Ben stepped around two cowhands and blocked his way. He had been Wyatt's classmate and closest friend throughout their years in grade school, and was always pleasant company. Although he was not in the mood for small talk, Wyatt could not ignore him.

"Don't try to high-hat me, tall boy!" Ben chortled. "I knew you before you got famous."

He slapped Wyatt's shoulder and pumped his hand, his full-cheeked face turning pink with excitement. Ben was the son of Walt Dorsey, owner of the Wildfire Saloon, but his father refused to allow him to work there. He was too well-educated and intelligent to waste his life as a saloonman, Walt believed, but Ben had no problem finding a job. His bright, outgoing personality made him a desirable employee, and at one time or another he had worked for almost every merchant in town. He was the man Justin had hired as manager of the ill-fated clothing store, Wyatt had learned from his brother.

Leaning back in mock admiration, Wyatt patted the front of Ben Dorsey's wool coat, that was straining at the buttons across his generous stomach. "I see you've lost weight, Ben."

"It's for the girls," Ben declared. "Women like a man with meat on his bones." He looked at Wyatt speculatively. "You recall Laurie Custer, the little hot-blooded blonde you was so sweet on in school? Well, old buddy, I married her while you were making the West safe for widows and orphans. How's that for a fat man?"

It was Wyatt's turn to laugh. "You don't lie any better than you ever did, Ben. I saw Laurie this morning, and she's still footloose and fancy-free."

"Son of a gun." Ben laughed again. "You were always a step ahead of me, Wyatt. Someday I'll catch up."

"Keep trying, Ben." Wyatt tried to hide his impatience, but his straying glance told Ben that he wanted to be on his way.

"I guess you've got things to do," Ben said. "Let's have a drink at my old man's place some time."

"I'd do that now," Wyatt said apologetically, "but I need to get to the bank and see if I can talk with Lloyd Rocker."

"That's my place," Ben said, smiling. "That's where I'm working. Lloyd hired me as his head teller. He'll be there."

"We'll have that drink soon," Wyatt promised, and Ben Dorsey walked away, shaking his head and chuckling.

Wyatt regretted he did not have more time to spend with Ben Dorsey. For a few minutes he was relaxed and at peace with himself, pleased by the knowledge that true friends could spend years apart and still feel comfortable when they met again. He was glad Ben did not mention his experience with Justin's store, and he was not offended by his friend's lighthearted reference to the reputation Wyatt had earned as a bounty hunter. He was sorry, however, that Ben had teased him about Laurie Custer. It conjured up in his mind the image of Laurie riding away from his cabin with Ward Chesser. He glanced at the Sunset Hotel farther down the street, and wondered if Laurie was in her room or somewhere with the Lazy L Ranch manager.

There was less traffic in town now as the sun moved

145

closer to the western horizon. Many of the ranchers and older couples, who had traveled as much as twenty miles for their weekly supplies, had completed their business and gone home. A score of younger cowhands were still in town, some gathering in small groups beneath wooden awnings, some strolling between stores with girls holding to their arms, and all of them detouring occasionally to visit the Wildfire Saloon or the smaller, noisier Bronco Bar.

Wyatt covered the distance to the Drovers Trust Bank without further delay. The window that faced the narrow passage between the bank and the Opera House was protected by a wire mesh, but Wyatt had a clear view of Lloyd Rocker. The banker was seated at his desk, an oil lamp overhead lighting the pages of the ledger book in front of him.

He looked up when Wyatt rattled the wire mesh, stared at him for a few seconds, and called, "What do you want?"

"I need to talk with you," Wyatt replied. "Can you give me a few minutes?"

Lloyd Rocker shook his head. "I don't know you. Come back Monday when there's some help around."

"You know me, Lloyd. It's Wyatt Kirk."

Putting his pen aside, the banker rose and came closer to the window. "By George, that is you, Wyatt! Come on around."

He met Wyatt at the rear door, swung it open, and locked it when Wyatt stepped inside. The banker led him down the hallway to his office, sat down behind his desk, and waved Wyatt to a chair.

Despite his familiarity with the place and his long acquaintance with Lloyd Rocker, Wyatt felt intimidated in the presence of the man who might determine the fate of the Keyhole. He was trying to think of a way to open the conversation when Lloyd Rocker surprised him with a blunt inquiry.

"I hear you tied a man with ropes and set his beard on fire. Did you do that?"

Wyatt stifled a curse. "I didn't know that tale got spread around this far. Is that important right now?"

"It is to me. I assume you're here to talk about the Keyhole's loans. They're in bad shape, and I've got several options as to what to do about them. I can't count on being paid by a man who's in jail, especially one who might end up dead. Does Justin realize he could be hanged if he's found guilty of the charge Herbert Naylor lodged against him?"

"It's soaking in on him," Wyatt replied. "He's scared."

"What're you going to do about him?"

"I'm going to get him out of jail, and I might make Herbert Naylor eat that warrant."

The hint of a smile played around the corners of the banker's mouth. "I'm glad you said it plain instead of hemming and hawing like you're stuck. That's important to me. If you hadn't showed up, I was going to file papers first thing Monday morning. Justin's in some kind of dream world, and I can't get through to him that the bank has to be made whole. If you're honest and law-abiding, maybe we can work something out. Before I talk business I have to know if I'm dealing with a hard-case who's going to kill me to get me off his back,

147

or whether your mean streak just comes and goes. Did you set a man on fire or not?"

Lloyd Rocker was willing to give Wyatt time to consider his reply. He took a slim panatella from a desk drawer, lit it, and puffed the cigar alive. The banker was a sharp-featured, silver-haired man who had long since abandoned his Eastern dress and retained only a hint of his clipped New England accent. Thirty years ago, he had disclaimed any interest in his Boston family's shipbuilding business and struck out on his own when hundreds of young people emigrated to the West in search of adventure and wealth. Over the years, Lloyd Rocker had talked often with Aaron Kirk, and the rancher had passed on to Wyatt his knowledge of the banker's background.

Rocker had been aboard one of the wagons that carried the forty-niners to California. He located a profitable claim, mined it for a while, then sold it for a small fortune. Later, he owned a hotel and saloon in Abilene. When the rowdy railhead town closed its borders to the cattle trade, Rocker drifted south. He bought and sold two cattle spreads in the panhandle country before he moved again to establish Rampart's only bank, that he had maintained as its principal owner for twenty years.

An open-necked flannel shirt, plain moleskin pants, and scuffed riding boots were an indication that Lloyd Rocker preferred the manners and dress of his adopted land to the vested suits and toe-capped shoes of Eastern bankers. While he waited for Wyatt's response to his curiosity, he leaned back in his chair and blew smoke rings at the ceiling.

"I've run into bounty hunters in my time, and most of them were as bad as the men they were after," Rocker said presently. "I'm trying to decide if you're like them or a cut above them." He dusted ashes from his cigar and continued. "Talking to your banker is like talking to your preacher. You've got to bare your soul to gain his trust. If you've got anything to be ashamed of, you'd better come right out with it so you won't be regarded as a hypocrite if your sins find you out later."

Wyatt thumbed his hatbrim higher on his forehead and looked the banker in the face. "I'm not ashamed of my work. The stories people tell about me get twisted around until there's not much truth in them. That beard-burning thing got started the day after I left town, except it didn't happen the way you heard it."

Long ago Wyatt had read a newspaper account of the incident that ignored the facts in favor of sensation-alism, and Lloyd Rocker was the first person to ask him about it face to face. Some of those who knew him best described the banker as independent; others called him an eccentric. He had been known to refuse a loan to a man who declined to answer questions that involved matters too personal to discuss. Under the circum-stances, Wyatt could not afford to alienate Lloyd Rocker, and he had no choice but to relate the events that eventually led him into the bounty hunting trade.

The day Wyatt left the Keyhole he had no definite destination in mind. He wanted to put distance between himself and his brother before their arguments resulted in violence, take time to clear his head and decide whether he should cool his anger and return to the ranch, or stay away forever.

He bought a ticket to Pilot Hill, boarded the stage-coach at midmorning with three other passengers, and paid little attention to his surroundings until they stopped at a road ranch to change horses and pause for a noon meal. Aside from a few polite exchanges, he spoke only a few words to his companions. The other passengers stayed behind at the road ranch to catch the north-bound coach, that would arrive later in the day.

Wyatt declined the greasy-looking meal served at the road ranch. He chose instead to have a drink, and the stage driver joined him while the wrangler was harnessing fresh horses outside.

The bar was about eight feet long, crowded into an alcove in a back corner of the room. There was barely room for Wyatt and the driver to squeeze in between four other men who were keeping the sweating proprietor busy filling their orders. One of them, a slope-shouldered man with a long red beard, turned half around and looked them over without any effort to conceal his curiosity. He paid the bartender for the bottle he had been sampling and took it with him when he left through a door that led to the hitching rails at the rear of the building.

"About five miles from the road ranch we got held up," Wyatt told Lloyd Rocker. "We were in rough country somewhere outside of Pilot Hill. I was half asleep when it happened."

The wheels of the coach were barely turning as the six horses struggled in their traces, Wyatt recalled, and the bandit had no trouble overtaking them. He had poked a six-gun through the coach's open window, told the driver to stop, and threatened to kill the passengers if the stageman reached for his shotgun.

The only other occupants of the stagecoach was an elderly couple who had introduced themselves as Mr. and Mrs. Skipworth. They told Wyatt they were on their way to visit their soldier son at Fort Clear. At the masked man's command the three of them stepped down beside the driver, all holding their hands high.

The bandit took the woman's handbag, then patted Mr. Skipworth's frock coat and snatched a leather wallet from the inside pocket. He rifled the woman's purse, scattering papers, a comb, and a lace handkerchief on the ground. It contained nothing of value, but he found a few bills in the man's wallet, stuffed them in his pocket, and threw the wallet aside.

Eyeing Wyatt warily, he ordered the driver to turn his pockets inside out. The effort revealed a twist of tobacco, two shotgun shells, and a pocket knife. The bandit saved Wyatt until last. Keeping his finger curled around the Colt's trigger, he ran his hand cautiously over the tall, dark-faced man with the pearl-handled Peacemaker holstered low on his thigh.

He backed away a few feet. "I ain't goin' to fool with you, mister. I felt a wad of money in your pocket. Don't even think of goin' for that pretty gun. Hand over the money real nice or I'll put a bullet between your eyes and help myself."

The bandit had been in too much of a hurry to go through the routine of disarming his passengers. He counted on the threat of death to keep them orderly.

Wyatt's Colt was six inches below the edge of his right pocket. He debated the time it would take him to grab the gun and fire while he tried to duck below the sight of the bandit's Colt. He decided the money in his pocket was not worth the risk. He gave the man the money.

The masked man took a step toward the boulders that had concealed him and his horse until the stagecoach had dragged almost to a standstill. He was covered from the bridge of his nose to the second button of his shirt by a soiled flour sack that had been torn in half, but he was not wearing gloves. Wyatt had seen those hands before and he knew the man's identity.

"I don't fancy bein' shot in the back," he said to Wyatt. "Lift that Peacemaker real easy and throw it over the top of the stagecoach. I want to see it sail far enough that it'll take you a while to find it, or I'll shoot it out of your hand."

Wyatt did as he was told. The bandit turned his attention again to Mrs. Skipworth. "You didn't have no money, lady, but you've got a nice piece of gold around your neck. Hand it over!"

The frail, white-haired woman summoned a spark of courage, vowing she would not surrender the oval-shaped locket that hung by a chain around her neck. She appealed to the bandit's sympathy, explaining that it had belonged to her deceased mother, but her plea was answered with a muffled curse. The robber lashed out with his free hand and left the mark of his fingers on the woman's thin face. "Maybe that'll change your mind," he snarled.

Sobbing, her hands trembling, she gave up the locket.

At that moment, Wyatt regretted that he had been so quick to part with his gun. The bandit ducked behind the rocks, mounted a waiting horse, and fled before Wyatt could find his gun.

Lloyd Rocker puffed on his cigar and listened silently while Wyatt recited the details of the holdup. The banker swore when Wyatt described the treatment suffered by Mrs. Skipworth. He said, "I hope you caught the son of a bitch!"

"I caught him," Wyatt said.

He remembered that the red-bearded man he had seen drinking at the road ranch wore an unusual ring. It was a gold band shaped like a coiled snake with its head raised in striking position. The robber was wearing the same ring.

Wyatt had ridden the stagecoach on to Pilot Hill, but he did not linger long. From the hundred dollars he had withdrawn from the Keyhole's bank account, he had sixty-three dollars left after paying his fare. Before he had boarded the stagecoach in Rampart, he stuffed a twenty-dollar bill into the toe of one of his boots for safekeeping. It was more than enough to pay for the rental of a horse at the Pilot Hill livery, and Wyatt rode out immediately to retrace the ten-mile trail to the road ranch.

"I got back there about ten o'clock that night, and the place was deserted except for the bartender and the red-bearded man with the snake ring. He was about to down a drink when I put a gun on him. I marched him outside and searched him. He had six dollars on him, and he swore he didn't pull the holdup. I knew he had hidden the money and Mrs. Skipworth's locket somewhere, and I meant to do whatever it took to get it all back."

"You set his beard on fire to make him talk," Rocker guessed.

"He thought I did, and probably told a lie about it," said Wyatt. "I put him on his horse, took him down the stage road a piece, and tied him to a tree. That's when the notion came to me."

Using his own neckerchief, Wyatt blindfolded the man and promised to burn the hair off his face unless he revealed where he had hidden his loot. The bandit laughed at him. Wyatt pulled the man's neckerchief down on his chest and struck a match to it. When the man felt the heat he thought his beard was on fire. He started screaming out directions to the deadfall where he had buried everything he had stolen from the stage-coach passengers.

"I pulled off his neckerchief and stomped out the fire before he was hardly scorched," Wyatt concluded. "That's all there was to it. The Skipworths were glad I found their money and the locket."

Lloyd Rocker nodded approvingly. "What did you do with the scoundrel after you got your money back?"

"I collected a five-hundred-dollar reward that Wells Fargo had posted for his capture. When I turned him over to a deputy sheriff in Pilot Hill, I found out he was wanted for four other holdups. The deputy put me in for the reward and gave me a bundle of flyers on people wanted by the law. I figured I could earn a few dollars that way until I landed something permanent. Later I tracked down a hired gun who'd shot somebody in the back, and I just kept at it. That tell you what you want to know?"

Lloyd Rocker rubbed out the fire of his half-smoked cigar and dropped the panatella into his desk drawer. "Tells me plenty. Tells me you're not short on guts. You don't have the kind of meanness in you that I was worried about. Some folks don't know the difference in being mean and being tough. I have no faith in people who won't stand up on their two legs and persevere when things go against them. Your pa would stand up against a grizzly bear. Maybe you're cut from the same mold."

Wyatt shrugged. "I hope we can stop talking about me and get down to business. How much money do I have in my account?"

The banker thumbed through one of the ledger books stacked at his elbow. "Well, I got in a hundred-fifty-dollar draft from a deputy down in Clayfield just yesterday."

"That's the balance of the reward for a killer named Ray Beemer. It almost beat me here."

Without looking up from the papers he was studying, Rocker asked, "Are you going to keep on with this man-hunting business?"

"I'm going to run a ranch unless you plan to sell it out from under me."

"I see," Rocker grunted. "Your account shows a balance of forty-six hundred and seven dollars, including interest. That's a respectable sum for three years of saving, but it's far short of what you'll need to clear the Keyhole's debts if you plan to use it to pull Justin's

155

chestnuts out of the fire."

"They're my chestnuts, too. The Keyhole's debts are my debts."

"Not exactly," Rocker said. "I had Justin bring me Aaron's will so I could set my legal grounds. The worst that can happen is that I'll force Justin into bankruptcy and sell off his fifty-five percent of the ranch. You'd have a new partner, but you'd keep your share of the Keyhole."

Wyatt's stomach felt like it was shrinking. "I couldn't live with that. I'm not about to let some stranger with the majority share tell me how to run the Keyhole. Pa worked all his life to build something we could count on, and I want to keep the Keyhole in the family. How much do we owe?"

The banker opened another book and ran his finger down a column of figures. "The whole thing is sixteen thousand four hundred sixty-five dollars and forty-five cents."

"Damn!" Wyatt rubbed a hand across his forehead to keep the sweat out of his eyes. "How much time can you give me?"

Lamplight glistened on Lloyd Rocker's silvery hair as he bowed his head and stared at his desk. He raised his piercing eyes, studied Wyatt's face, then looked again at the ledger sheet.

"I can't wait long," Rocker said. "I've been too lenient already. When Justin didn't make any payments, not even the accrued interest, the whole balance fell due. Now it's six months past due. I'm sure you understand how the bank business works. The money I

156

loaned Justin wasn't mine. It belongs to the depositors who trusted me with their money. If all of them wanted to withdraw their savings tomorrow, I'd need that money from Justin to accommodate them. I don't sleep well for thinking about such a possibility when my cash flow drops off because of bad debts."

Wyatt did some hasty calculations in his head. "If I gave you my savings, we'd still owe about twelve thousand. I can't settle that overnight. There might be a way to pay over half of it if you can wait for me to pull some strings."

Lloyd Rocker put a finger to his lips and sat silently for a full minute. "I'll need to think about the situation for a few days. Justin doesn't have the guts to face his problems. I can't even get him in here to talk about the mortgage. If you're taking over at the Keyhole, it changes the picture some. We can talk as long as you want, but I can't make any commitments today. Come in one day next week and we'll get down to brass tacks."

He leaned forward with a sudden thought. "Do you want to apply your savings to the loan?"

Wyatt had moved around too much to receive statements of his account, but he had hoped he had accumulated enough reward money to finance a scheme that would even the score with Herbert Naylor and result in a profit for the Keyhole at the same time. If he could arouse the Lazy L owner's competitive nature one more time, he might have enough to make the plan work.

He said, "I need that money to make money."

Lloyd Rocker looked disappointed. "You'd help my

thinking if you'd tell me what you've got in mind."

Wyatt's plan was a gamble, and any chance for success depended on secrecy. He needed an accomplice, someone to test his thinking, but it would be a mistake to confide in Lloyd Rocker. It was not the kind of endeavor a banker would approve.

He said, "I'm going to do my best to hold onto the Keyhole, and I think I know how to start. First, I'm going to do some rustling. After that I'm going to have a bargain sale on some good longhorn cattle."

THIRTEEN

It was almost dark when Wyatt returned to the Keyhole headquarters. His bones ached and his stinging eyes reminded him he had not slept in sixteen hours. Fatigue numbed his muscles, but his spirits were higher than they had been when he rode away from the ranch that morning.

He headed for the house to speak with Wilma, but changed directions when he saw her run toward him from the cookshack. She had an apron around her waist, and strands of moist blond hair fell around her cheeks. Her hands were white with floured dough.

"We were trying to hold off supper until you got back, but the men were beginning to gripe about waiting so long," she said as she stopped in front of him. "I've been helping Caleb make biscuits to go with the stew."

She brushed flour from her hands and wrinkled her brow. "How's Justin? Is he coming home? Did he ask about me? What—"

"Whoa! Slow down." Wyatt sat in the dun's saddle and looked down at her, pleased that Wilma was making her first effort toward fulfilling her promise that she would change her ways and settle down in the role of a ranch wife. He had never known her to help with the cooking for the Keyhole crew.

"Justin sends his love," Wyatt told her. "He's out of sorts, but that won't last much longer. Mace won't give any ground, but maybe I can get Herbert Naylor to drop the charge. I'm going to try. If it works, Justin will be home in a couple of days."

"How are you going to change Naylor's mind?"

Wyatt's reply was curt and stern. "Ranch wives don't meddle in a man's business. Remember that. I told you I'd do something, and I will. While we're at it, I'll tell you something else. From now on I'm the boss at the Keyhole, no matter what Pa's will said. You might as well get used to that idea, too."

She nodded agreeably, but there was a flash of defiance in her eyes. "Justin won't argue with you. He's in over his head and he knows it. I'll do what I can to help, but I'm not going to bow and scrape every time you speak, Wyatt Kirk! I'm tired of hearing that women can't share a man's problems. One day Texas won't belong to men alone. If some gun-happy fool don't kill you first, you'll see women ranch owners, women lawyers, women doctors, and maybe a woman sheriff. I'll do all I can to hasten the day."

She dropped her arms to her side and took a deep breath. "Put your horse away and come on to supper."

He drew his chin close to his chest and pretended

shock. "Yes, ma'am," he said in the manner of a young-ster obeying the commands of his mother, and reined his horse around. Wilma had summoned from deep within herself a new and different strength since their early-morning encounter.

Despite his cynical attitude, Wyatt was not offended by her prediction that the role of women in the West would change as the country grew. In fact, he hoped she was right. It would suit him fine if someday he had a daughter who would become a doctor or lawyer. He had come home with the hope that the Keyhole would pro-vide enough wealth to afford the kind of education that would enable his future children to have a choice between the cattle business and some more prestigious vocation.

After refreshing himself with cold water from the well pump, Wyatt joined the ranch hands at the cookshack. Caleb Frye, his bald head shiny with sweat, greeted him at the doorway and said, "Having you at the table brings back old times."

The others were lounging on the benches on either side of the long table in the center of the room. They got to their feet as Wyatt entered. Wilma had begun setting food on the table, but she moved aside while introduc-tions were exchanged.

Aside from Caleb, the only familiar face belonged to Bill Bartlett. The red-haired, freckle-faced cowboy, showing no ill effects from the broken leg he had suf-fered long ago, was the first to shake hands. Sam Hopson, who had succeeded Newt Hardy as the Key-hole foreman, hung back a moment, appraising Wyatt with the caution of a man approaching a strange dog. He was a head shorter than Wyatt, slender and wiry, with sparkling white teeth and dark curly hair that grew to a widow's peak on his forehead. The viselike grip of his handshake indicated it would be a mistake to underestimate the power in his stringy muscles.

"There ain't much family resemblance between you and Justin," he remarked, unsmiling, and went back to his seat at the table.

It was left to Len Tolbert to voice what the others were not bold enough to discuss. Len was the baby of the crew, not yet twenty, and he seemed unsure of how he should treat Wyatt Kirk. He took a step forward, then stopped, fingering the brim of his hat. He tossed his head to shift the cotton-colored hair that kept falling across his nervous blue eyes. Finally, he shook hands and introduced himself in a shy, reedy voice.

"I'm new here and just learning the cow business," he said. "I hope I'm not stepping out of place, Mr. Kirk. I need to send some money to my folks up in Kansas, and we ain't been paid in over a month. I was wondering—"

"I'd wonder, too." Wyatt patted Len Tolbert's shoulder. He swung his glance toward the men at the table and saw that they were watching with interest. "I've got some money, but I can't get to it right away. Give me a week or so, and I'll get you paid."

There was a hum of muted voices as the men at the table spoke among themselves. The cotton-haired youngster nodded and started back to his seat. He looked over his shoulder and grinned as Wyatt said,

"Don't call me mister, Len. It makes me feel old. Call me Wyatt to my face and anything that comes to mind behind my back."

A half-hearted chuckle sounded around the table, and Wyatt felt that the crew was ready to accept him as one of them. After the men were served, Wilma filled a plate and went outside to eat alone on the bench next to the bunkhouse wall. Unaccustomed to her presence, the crew had been unusually quiet and respectful while she was in the room, but now they relaxed and grew talkative.

Wyatt sat next to Sam Hopson, saying little while he listened to the conversations about weather, drunken fights and crooked gamblers, and some good-natured teasing aimed at Len Tolbert. The food was good, and Wyatt ate as much as his stomach would tolerate, hoping the nourishment would renew his strength.

When the meal was finished, and the men began to push back from their plates to smoke and talk, Wyatt asked Sam Hopson to walk outside with him. They nodded to Wilma, who was still picking at her food, and went to the corner of the bunkhouse.

"I figured if we're going to have any hard words between us, we ought to have them in private," Wyatt told Hopson. "I've got nothing against you, but I want to bring Newt Hardy back as the Keyhole foreman if I can get him."

Sam Hopson's white teeth sparkled against his swarthy skin. He hooked his thumbs in his Levi's pockets and scraped up dirt with the toe of one boot. "Hell, partner, I'm not goin' to raise a ruckus about that.

When I sign on with a spread, I ride for the brand—do whatever the boss tells me. I reckon that's you now."

"That's right. I'm the boss. If Newt won't come back, I'd like for you to stay on as the Keyhole ramrod. Will you do that?"

Sam Hopson reached for tobacco and papers. He rolled a cigarette, lit it, and blew out a puff of smoke while he considered Wyatt's question. He said, "That depends on which hat you're wearin'—man-hunter or rancher. It's known around here that you've been claimin' bounty on some folks. I got nervous when you called me out. I might as well tell you that I was mixed up in a little difficulty over in New Mexico Territory some years back. There may be a notice out on me, maybe not. I don't know. One of the hard-cases who was ridin' for the spread I was workin' for got into a hassle with me. He called me a name I don't take from nobody. It ended up in a gunfight. He had a fair chance, but he didn't make it. That's when I drew my time and left."

Wyatt gave Sam Hopson a closer look, his glance lingering on the bone-handled Colt .45 in his tooled leather holster. "Are you pretty good with a gun?"

"Real good," said Hopson.

The man's frankness surprised Wyatt, and he felt his skin tingle with apprehension. "Are you looking for a reputation?"

"Runnin' from one. I sure don't want to try to take yours, if that's what you're askin'. Somebody will, though, if they've heard as much about you as I have."

Wyatt shrugged. "We'll get along, Sam. Don't say

anything to the others until we know about Newt. I'm going to head for my cabin in a few minutes, but I want Caleb Frye to run an errand for me. Will you send him out?"

"Sure." Hopson took a deep drag on his cigarette and let the smoke trickle through his nostrils. He took a step and stopped. "You've got a spread here that'll make you rich if it's run right. Caleb says you're a good cattleman. I'll stick with you as long as you want me. You need anything from me, just tell me."

"Appreciate it," Wyatt said.

His instructions for Caleb Frye were brief and well received. He asked Caleb to leave at first light the next day and carry a message to Newt Hardy at the Arrowhead Ranch.

"It'll take you four, five hours to get there, so I'll leave later in the day. Tell Newt what I want and ask him to meet me in Rampart to talk about it. The Wildfire Saloon closes until after church, but it'll be open in the afternoon. I'll meet him there."

Caleb smiled his approval. "By God, things are looking up around here. I'll leave plenty early."

Some of the church crowd was still in town when Wyatt rode into Rampart. Women strolled along the boardwalk in groups of twos and threes, pausing to point at displays inside the stores. The only places open for business were the two saloons and Brock's Apothecary. The women entertained themselves with window-shopping while the men lounged on the benches in front of the Sunset Hotel or slipped away for a drink.

The day had dawned clear and hot, and Wyatt could feel the heat bouncing off the buildings as he rode down Front Street and headed for the Wildfire Saloon. He had gone to bed early the night before, but his sleep had been disturbed by ghosts of both the dead and living. Justin appeared in his dreams, standing on a scaffold with a hangrope around his neck, then Sheriff Lester Mace showed up with a prisoner in handcuffs and shouted, "Wait, you've got the wrong man!"

In the misty world of his subconscious, Wyatt had a hard time recognizing Lester Mace's prisoner. At first he saw a glistening white skull, then out of the fog came flesh and color and he recognized the thin, sharp-chinned countenance. It was Dr. Evan Halsey with his blond brush mustache and pale eyes that were like a flickering blue flame as they glared at him through gold-rimmed spectacles. Lester Mace spoke again, but the words were drowned out by the voice of Wyatt's father, who shouted, "Hell, I ain't dead. I tricked you. I played dead to get my wife off my back!"

With the sound of Aaron Kirk's voice ringing in his mind, Wyatt had sat up in bed and gazed around the dark bedroom, expecting to see his father standing nearby. It took him a moment to separate the dream from reality, and afterward it took him a long time to go back to sleep. He kept thinking about Lester Mace's story of the killer who had faked his own death, and the sheriff's speculation that Justin Kirk's current problems might be connected to events of the past.

Was it possible that Dr. Evan Halsey was still alive, and involved in Herbert Naylor's apparent vendetta against the Keyhole Ranch? Wyatt mentally explored the possibility of Halsey being alive, saw no logic in it, and exhaustion finally let him sleep.

He had awakened before sunrise. He was not pressed for time and he was still tired. He went back to sleep and got up two hours later than was his custom. From the supplies Laurie Custer had left in his cabin, he drank half a pot of coffee and ate a big breakfast of beans, bacon, and canned apples.

After shaving and bathing in the creek, he chose clothes that would be more appropriate while he mingled with those who would be dressed in their Sunday best. He wore a pair of striped gray moleskins, a blue cotton shirt and a black polka-dot neckerchief. The pearl-handled Peacemaker looked out of place with such attire, but Wyatt would not appear without it until he was sure he could walk the streets of his hometown without being challenged by a gunfighter who resented his reputation.

Word of Wyatt's return to the Keyhole had spread across the range, and it was no longer a surprise for him to be seen in town. He was relieved to note that he drew no special attention when he anchored his buckskin at the tie-rail in front of the Wildfire. He stayed outside long enough to survey the other horses that were tied in front of the saloon. Most of them had small bundles or rolled tarps tied behind the saddles, and he wondered if one of them belonged to Newt Hardy.

Slanting rays from the sun speared through the front windows and reflected upward from the planked floor, and the interior of the Wildfire Saloon was almost as bright as the outdoors. Wyatt saw Newt Hardy as soon he went through the batwing doors. Newt was sitting with Caleb Frye at a table a few feet from the left corner of the bar, and was in the process of pouring himself a drink from a full bottle when Wyatt entered.

Walt Dorsey watched each customer who entered his saloon, and he spotted Wyatt immediately. Wiping his hands on his beer-stained apron, Walt stepped from behind the bar and came toward him with a smile on his round, florid face. He held out his hand and said, "It's good to have you back. My boy Ben told me he saw you, and that you ain't changed a bit."

Wyatt chuckled as he shook the saloonman's hand. "He didn't look hard enough. Ben was always easy to fool."

Walt Dorsey slapped Wyatt on the back. "The first drink's on me. Come on over to the bar."

"Appreciate it, but I see Newt Hardy and Caleb Frye have a bottle on their table. I'll let Newt pay for it."

"Whatever." Walt laughed, and went back to his post.

The three men at the bar had kept their eyes forward until the saloonman spoke Wyatt's name. They turned slowly around. One of them was Laurie's father, Jacob Custer. Wyatt also recognized the other two—Jeff Inman of the J-Bar and Syd McBride of the Half Moon Ranch. Inman's J-Bar was the Kirks' neighbor to the west, but the lay of the land put ten miles between their homes. Wyatt had seldom seen him except when they were swapping strays at roundup time, but he remembered him as friendly and pleasant.

Inman and McBride spoke politely, shook hands, and

went back to their drinks. Jacob Custer, a solidly built, square-faced man with an easy manner, took Wyatt by the arm and eased him a step away from the others.

"My wife and I visited with Laurie for a few minutes after church," he said quietly. "She was in such a tizzy, we went off and left her alone. She was expecting company to eat the noon meal with her at the Sunset dining room and acted like she didn't want us around. I'll declare, Wyatt, sending that girl off to college was the worst thing I ever did. She ain't been the same since."

Wyatt was uncomfortable with the conversation. He said, "I don't know, Jacob. She seems happy with her work and her poetry."

"Happy one minute, moody the next," Custer said. "She ain't happy today. She said you and her didn't get on good when you met at your cabin. She said you had words with a friend of hers—that Chesser feller who works for Herbert Naylor at the Lazy L—and things went from bad to worse."

"It didn't go good," Wyatt said, his glance flitting impatiently past Custer and toward Newt Hardy's table.

Custer wanted to share the worries on his mind. He said, "I don't know Herbert Naylor, but I don't like him. Nobody likes him. Us ranchers have had a hard time getting a fair deal from the cattle brokers since that fool cut his prices. A couple of us rode over to talk to him about sticking together on prices, but he wouldn't even come out of the house—sent Ward Chesser to do his talking, and we got nowhere. I don't like nobody from the Lazy L, and I wish Laurie wouldn't fool around with Chesser. She's waiting for him now. You ought to go over to the Sunset Hotel and make up with her before he shows up."

"I don't have time today, Jacob. I've got some other things that have to be done."

Custer pulled at his hatbrim and forced a smile. "Hell, I shouldn't be unloading my mind on you at a time like this, what with Justin in jail and—"

His face assumed a flustered expression and he left the sentence unfinished.

"It's all right," Wyatt said. "We'll talk again."

Chairs scraped as Caleb Frye and Newt Hardy rose when they saw Wyatt crossing the floor. The Keyhole cook nodded and Newt Hardy reached across to shake Wyatt's hand, running his eyes over him as though he were sizing up a stranger. He sat down, motioning Wyatt to a chair on his right. Still standing, Caleb picked up his glass and downed the rest of his drink. He wiped his lips with the back of his hand and said, "I guess I'd better be getting on. I was keeping Newt company until you got here, Wyatt."

"I'll be along shortly," Wyatt said.

The cook started away, then came back. "When Wilma found out I was coming to town, she sent Justin some fresh duds. I didn't stop on my way to get Newt, but I'm going to take his things to the jail on my way home. You want me to tell him you're here?"

"No. He'll be upset because I didn't come to see him. I might sound cold, but I'd rather get him out of jail as listen to him fret about it. Newt and I need to talk, and then I'll know what I'm going to do."

Newt Hardy had brought an extra glass to the table.

He pushed it across to Wyatt and pointed at the whiskey bottle. He was a big man—big shoulders, big arms, big muscles, and a big voice. Ignoring the glass, Wyatt took tobacco and papers from his pocket and grinned at Newt Hardy.

"You going to talk or just sit there and frown at me?"

The chair squeaked as the big man leaned back and shrugged. He pushed his black hat away from his face, then lifted his hands and rubbed his fingers across his bluish-green eyes as though they were bothering him. He had the eyesight of an eagle, but Newt had a habit of rubbing his eyes when he was angry or puzzled.

"I let everybody have their say before I talk," said Newt. "I figured you'd want to get Caleb out of the way first. He says you want me back at the Keyhole."

Wyatt nodded. "The word's all around about how much trouble we're in, so I know you've heard. I need a ramrod who'll keep his mouth shut and do what I say. I know I can trust you to do that. Your old job's waiting for you if you'll take it."

Leaning forward to rest his arms on the table, Newt tried to lower his voice, but it still rumbled in his chest like a kettle drum. "Depends on what you're going to tell me and what you want me to keep my mouth shut about."

"I'm going to show Herbert Naylor how it feels to have your dirty tricks bite back." Wyatt struck a match to his cigarette and spoke through a swirl of smoke. "I've got two schemes in mind, but I can't tell you about them unless you're working for me."

Newt Hardy rolled his empty glass between his palms

and scowled. "I can't work for Justin—don't understand him. You going to run the Keyhole?"

"You can bet on it. I'm the only boss you'll have."

Newt poured himself another drink and gulped it down. "Herbert Naylor's kind ain't good for this range. I think the man's loco, but that's neither here nor there. If you're going to buck him, I'll side with you. You've got yourself a ramrod."

Wyatt sighed with relief. "Good. When can you start?"

"I brought my gear with me just in case." Newt said. "I tied up in back and my horse is tired of standing. Let's go home."

He scooted his chair away to stand up. Wyatt held up a hand to delay him. "You know the layout at the Lazy L, and I want you to steal something for me on the way. Are you up to that?"

The big man cocked his head and waited to see if the question was the beginning of a prank, but he saw that Wyatt was serious. He said, "Not if it involves horses, cows, or any man's personal traps. I've carried stuff off some spreads accidental, but it wasn't nothing of value. I won't hire on as a thief."

"We're not talking big value," Wyatt assured him. "I want a Lazy L branding iron. We'll borrow it and take it back."

For the first time during their meeting a thin smile softened the coarse features of Newt Hardy's broad face. "I think I know what you're up to. I'll get you the iron. When do we start shoving it down Naylor's throat?"

"First thing in the morning," Wyatt replied hopefully.

FOURTEEN

During his ride from the plateau country, Wyatt had spent less than twenty dollars from the fifty he had collected as part of the reward on Ray Beemer. He reached in his pocket to pay for the bottle that Newt Hardy carried to the bar on their way out of the saloon. Newt waved him aside.

"I'm taking the bottle with me and I'll pay the freight. We might get snakebit on the way home."

Walt Dorsey took a bill from Newt, gave him change, and waved to Wyatt. "I'll get into your money another time."

"Probably," Wyatt said, and went outside with Newt Hardy. They had just reached the street and Wyatt was about to untie the buckskin when Newt nudged him and said, "Look who's coming."

Following Newt's glance he saw a short, plump woman in a gingham dress and gray bonnet walking toward the Sunset Hotel. She had one arm hooked through the handle of a woven basket that was partially covered by a red-checked cloth, and was using her free hand to wave to the people she passed on the street.

"Who is it?" Wyatt asked.

"Maggie Gregg. She was your ma's housekeeper for a while. Don't you remember her?"

"Good Lord," Wyatt murmured. "I didn't think I'd ever forget Maggie. She was the best thing that ever happened to the Keyhole. She still work at the Sunset?"

Newt Hardy nodded. "She's still there, which is a

wonder to some people. She don't need the money but I reckon she likes to keep busy. Maggie caused quite a stir in Rampart a while back and it ain't died down yet."

"What did she do?" Wyatt asked, puzzled. "I can't imagine Maggie bothering anybody."

"I guess you wouldn't know about it." Newt lowered his voice as Maggie Gregg came closer. "It happened eight or nine months ago. The only thing she bothered was everybody's curiosity. She suddenly come into a big sum of money. The gossips are still wondering about it, and I'd guess Maggie is, too. She swears she's never found out where the money come from, and Maggie ain't known for telling lies."

A dubious look clouded Wyatt's eyes. "Sounds like somebody started a rumor that got out of hand. I've never heard of such a tale turning out to be true."

"It's true all right," Newt declared. "Maggie don't mind talking about it herself. She got a package at the post office with no return address on it. There was five thousand dollars in it and nothing to say who sent it or why. Some thought it might have come from your ma. Maggie talks about Liza Kirk a lot, and I know they was real close when Maggie worked at the Keyhole."

"Ma's been dead since I was sixteen. She died of pneumonia a year or so after she moved in with her sister in Sacramento. You were there when the letter came."

"I know, and Maggie knows that, but everybody don't," Newt said. "People like to make up their own answers to mysteries."

Wyatt shook his head. "It's going to take me a long

time to catch up with what went on around here while I was away."

Maggie Gregg glanced toward the horses tied at the Wildfire hitching rail, looked away, then stopped and stared at Wyatt and Newt Hardy. She left the boardwalk and hurried toward them in her short, choppy stride. Shifting her straw basket, she laughed joyfully and put an arm around Wyatt's waist, hugging him lightly.

"Lordy!" she exclaimed. "What a sight for sore eyes. It's my other boy, come home at last."

Apple-cheeked women seemed always to be smiling, always gentle and affectionate. Maggie Gregg was like that. Drawing away from him, she pushed a crinkly wisp of coppery hair beneath the brim of her bonnet and raised her eyes to Wyatt's face. "You don't remember me, do you?"

"I knew you the minute I laid eyes on you," Wyatt lied. "I'd give a dollar for a dish of that apple cobbler you used to make." He pointed to her basket. "You going on a picnic?"

"Goodness, no! I've been down to the jail visiting Justin. I cooked him a good meal, and he barely picked at it. He wouldn't talk to me, sat there staring like he didn't know me. Justin never was the friendly kind, like you. Today he acted plumb addled—about as bad as Bertetta Halsey when . . ."

Maggie's hand fluttered in the gesture women used when they felt their conversation was beginning to ramble. She looked aside and said, "I'll swear, Newt, you get bigger every time I see you."

With her chin uptilted, the brim of her bonnet still fell

below the level of Newt Hardy's chin. Acting bored, Newt said, "You keep telling me that, Miss Maggie. I must be the only fifty-five-year-old man in Texas who's still growing. You're looking right pert, yourself."

"Pshaw!" Maggie murmured, "You're six years older than me and you look ten years younger. I don't know how you do it."

There was truth in Maggie Gregg's observation. Newt's broad face, with its firm jawline and blocky chin, was unlined. His tight-lipped mouth gave him a taciturn look, but Newt spoke easily with his friends and usually faced those he disliked with a stony, silent stare.

He chuckled at Maggie Gregg's flattery. "I keep my good looks because I don't worry about things that make you old. I drink, smoke, cuss, and eat too much. I reckon God feels sorry for a sinner like me and ignores my bad habits."

Maggie's eyes settled briefly on the bottle that Newt held at his side. She made a clucking sound with her tongue. "It'll catch up with you all at once someday." She moved the basket to her other arm and said to Wyatt, "You've got to help Justin. People are picking on him and it's not right. I know you'll do something. Aaron would, God rest his soul."

"Yes, ma'am," Wyatt said absently. His mind was on something Maggie Gregg had said earlier. Justin's state of mind had reminded her of Bertetta Halsey for some reason. She started to speak about it, but had left the remark unfinished.

The mention of Dr. Evan Halsey's wife sent Wyatt's blood racing and his mind groping for a vagrant suspicion that lurked just beyond his grasp. Maggie worked as a part-time cook and cleaning woman at the Sunset Hotel, and he wondered if she knew more about Aaron Kirk's death than she had ever told.

"Yes, ma'am," Wyatt repeated. "I'm going to see that Justin gets out of jail and has his name cleared." He looked down at the chubby little woman and smiled. "What was it about Justin that reminded you of Bertetta Halsey? You didn't say."

Maggie Gregg glanced over her shoulder as though she wanted to be on her way. "Land sakes, I don't know. Some days I'm so absentminded I start to say something and forget what I was talking about. Maybe it'll come to me later."

A guarded look had come into Maggie's eyes, but Wyatt pretended to be unaware of it. "It's not important. Were you and Bertetta Halsey good friends?"

"Not exactly. I used to clean Doc Halsey's office for him in the evenings after he closed up. Sometimes Bertetta stayed around and talked. She was a nice lady, pretty as a picture, and real friendly. Not like her husband. Doc was a cold fish—didn't have anything to say to anybody unless he was asking about their pains and bowel habits. Bertetta was an unhappy woman. I think he was mean to her. They're not here anymore, you know."

"Yeah, I know," Wyatt said. "Nobody knows what happened to her, but the sheriff gave me some news about Doc Halsey. He was killed by a bushwhacker outside of Rumford."

Maggie Gregg's cheeks turned red. "He's dead? Doc

Halsey's dead? I didn't know that."

Wyatt nodded, studying the sudden twinkle that brightened Maggie's eyes. She lowered her head, preoccupied momentarily, then said, "Well, now, that puts a different light on . . ."

Again, her thoughts seemed to stray and she did not continue. She adjusted her bonnet and gave Wyatt's arm a squeeze. "It's time for me to go to work. I know you're a good boy, Wyatt, and I don't believe the things I've heard about you. I'm glad you're home to look after your pa's ranch."

Wyatt held to her arm as she started to turn away. "You looked relieved when you heard Doc Halsey is dead. What—"

"I know what you're angling at, Wyatt." Her expression became stern. "I talked to Lester Mace about Aaron Kirk's death a long time ago. It happened on my prayer-meeting night. I didn't see anything that went on at the hotel that night, because I wasn't working. That was a bad, bad time for everybody and I don't like to call it up in my mind. It's over and done."

She backed away. Her hand fluttered in a quick farewell and she hurried toward the Sunset Hotel.

Except for their exchange of small talk, Newt Hardy said nothing until the woman was gone. He watched her back through narrowed eyes and said, "I've got a hunch the sheriff didn't talk to Maggie long enough."

Wyatt agreed. "She might not know much about Pa's killing, but my guts tell me she knows what happened to Bertetta Halsey. Justin's scared, half out of his mind, and ashamed of his failures. Maggie saw him that way and it reminded her of Bertetta. I'd like to know why, but she's not going to talk any more today. I'll let it pass for a few days, then try to see her again."

He picked up the buckskin's reins and let his breath out through tight lips. "I get a feeling there are loose strings all around me that tie together somehow, but I can't put my finger on what they are."

"Beats me," Newt Hardy said. "Sometimes somebody says a word or makes a move that hits your mind like a lightning bolt. The thing you're pondering gets clear as daylight all of a sudden. You'll have to think about loose strings while I'm sneaking around Naylor's spread to get us a branding iron. We can't do but one thing at a time."

"You're right. That's the most important chore today. If you get caught, it'll tip our hand."

"I ain't a expert thief, but I'll manage. I didn't have much truck with anybody at the Lazy L except Jesse Estep. Naylor's got a crew of six, seven men, but Estep and me were the only ones who worked like cowhands. He's a good man. The rest of the lot struck me as loafers and ne'er-do-wells. I'll visit with Estep awhile, tell him I'm coming back to the Keyhole to be his neighbor, then pick up a branding iron from the side of the toolshed when I leave. Nobody will give me a second look."

Leading the buckskin, Wyatt walked with Newt Hardy to the rear of the Wildfire Saloon. Newt checked the lashings on his bedroll and climbed into the saddle of his black stallion with the ease of a bronc buster. They rode out of town toward the Keyhole and Herbert Naylor's Lazy L.

Although Naylor had lived on the Rampart range for almost a year, no one knew much about him. During the hour he spent at the Drovers Trust Bank, Wyatt tried to get Lloyd Rocker's opinion of the man, but had little success. Ethically bound by rules of confidentiality between banker and depositor, Rocker would speak about Naylor's finances only in general terms. He was not quite so discreet in his view of the man's personal conduct.

"He's got more money in this bank than anybody has ever had, but he's got no regard for it," Rocker stated. "He throws it around like cow chips, wastes it on whims. The way he lost his own money to shut Justin down was mean and senseless."

The banker paused, pursing his mouth in disgust. He appeared to be waiting for a response and Wyatt said, "That's water over the dam, but he didn't stop there. He's still making trouble."

"The man's two-faced," Rocker had growled. "He claimed he wanted to make Rampart a better town, but it was all talk. A week after Justin went broke, Naylor closed his stores, too. Big freight wagons from Missouri rolled into town and took his stock back where it came from. I can't speak well of a man who uses his wealth as a weapon, even if he is a good customer."

At least Wyatt had learned more about Naylor's cut-throat methods than Justin had cared to tell him. The feed store, Lloyd Rocker declared, was the victim of old competition rather than new. Ranchers had depended on Charlie Blake's livery stable to supply their needs for years, and they continued to do so.

In the last few minutes of his visit at the bank, he was encouraged by Rocker's sympathetic tone. "You'd be a lot more in debt if the bank hadn't financed Justin's buildings," Rocker had said. "I put up the money for them and held a mortgage for security. When Justin went broke, I took them back and marked the slate clean. That doesn't bother me. Someday I'll sell them, get new businesses in them, and that'll be good for Rampart. That's what a bank can do that Naylor didn't do—help a town grow."

The image of Herbert Naylor as portrayed by Lloyd Rocker was still in his mind, and Wyatt hoped to get a different perspective from Newt Hardy. Newt had spent a month at the Lazy L, and Wyatt wanted to know if he had heard any hint that would explain Naylor's grudge against Justin and the Keyhole.

It was hard to talk from a rocking saddle, and Wyatt waited for a quieter time to ask Newt about his experiences at the Lazy L. An hour out of Rampart, they drew rein in a cedar grove and stepped down to stretch their legs. The sun was low in the western sky, but its fire was not yet gone and the air was hot and still. Newt took off his hat and fanned his face. He rolled the hatbrim with his fingers and gazed across the grasslands that rolled away from them toward the hills in undulating swales.

Newt was in a sentimental mood and his bass voice was soft and thoughtful. "Your pa was like family to me, and I'm glad you asked me back. I never wanted to leave the Keyhole to begin with."

"I want you to help me hold onto it," Wyatt said.

"I thought you had some notions about how to do that.

Ain't that why I'm on my way to steal a branding iron?"

Wyatt nodded. "It's a start. I've got a notion I can get the Lazy L to help me raise some cash later on. Lloyd Rocker's going to sell us out if we don't knock a big hole in what we owe him. I figure Naylor's waiting for that to happen so he can get his hands on the Keyhole."

Newt rubbed a hand through his hair and put his hat on. "I don't think so. Before I drew my time at the Lazy L, I put that question to Ward Chesser straight out. That was before he accused Justin of rustling, but I had my suspicions about Naylor. Too many things went wrong after Naylor showed up in these parts. I told Chesser if Naylor was trying to push Justin out of the county he ought to do the up-and-up thing and make a cash offer for the Keyhole that was too good to turn down."

"That's plain, but Justin couldn't sell unless I agreed."

"Didn't matter," Newt said dryly. "Chesser told me I'd better watch who I was pointing fingers at, then grinned like he was smarter'n me. He said I couldn't read signs worth a damn, and that Naylor don't want to own the Keyhole or any other ranch."

"Maybe you should have had that talk with Herbert Naylor. Maybe Chesser doesn't know what Naylor's thinking."

Newt's chuckle was a scornful rattle. "Nobody except Ward Chesser talks to Naylor. He don't have no truck with the cowhands. Chesser handles the complaints and gives all the orders. The only time I was close to Naylor was when I'd be around the corral when he came out to get his horse. Most days he'd mount up about dusk and ride off toward the badlands. He don't carry a handgun, but I noticed he carried a Winchester in his saddle boot. Maybe he—"

"You've never met the man?" Wyatt asked incredulously.

"Never did. Ward Chesser hired me and let me know I wasn't to bother Naylor about anything. Chesser's hard to read. He likes to brag about Naylor's money like it's his own. Naylor got rich from a big wagon factory he owns in Missouri. It's been in the family for years. According to Chesser, Naylor's outfit built about every prairie schooner that ever shoved off from Saint Jo for the Oregon Trail or the California gold diggings."

Wyatt remembered Ward Chesser's swaggering manner. The foreman's ego and confidence had been bolstered by the trust and authority bestowed upon him by Herbert Naylor. Newt's impressions of Chesser made Wyatt want to learn more about the man.

"Is Chesser related to Naylor or his wife in some way?"

Laughing again, Newt said, "We'd sure as hell have heard about it if they was. Chesser couldn't claim kin, but he let the crew know that his folks and the Naylors are old friends. My guess is that Chesser was the black sheep of the family. He hinted that he had a falling-out with his folks and headed west on a wagon train when he was a kid. He's been in Texas a long time, but I reckon Naylor knew where to find him. I think Chesser has been running with a bad crowd along the way. He talks about learning good lessons from long-loopers and fast gunmen."

Wyatt started toward his horse, his head down. "We're up against a strange pair. I don't care about Chesser. I want to take Naylor down a peg."

"You'd better care about Chesser," Newt warned. "He runs the show for Naylor. If you meet him, you'd better watch your back."

"Now you tell me." Wyatt grinned, somewhat embarrassed. "We've met and I wasn't smart enough to watch my rear."

He told Newt Hardy about his fight with the Lazy L man at the cabin on Castle Creek, choosing his words carefully in explaining Laura Custer's part in it. Despite his own suspicions, he did not want Newt Hardy to harbor any doubts about the girl's reputation.

Grinning, Newt said, "I'm glad you gave Ward Chesser a good thrashing. I wish I could have the pleasure myself."

"That was personal," said Wyatt. "It didn't do anything to help the Keyhole. I can't make heads nor tails of what's going on around me. Lester Mace tells me Evan Halsey was bushwhacked, and now he thinks Doc's ghost might be hounding the Keyhole. You tell me Naylor don't want the Keyhole graze, but he's been a thorn in Justin's side for months. Maggie Gregg gets mysteriously rich, and today she starts talking in circles about Bertetta Halsey and Pa's death. I keep trying to make something out of all these separate happenings, but I can't."

Newt Hardy rubbed his fingertips across his eyes and spat into the grass. "You can get hornets in your head trying to make something out of nothing. If you poke at a fire you get sparks. That starts another fire that'll burn the rubbish away so you can see the lay of the land. You'll get sparks when we set up a way to get Justin out of jail. Let's do that and see what happens."

FIFTEEN

At the toe of the ridge that sheltered one side of Castle Creek Basin, Wyatt and Newt Hardy parted company. To bring Newt closer to his destination, they had chosen a route that brought them into the broad valley where most of the Keyhole cattle grazed, rather than the shorter trail that crossed the hills west of the ranch.

"I won't be long," Newt said as he turned his horse toward the Lazy L Ranch. "You tell Caleb Frye to save me some supper."

"I'll tell him. He'll be glad you're back."

By the time Wyatt reached the Keyhole ranch yard the sun was gone, leaving in its wake a finger of scarlet along the western horizon as twilight's lavender hues tinted the buildings and the land around them. It was almost dusk, an hour past suppertime, but the air was heavy with the odors of fried potatoes and steaming meat.

Caleb had seen him coming and was waiting in the doorway of the cookshack when Wyatt dropped the buckskin's reins and dismounted. The cook's stooped shoulders seemed to sag lower as he looked across the yard for another rider and saw none. "Newt turned the job down, huh?"

Wyatt sank to a seat on the bench beside the doorway.

184

"He'll be along directly. He needed to run an errand, but he'll be here."

"That's good." Caleb peered closely at Wyatt, running his eyes over the round-jawed face and the weariness in the china-blue eyes. "You look beat. You're going to wear out your horse going back and forth to town."

"Looks like it," Wyatt said. He glanced across the yard at the log-walled ranch house, thinking of the loneliness and sadness he had felt when his mother left, and how empty the place had seemed when his father's voice and carefree laughter could no longer be heard within its walls. The red sky was reflected in the windows of the ranch house and smoke curled from the stone chimney, flavoring the air with the smell of charred wood.

He felt Caleb's eyes on him, and looked up. "Have you got something on your mind?"

"Not a'tall," Caleb said. "I was wondering if you want to eat now or wait on Newt?"

Rising, Wyatt stretched his arms and shook his head. "I'd like the company, but Newt won't be here for two or three hours. He'd like to talk with the crew, but they'll probably be in bed."

"Seeing as how they turn out at five in the morning, they don't like to stay up much past nine." Caleb said. "They'll be up longer tonight. They're all keyed up. Ever since you talked to them, they've been walking around like men waiting for a gun to go off. They think something's about to happen and they can't wait to see what it is. I told them you was meeting Newt in town. That made them feel sure there was something afoot.

They're going to be disappointed if they don't get some word tonight from you or Newt."

"Sometimes you talk too much, Caleb." Wyatt smiled to soften the criticism. "I'm not going to talk with the crew, but maybe Newt will get here in time to give his own orders. He knows what I want done. I'll eat and go on to Castle Creek."

Looking relieved, Caleb led the way into the cook-shack. Wyatt paused and looked back at the smoke rising from the ranch-house chimney. "I reckon you didn't have any help today."

"Sure did," Caleb said. "I only beat you home a couple of hours, and Miss Wilma had most of the cooking done. She stayed around until the men were fed, then went home to fix something for herself. She's real blue tonight. I brought her a message from Justin and she started crying. She misses him real bad. She's afraid Herbert Naylor has enough power to get Justin hung."

"She's wrong," Wyatt said. "Nobody has any power over Lester Mace except Lester Mace. I'm not going to let Justin hang."

While Caleb filled a plate with food, Wyatt rinsed his hands and face at the tin pan that the cook kept on a washstand in a corner of the room. Caleb followed him to the table with a coffeepot in his hands. He filled a heavy mug, set it beside Wyatt's plate, and returned to the stove. In the past few years Wyatt had grown accustomed to spending much of his time alone, and he welcomed the peaceful atmosphere while he ate.

There was stillness around the ranch, but not complete

silence. Far off a crow cawed a farewell to the dying day, and Wyatt heard the mournful notes of a harmonica coming from the bunkhouse thirty feet beyond the cookshack. It was a familiar sound, one he had heard often before he went away, and he knew the musician was Bill Bartlett.

Wyatt finished his meal, complimented Caleb on his cooking, and went outside to get his horse. Caleb followed, watching silently as Wyatt climbed into the buckskin's saddle.

"If there's any special chore you want done, let me know," Caleb said. "I want to help with whatever it is you're doing."

"I'm glad you brought it up." Wyatt's eyes narrowed thoughtfully. "I might need you to fetch the sheriff out here."

"The sheriff? Do we need the sheriff?"

"Yeah," Wyatt said. "I've been checking our stock on my trips back and forth. I think somebody's stealing Keyhole cattle. Newt and I are going to check it out tomorrow."

Caleb frowned and rubbed his chin. "I don't know how you'd pick up that kind of sign so easy, but if you want the sheriff I'll get him. I'll head for town at first light."

"Not tomorrow," Wyatt said. "We need time to find the proof. It'll probably be the day after tomorrow. I'll let you know."

"Good enough. I'm glad I'm going instead of you. It ain't a good idea for you to spend too much time in Rampart."

187

"Why's that?"

Caleb avoided Wyatt's eyes and spoke rapidly in the manner of a man who thought his opinion would touch a raw nerve. "You're too famous. I'm afraid somebody's going to run into you and get a hankering to test you. It might be a gunman who's faster than you. If anything happens to you, the Keyhole will go under. Me and the others will be out of a job, and I'm too old to go looking."

"Don't worry about it." Wyatt lifted the buckskin's reins and prepared to leave. "Justin's the one who's in trouble. Let's worry about him."

He rode away from the ranch yard without speaking to anyone else, but Caleb's words stayed with him. Wyatt tried not to think about the reputation he had earned as a gunfighter, but others were constantly reminding him of the dangers attached to it.

It was not a concern that would keep him awake on this night, however. He was too tired to worry about anything and he looked forward to a long night's sleep.

The rifle shot broke the stillness along Castle Creek just as Wyatt came within sight of his cabin. The crackling explosion echoed through the hills and he heard the whine of a bullet cutting through the night air.

His reflexes propelled him from the saddle. He landed on his feet, then dived to the ground. He rolled away from his horse, looking for a place to hide in the shadows cast by the sliver of early-rising moon that was peeking over the rocky ledge east of Castle Creek. A second shot followed close behind the other, and Wyatt was still exposed. The trees along the creek were too far away, and the closest cover was a clump of hackberry fifty yards away. Wyatt's muscles strained to shrink him into a smaller target. He lay still, deciding it was safer to stay where he was than to stand up and run across the open land.

He propped himself up on his elbows and became aware that his Peacemaker was gripped in his hand. He had drawn the gun instinctively as he leaped from the buckskin's saddle. He stayed on the ground for five minutes, his eyes searching the skyline for the flash of a gun, his ears straining for any sound that would locate the sniper. Silence returned to the basin. Wyatt could again hear the rippling of water running over rocks in the creekbed and a bullfrog croaking on one of the banks.

He stood up, holstered his gun, and walked back to his horse. The striped moleskins that he had thought suitable for a Sunday visit to Rampart were covered with briars and dust, and he was sorry he had worn them. He slapped at his thighs to get rid of some of the dirt and took a final look around the area.

The gunshots had followed the pattern Wyatt had been told about. They came from far away and had been aimed high over his head. They were not meant to kill, but to annoy and frighten those who rode the Keyhole range. A search for the sniper would be useless, and Wyatt did not waste his time trying.

Wyatt recalled what Newt Hardy had told him about Herbert Naylor. The Lazy L owner rode away from his ranch often in the early evening with a rifle in his saddle boot. Newt's appraisal of Naylor would indicate that he was not a man who would do his own dirty work. He would assign those duties to a hired hand such as Ward Chesser. It was possible, however, that shooting at unsuspecting riders from the cover of darkness gave Naylor a sense of power that he enjoyed.

Anger replaced Wyatt's fear, and he rode home with less concern for danger. He despised bushwhackers and felt the same about snipers who left a man wondering if he was going to be killed or simply harassed. He was comforted by the knowledge that he and Newt Hardy were ready to strike a blow against the Lazy L. He looked forward to tomorrow, and thoughts of what lay ahead eased his mind as he stretched out on his bed. Fatigue was his ally, and for the first time in weeks he slept through the night without awakening.

Sheriff Lester Mace sat his horse on the brink of a twisting arroyo and gazed down at the five cows and five calves that were strung out along about fifty feet of its length. He was flanked on the left by Newt Hardy and on the right by Wyatt Kirk. They were only a few hundred feet east of Castle Creek, but the arroyo was on Lazy L land.

"So you sent a man lookin' for strays and this is what he found," Mace said. "You're a clever man, Wyatt. Caleb Frye told me you were goin' over for a show-down with Naylor and that you'd promised to take me with you. You knew I'd come runnin'."

"I've got good reason to talk with Naylor, and you've got a good reason to go with me," Wyatt replied. "You'll have to get closer if you want to inspect the brands."

The sheriff rose in his stirrups, squinting his steel-gray eyes. "That first cow there's wearing a Keyhole brand. Her calf looks like it's got a letter on its hide that's layin' on its back. I'm sure it's a Lazy L, and I'm sure you put it there."

Wyatt met the sheriff's cynical stare with an expression of wide-eyed innocence. "You're not a mind reader, Lester. You've got to go by evidence. I want you to be convinced beyond a shadow of a doubt. Come on."

They rode down the slanted walls of the wash together, their horses' hoofs sliding and sending small stones rolling ahead of them. The cows skittered away as the riders came close, swinging their horns to protect their offspring. Newt Hardy's hulking body was enough to intimidate even a longhorn. Sitting tall in the saddle of his stallion, he grabbed the rope from his saddle horn and fashioned a loop. He swung the rope in front of the cows to hold them back while Wyatt and Mace looked at the calves.

After fifteen minutes Lester Mace had seen enough. He circled a finger over his head and pointed upward as a signal that he was leaving the arroyo. He took his horse up the eroded slope, rode on for twenty yards to escape the noise of bawling calves and thrashing feet, and waited for Wyatt and Newt to join him.

"I don't like bein' caught in this kind of snarl," the sheriff grumped. "Ain't been long since Ward Chesser brought me out here to look at some Lazy L cows that had calves wearin' Keyhole brands. Now you're showin' me Keyhole cows with calves wearin' Lazy L brands. I should have guessed you'd do somethin' like this. You're makin' me look like a fool, Wyatt."

Wyatt locked his hands on his saddle horn and looked straight ahead. "I don't like to throw off on old friends, but you made yourself out a fool when you arrested Justin. My evidence is just as good as Herbert Naylor's."

"So it appears. What do you want me to do?"

Wyatt looked at the sheriff with a cold smile. "I want to swear out a warrant against Herbert Naylor for rustling."

"Figured you would. I didn't come out here with a handful of blank warrants in my saddlebags. You'll have to go into town with me to do the paperwork."

Wyatt's plans had been formulated days ago—long before he and Newt Hardy worked throughout the afternoon rounding up their own cows and branding them with the Lazy L iron Newt had sneaked away from Naylor's ranch. He had reviewed them several times while he waited beside Castle Creek for Newt to take the branding iron back to Naylor's spread under the cover of darkness and return to tell him the mission had been accomplished without incident.

He knew how he wanted this day to end, but he pretended to consider the delay that would be incurred by Lester Mace's dedication to legal proceedings. He glanced at the mid-afternoon sun that was baking the back of his neck, and appeared to be pondering a problem.

He said, "Maybe we ought to see how Naylor's going to take this first. When you tell him the evidence you've

192

got against him, he might want to give himself up and call in a lawyer. We could do the paperwork then."

"I see," Mace said without looking up.

Wyatt kept talking. "If Naylor can point to one of his men who was trying to steal my calves, you can arrest the cowhand. Otherwise you'll have to hold Naylor responsible. The calves were on his land. That makes him as much of a rustler as Justin, and you can tell him that."

A half grin pulled at the corners of Mace's mouth. "I knew you'd want to be fair. I know exactly what you've got in mind. I hope it works out for you."

"Naylor might want to bring one of his branding irons out here to see if it matches the brands," Wyatt said.

Cocking his head as though the comment was without merit, Mace said, "I doubt it. You're a careful man. I'd bet my saddle it would match. Naylor's smart enough to know when he's been whipsawed and he won't get into that. Let's go see if he wants to be arrested peaceful-like or wait for me to serve papers on him."

"I can't wait to see Naylor's face." There was no smile on Wyatt's face and no gloating in his voice. He sounded nervous. "I want to see what kind of man we're dealing with."

They wheeled their horses together, facing them in the direction of the Lazy L Ranch. The lawman hesitated and looked back at Newt Hardy, who sat with his lips clamped tight and appeared disinterested in their plans.

"You goin', too?" Mace asked.

"I'd give a day's pay to be there, but I ain't got time

for pleasures. Wyatt got up with his working britches on yesterday morning, and we ain't had time to breathe since. He wants us to round up four hundred head to sell as soon as we can. He's asking a three-man crew to do what five ought to be doing. I'll be chasing cows while you're gone."

Newt rode away abruptly with Mace still staring at his back. There was no way to read the thoughts behind the solemn look in the sheriff's eyes, but Wyatt knew him well enough to know that Mace found Newt's excuse hard to believe.

He nudged his horse into a canter and Wyatt's buckskin matched its stride. They rode in silence for more than a mile before the lawman said, "From what I've heard, I had the notion Keyhole cattle was in short supply. I didn't figure you'd be sellin' off more stock."

"Things are better than I thought." Wyatt said, keeping his eyes straight ahead. "Lloyd Rocker's pushing me for money. I have to do something. I sent a telegraph to a broker in Caprock Junction while I was in town Saturday. I'm offering him a herd at fifteen dollars a head and that ought to get his attention. If I can pay the bank six thousand dollars, Lloyd Rocker might give me some time on the balance. It's going to be hard to build the Keyhole back to what it used to be."

"Uh-huh." Mace grunted. "That's givin' cattle away—ten dollars below market price. I reckon you're makin' sure Naylor won't undercut you this time. I wouldn't count that money just yet. Naylor acts like a man who's tryin' hard to get rid of all his money. It wouldn't surprise me if he undercuts you again like he did with Justin."

"Maybe I'll stick with him," Wyatt said. "We'll see."

Swearing under his breath, Lester Mace kicked his horse into a gallop. Before Wyatt could react, the sheriff was twenty yards ahead of him. Spurring the buckskin to catch up, Wyatt pulled alongside and shouted, "What the hell happened?"

"Nothing happened. I just want to get to Naylor's place and get this over with. The more I talk to you, the more I get the feelin' that I'm goin' to be sorry you ever came back to Rampart."

"Naylor's the one who's going to be sorry," Wyatt yelled above the clatter of the horses, and they did not speak again until they came within sight of the Lazy L headquarters.

SIXTEEN

During his younger days, Wyatt had accompanied his father on occasional visits to the Lazy L, and he expected the surroundings to be familiar. Much of the place was as he remembered it—the arch-roofed barn at the edge of an open field, the scattering of corrals and outbuildings, and the row of tall pines that formed a windbreak along the western edge of the ranch yard.

The house had changed, however. Under Matt Latham's ownership, the Lazy L had prospered and grown, but his lifestyle continued to be much as it had been when he bought his first section of grazing land. He lived comfortably, but he and his wife had been content with their modest house of hewn logs with its distinctive stone chimneys rising above each end of the gabled roof.

Part of the original building was still visible, but its appearance was remarkably different. A square-topped portico, supported by sandstone columns and trimmed at the top with gingerbread woodwork, provided a new entrance. A wing of rooms had been added to form an "L" and double the size of the house.

"Money shows, don't it?" Lester Mace murmured as he and Wyatt drew rein beside one of the corrals. "This is the first time I've been out here since Matt Latham left."

"Big business, I reckon," Wyatt said. "Naylor's probably trying to run his wagon factory from Texas, and he needed office space for himself and Ward Chesser. I don't care about his money. I want to put him in jail for rustling."

The sheriff settled his steely eyes on Wyatt's face. "You let me do the talkin' when we get to the house. We'll run into Ward Chesser first, and I understand he's somethin' of a hothead. I don't want you startin' anything with him."

Wyatt smiled, but it was without amusement. He said, "It's already started. I had a fight with Chesser the day I got home. He might want to keep it going. He said something about knowing people who could take care of me if he couldn't."

"What? I'll be damned if you don't worry me more every—"

"It was a personal matter," Wyatt interrupted. "Laurie

196

Custer's been staying at my cabin on weekends, and I found Chesser hanging around there. We had words over Laurie."

"I don't want to hear about it," Mace said sharply, and started slow-walking his horse toward the house.

The portico extended out from the house far enough to cover the driveway and hitching rail in front of the porch. Wyatt and Lester Mace dismounted in the shade of the overhang. Their feet had barely touched the ground when the door swung open and Ward Chesser stepped outside. Like a sentry on guard duty, he spread his legs, folded his arms across his chest, and looked at the visitors with displeasure.

"What can I do for you?" he asked bluntly.

Wyatt was in the process of tethering his horse to the wooden bar, and he waited for Lester Mace to respond. The sheriff took his time, looping the reins of his chestnut around the hitching rail with studied care. He turned slowly to face Chesser and said, "I've got business with Naylor. Ask him to come out a minute."

Chesser unfolded his arms and set his hands on his hips. The marks of his fight with Wyatt were still visible on his face. A crusted scab showed where Wyatt's fist had smashed his mouth, and there was a lumpy splotch of discolored skin below his left eye.

"I handle all of Mr. Naylor's business. You can tell me what's on your mind."

Lester Mace was not a patient man, and sometimes he had to work at it. He set one scuffed boot half a step in front of the other and slouched so that his weight was on his back leg. He ran his eyes over Ward Chesser's compact form, starting at his tooled boots, moving over the fawn-colored wool pants, lingering a second on the oak-handled Colt in its polished holster, and finally settling deliberately on the man's face.

"You can't handle this," Mace said. "I came to see Naylor."

Defiance sparkled in Chesser's eyes. He moved his hands again, hooking the thumb of his right hand in the waistband of his pants with his fingers extended above his gun butt. "Mr. Naylor's a busy man. He pays me to keep people from bothering him. You'll have to talk with me or go on your way."

His stance still half-slouched, Mace spoke in a drawl so slow it sounded like a man rousing from deep slumber. He said, "If you're partial to keepin' all your parts, mister, you'll get your fingers away from that six-gun or I'll shoot 'em off. I'm the law and I don't deal with handymen. Either you get Naylor out here in the next minute or I'm goin' in and get him myself."

Chesser slid his hand slowly away from his hip and fiddled with his belt buckle. The sheriff was treating him like a messenger boy, and the sullen expression on Chesser's face was a sign of frustration. He was offended, but he was not foolish enough to pull a gun on a man with a badge. He tried to preserve a measure of authority by changing the subject.

He tilted his head in Wyatt's direction and asked, "What's he doing here?"

Mace ignored the question. He took a threatening step toward the porch and said, "I'm through talking to you, mister."

"Let it go, Ward! I'll handle it."

Wyatt saw a shadowy form move in the gloom beyond the doorway a second before the calm, crisp voice sounded inside the house. He found himself holding his breath expectantly as he waited for the man to show himself, and presently he got his first look at Herbert Naylor.

He stepped onto the porch and moved Ward Chesser aside with a wave of his arm. He was a man in his sixties, but his strength showed in the spring of his step and the erect posture of his six-foot frame. His face was angular, with prominent cheekbones, a long jaw, and a wide mouth with a lower lip that protruded like the spout of a coffeepot. His eyes were dark brown, almost black, and there was a look of sadness in them. He wore jodhpur-style riding breeches that bloused away from his thighs like khaki-colored wings, tapering close from his knees to his ankles to fit into polished black leggings. His black plainsman's hat, with a wide flat brim, was set squarely on his head, and the hair that showed around its edges was close-cropped and iron gray.

A brown leather belt circled Herbert Naylor's waist, but he did not wear a gunbelt. He carried a hickory-handled riding crop in his right hand and he tapped it lightly against his palm while he waited for Lester Mace to speak.

"Looks like there's been some more cattle rustlin' goin' on out this way," Mace began tentatively. "Couple hours ago I saw five calves whose brands don't match what their mothers are wearin'. They were on your land."

Herbert Naylor cast a quick glance at Ward Chesser. He arched his gray eyebrows and slapped the riding crop against his leg.

"You've found another group of my calves with a Keyhole brand on them? Is that it, Sheriff?"

Mace shook his head. "Not this time. I saw Keyhole cows with calves that had been branded with a Lazy L."

He described the location of the arroyo he had visited, assured Naylor that he had inspected the site carefully, and invited the rancher to go see the calves for himself.

"That won't be necessary." Naylor spoke without animation. He faced Mace with a vacant stare, as though his thoughts were miles away. "If you say you saw the calves, I'm sure they're there. I'll take care of it. I'll have my men bar the brands and drive the cows back to Keyhole range. They can be rebranded."

Barred brands were often agreed upon between honest men. A slash was burned across the original mark when roundup mistakes were made or ranchers traded breed stock among themselves. Lester Mace had never heard of a rustler making such an offer, but he knew Wyatt had planned too carefully to accept the proposal.

"It ain't that simple," Mace said. "That's what Justin Kirk suggested when Ward Chesser found them calves on Castle Creek. You turned him down."

He nodded in Wyatt's direction and said, "This feller with me is Justin's brother. You bein' the owner of this spread, he's chargin' you with rustlin'. I'll have to take you in if you're willin' for the three of us to go together and let Wyatt sign the papers when we get to town. If you don't agree, I'll have to ride to Rampart, get a warrant, and come back for you. I'll be in a mighty testy mood if you put me to all that trouble."

Wyatt had remained with his horse, standing at the buckskin's head with his rear braced against the hitching rail. He had seen Naylor cut a quick glance at him when he came outside. Naylor had ignored him afterward, but now the red-faced rancher looked squarely into his eyes.

"I've heard about you," he said. "You're the man who beat up my manager. Ward says you jumped him from behind."

His china-blue eyes darkened as they met Naylor's accusing stare. Wyatt held his temper and said calmly, "Ward's a liar."

From the edge of his vision he saw Ward Chesser's hand move toward his gun again, then drop to his side.

The pouches under Herbert Naylor's eyes seemed to grow larger, but his sad-faced expression did not change. "I also hear you're a roving gunfighter. I presume you've come home to protect your older brother. There's one thing about hired killers—anybody can buy one in this part of the country if you've got the money."

Wyatt meant to shrug the man's comments aside, but Lester Mace came to his defense. "I've known Wyatt since he was a pup, and he's not much for goin' against the law. He's been workin' as a bounty hunter, which some call honorable and some call killin' for pay. I lean toward the honorable side. That's got nothin' to do with our business here. If you want to pack some clothes—"

"I don't intend to go to jail, Sheriff!" Naylor said

firmly. "None of my men branded those calves and I think you know it. Wyatt Kirk or some of his crew put those brands on his own calves to set me up. You're not talking to a slick-faced greenhorn. I've had dealings with lawyers, sheriffs, and judges all my life. I assume you know that falsifying evidence is a crime."

Lester Mace poked a finger against his hatbrim and raised it higher on his forehead. He glared at Naylor's shiny black leggings and flaring pants with a look of disgust.

"There's been a lot of falsifyin' goin' on around here lately, and it ain't up to me to sort it out," Mace said flatly. "I'm leavin' that for the judge to settle. You can tell him how smart you are about the law. I'll walk you over to the barn to get a horse, or a carriage, or whatever suits your pleasure, but you're goin' to jail unless you can change Wyatt's mind about pressin' charges."

A nod of his head, a curl of the drooping lower lip, and another impatient slap of the riding crop were the first signs that Naylor finally understood Wyatt's motive in coming here. He said, "When I heard this bounty hunter had come home, I guessed he'd have more spunk than his brother, and I was right. I suppose if I drop my charges against Justin he'll drop his."

The sheriff looked at Wyatt, then at Naylor, as if such a thought had not occurred to him. "We didn't discuss it, but maybe that'll work. It's up to Wyatt."

"Suits me," Wyatt said.

"Sure it does." Naylor's sneering tone was the only emotion he had shown since the visitors arrived. "Consider it done."

Mace nodded. "I'll tear up your warrant and send Justin home. I hope this is the end of this feud."

"There is no feud." Naylor stood erect, his face solemn and sad, but there was fury in the dark eyes. "I don't like to be bested in a business deal. You'll hear from me again, Wyatt Kirk."

Mace had already started toward his horse, but he turned in midstride and gave Naylor a warning look. "This ain't business, mister. You're foolin' with a man's life."

"That's what I meant to do, but it's business with me. It's serious business."

Naylor started to say more, but he threw a quick look over his shoulder as a woman appeared behind him and took hold of his arm. She was dressed in a black dress that fell to her ankles, and there was a dark shawl across her head. Her face was pale, delicately formed with full pink lips and long-lashed brown eyes. She was not as old as Herbert Naylor, but the silken hair that curled beneath the folds of her shawl was snow-white. Her smooth skin and striking eyes reminded Wyatt of a younger woman, and for a moment he thought he had seen her somewhere before.

"What is it, Bert?" she asked excitedly. "What are these men doing here? Tell them to go away, tell them—"

"It's nothing to worry about," Naylor said. He slipped one arm around her shoulders and looked into her face. "They're just riding through, and stopped to pass the time. Go back inside, Etta. I'll be there in a minute."

She gave her husband a wan smile and turned back

toward the doorway. "Thank God, it's just drifters. I heard you talking to someone, and I was afraid you'd found out something else that terrible man Burdine Fisher did on Ward's orders. My conscience has hurt ever since we found out—"

"It's nothing like that, Etta. Go on now."

Fifteen feet away, Wyatt Kirk had one foot in the stirrup and was ready to step into the buckskin's saddle. His foot fell back to the ground. His breath hung in his throat, and he looked at Herbert Naylor with a stunned expression squeezing the pupils of his eyes to pinpoints.

Bert and Etta!

The words came together in his mind and formed another name—Bertetta!

Until a moment ago he had never seen Naylor's wife, and he had no reason to be reminded that Bert was a common nickname for men named Herbert. Proud parents had been known to combine their own names to invent one for their offspring, and Bertetta Halsey's name was too unusual to have come from any other source. Words spoken two days earlier by Newt Hardy came back to him. Sometimes a single word or a single action, Newt had said, could spark a man's thoughts and present an answer to a baffling puzzle.

Shrugging aside Mace's frown of caution as he passed by him, Wyatt strode to the porch and called Naylor's name. Ward Chesser had gone into the house and Naylor was a step behind him.

Swallowing to keep his voice calm, Wyatt said, "Even if we're not on friendly terms I can't leave without being decent enough to inquire about your daughter.

How's she getting along?"

Naylor's face paled. "My daughter—what daughter?"

"Bertetta Halsey—the doctor's wife. I was acquainted with her, and I was wondering why she didn't come here with you."

It was a shot in the dark, a conclusion hastily drawn, but Wyatt saw that it was working. Herbert Naylor's hands twitched and his stare became so fixed Wyatt thought the man had gone into a trance. He glanced at the doorway, started to move toward it, then stepped off the porch. His feet stomped the ground fiercely and he did not stop until the hard brim of his plainsman's hat was six inches from the brim of Wyatt's Stetson.

"So she told you my name." The riding crop made a swishing sound as Naylor swung it back and forth at his side. "My family is not a subject for public discussion, and I'll thank you to mind your own business."

Naylor turned his back and Wyatt thought he had heard all the man was going to say. Naylor threw his riding crop to the ground. His arms were stretched stiffly along the seams of his pants and his fists were clenched. His body shook with fury and he whirled to face Wyatt again.

He spoke through clenched teeth. "I ought to set my men on you and have them horsewhip you, but I won't. Since you're the blood kin of the man who put her where she is, I'll tell you about Bertetta. She's in a rest home in Saint Joseph. She sits in a rocking chair all day and stares out the window, except when she gets up to look at herself in a mirror."

Naylor was talking so fast he had to stop and catch his

breath. He shuddered and said, "Bertetta's face has scars that run from her cheek on each side to the tip of her ear. That sorry son of a bitch Evan Halsey did that to her. She looks at herself and cries, but that's the only sound anybody ever hears from her. She hasn't spoken a word in nearly three years, not even to me and her mother. Bertetta is a living dead woman. You asked and I'm telling you. That's how Bertetta is doing, and it's your father's fault."

Wyatt grimaced despite his effort to appear unmoved. His thoughts tracked back to the day Hap Gilley had brought the news of Aaron Kirk's death. Hap had spoken of a trail of blood leading down the rear steps to the alley behind the Sunset Hotel. Dr. Evan Halsey had used his scalpel first to slash at his wife's face, then killed her lover after she escaped.

"My pa didn't hurt your daughter," Wyatt said defensively. "Doc Halsey did that."

Sadness and grief had been Herbert Naylor's companions for a long time, and his misery continued to spill from his lips in a torrent of words as he breathed his hot breath in Wyatt's face. "Bertetta would be herself if Aaron Kirk had left her alone. Women like Bertetta are hungry for love. She didn't get any attention from her stiff-necked husband, and your father filled her head full of sweet talk and romantic dreams. He took advantage of her. When Evan caught them together he cut her up. She was so beautiful and now she thinks she's ugly. It's not as bad as she thinks, but she's ashamed to be seen and she's shut out the world. I miss her. Etta goes back to see her, but I can't stand it anymore."

Wyatt wondered how Naylor was so familiar with the details of events that had occurred long ago if Bertetta Halsey had cloaked her life in silence. Naylor soon answered that question, and many more that had been debated in Rampart since the townspeople awoke one morning to learn of the bloody killing at the Sunset Hotel.

Bertetta Halsey had not been mute when she first arrived at her parents' home in Missouri. She told them about her affair with Aaron Kirk and how Evan Halsey had surprised them in the middle of the night. They were asleep, but Bertetta had been awakened by excruciating pain when her husband's scalpel scraped across her face. Instinctively, she leaped from the bed and ran for her life, wrapping her nude body in a sheet that she took with her.

Bleeding and hysterical, she sought the nearest refuge, Naylor related. "She knew a cleaning woman who had a house across the alley from the rear of the hotel—a woman named Maggie Gregg. The woman took her in and kept her hidden until Evan was gone. They saw him run into the alley, look around, then hurry toward his office. He had killed Aaron Kirk, and had to get away before the commotion started. He had to give up looking for Bertetta. He would have killed her, too, if he'd had the time."

With Bertetta advising her, Maggie managed a superficial treatment for the woman's wounds. Fearing for her life, Bertetta's overriding thought was to get out of town and away from her enraged husband. She knew it was too risky to spend another night in Rampart.

Maggie hitched up her carriage and drove to the town of Spurlock, arriving in time for Bertetta Halsey to board the midnight stage.

Along the way, they had made a hurried stop at the Halsey home on the edge of town. Bertetta located a medical bag and covered her facial cuts with an ointment to stop the bleeding. She packed a few clothes in a valise and took a bundle of banknotes from a cabinet in the parlor. For the stage ride, she covered her head and most of her face with a shawl to conceal her wounds.

Herbert Naylor's voice grew more frenzied as he told the story of Bertetta Halsey's torturous journey home. He paced back and forth in front of Wyatt, his lower lip quivering.

"Days on stagecoaches, days on trains, then stagecoaches again," Naylor said, and his voice had a sob in it. "She found a doctor in some town who stitched up her face and made it better. It was healing when she got home. She told us her story and went to bed. We couldn't get her up the next day, or the next. We called in a doctor who gave her stimulants and finally got her awake. She might as well have been dead. She never spoke a word or acknowledged our existence after that."

Naylor stopped pacing and dabbed at his eyes. "My beautiful little girl—my beautiful little girl—"

His words waned and he stared silently at the ground.

Wyatt cleared his throat. "It's been bad for all of us. Bertetta is sick and my pa's dead. Maybe fate has a way of making things even. Doc Halsey's dead, too."

Naylor's head lifted and he laughed. It was a quiet,

rattling laugh full of venom. "I know," he whispered. "I've learned the ways of Texas. If you hire the right people, they'll ride a horse into the ground to find out what you want to know or do what you want done. You'll learn things about me. I use my money to reward those who do me favors and to punish those who do me wrong."

Wyatt's eyes narrowed. Naylor's face had a strange look, and his chuckling was unnerving. The man had lost his composure and Wyatt wanted to get away from him.

"You ought to go home and look after Bertetta," Wyatt suggested. "Texas is no place for you. You're not a rancher."

"Look after my daughter, you say? What can I do? My wife was losing her mind, and I had to get her away for a while. I thought about it, and then it hit me. I needed to get away from Saint Joseph. I needed to get close to Aaron Kirk's kin. I'll go back to Saint Jo, but not until I finish what I came for."

For a moment Wyatt had tried to comfort the man, but the Missourian had no interest in his views. He did not explain what he meant to finish before leaving Texas, but Wyatt understood the veiled threat. Naylor's hate sparkled in his eyes and Wyatt knew he was facing a vengeful enemy.

"You've been hounding the Keyhole since the day you got here," Wyatt said grimly. "You don't give a damn about the cattle business. You're here to punish me and Justin, to make us worry and fret and end up losing a ranch that's the only future we have. You can't blame us for what happened to your daughter. We had nothing to do with it."

Naylor's head jiggled up and down. His lips moved silently, as though he were reciting secret vows to himself. "I hurt inside. It's not right for me and Etta to bear this suffering alone. The Bible agrees with me. There's a verse in Exodus where God says the sins of fathers will be visited upon their children. Aaron Kirk's not around to pay for what he did, but his sons are. His sins are your sins now."

Wyatt backed away and fixed his eyes on Naylor's sweating face. He said, "I think you're loco, mister. Maybe you backed Justin into a corner, but I don't scare easy. I'm selling off a herd next week that'll cut our bank debt a bit, and I'll go on from there. The Keyhole will be around when you're dead."

Naylor's face froze again in its mask of sadness. "I can see you're tough enough to buck me. Maybe Justin would suffer more if he didn't have a brother. I can arrange that, you know."

SEVENTEEN

Both men knew there was no point in further conversation, but they parted slowly, each reluctant to appear outdone. Naylor was the first to move. He wheeled and went toward the house, beating his riding crop against his leggings as he went. Wyatt watched him until he disappeared inside, then walked to his horse.

Sheriff Lester Mace had waited aboard his horse, curious about the reason for the delay. He began asking questions as soon as Wyatt was within hearing range. "Let's get away from here and we'll talk," Wyatt said, reining the buckskin away from the hitching rail.

"I thought you won a big hand when you pushed Naylor into dropping his charge against Justin. There's more to it?"

"More than I bargained for, maybe." Wyatt replied. "I couldn't quite make up my mind that Naylor was behind all the Keyhole's troubles because I couldn't figure out any reason he'd want to hurt us. Now I know."

Wyatt was in too much of a hurry to put the Lazy L behind him to say more. Two miles from Naylor's headquarters, eyeing the sheriff's annoyed expression, Wyatt led the way to a clump of trees. Leaving the buckskin's reins trailing, he sat down on a fallen log, stretched his legs in front of him, and rolled a cigarette. He needed the smoke to calm his nerves. Lester Mace joined him, fidgeting while Wyatt puffed the cigarette alight.

"What went on back there?" Mace's harsh tone was a sign of worry. "I saw a heap of jawin' passin' between you and Naylor."

"I was struck by a name," Wyatt said, explaining how he had concluded that Bertetta Halsey was Herbert Naylor's daughter.

Mace slapped his knee. "That went right over my head. He's sure kept it to himself, knowin' Bertetta had friends here. It's interestin', but it don't have nothin' to do with what's been goin' on."

"It has everything to do with it. He blames Pa for what happened to Bertetta, but since he can't get to him, he wants to punish me and Justin as the next best thing."

Still awed by Naylor's frank admission of his motives, Wyatt's voice was a monotone as he related the man's description of his daughter's illness and his determination to avenge her plight. "Naylor moved to Rampart for one reason—to get at me and Justin. He doesn't want the Keyhole like I suspected, but he doesn't want us to have it either. He figures the best way to hurt Aaron Kirk's sons is to cause them to lose what their pa treasured most—the Keyhole Ranch."

Mace swore softly. "I've never run up against anything like this. Did he admit he's been poisonin' your cows, takin' potshots at you in the dark, and set out to frame Justin for rustlin'?"

"Not in so many words. He's too clever for that, but it's his doing. He quoted the scriptures for me, a verse about the sins of fathers being visited upon the sons. He's here to visit hell on us, and I've got a hunch it's going to get worse."

"Uh-huh," the sheriff grunted. "Every time I've met a man who finds something in the Bible to excuse his meanness, I've found a man who won't listen to reason."

Wyatt remembered the quivering of Herbert Naylor's lips and the zealous light in his eyes. He said, "The sight of me, or something I said, turned him wild and he spilled his guts. He knows Doc Halsey was killed. He might have had a hand in it. His wife said something strange—something about Ward Chesser giving orders to a man named Burdine Fisher. She was upset about it. Have you ever heard of Burdine Fisher?"

"Not that I recall, but I'll try to check on him." The sheriff stood and hitched at his gunbelt. "I've done all I can do here. I need to be gettin' back. I'm bein' pushed out of this squabble. There's no open sign that Naylor's breakin' the law and that ties my hands. He admitted things to you, but if I asked him he'd say you lied. I hate to say it, but I'm afraid you and Naylor are goin' to have to settle your quarrels between yourselves."

Wyatt rose and crushed his cigarette out beneath his foot. "I figured that from the start. I'm going to beat Naylor at his own game. If I do that enough, he'll give up and go home."

"You've got some kind of hole card to play that you're not goin' to tell me about," the sheriff mused. "That's all right. I don't care what you do with Naylor as long as you use your head instead of your gun. I don't want any killin'."

His head down, his palms sweating, Wyatt fell in step beside the sheriff as they went to their horses. "There'll be killing. Naylor's mad enough to kill me right now. He said Justin might suffer more if he didn't have a brother. That's killing talk. That set me to thinking he found him a hired gun to take care of Evan Halsey. He may bring in one to get me."

"Not likely." Mace scowled, and shook his head. "He's been playin' a different kind of game and he'll keep at it."

Wyatt was not sure the sheriff's assumption was right, but he did not dwell on the thought. He had drawn another conclusion from Naylor's frantic tirade as they stood face to face, and he shared it with Lester Mace.

"I think Maggie Gregg's secret money came from Naylor—a reward for helping Bertetta get out of town."

"Probably," Mace agreed. "It's the kind of thing a rich man would do. Maggie got around my questions by sayin' she didn't work the night Aaron was killed. She didn't tell me what went on at her house. She's the kind who'd risk her life to help a friend, but that don't matter anymore. Naylor's told it all, and I'm not goin' to bother Maggie about it again."

When they were back in their saddles, the sheriff asked if Wyatt planned to go to Rampart with him and ride back home with his brother. Wyatt declined. Justin's horse was at the livery, its board paid by the county. Justin valued his pride and dignity, and he would prefer to greet his family at home rather than in front of a jail cell.

"You two ain't very close, are you?" Mace drawled.

"We used to be. We will be again now that he's learned some lessons and I've learned to handle my temper a little better. I've got things to do here. I've got to get cattle rounded up for a sale. Newt Hardy and his crew need my help."

The sheriff gave Wyatt a long, searching look, but he could read nothing from the grim face. He kicked his horse into a lope, and they rode on toward the Keyhole boundary on Castle Creek. At the mouth of the basin, Lester Mace picked up the trail to Rampart and Wyatt went across the prairie to join his crew.

The roundup had begun at dawn the day before, progressing according to the plan Wyatt had outlined for Newt Hardy. The seasoned riders knew hard days lay ahead of them. Searching out half-wild steers from thousands of acres of rangeland and driving them a few at a time to a common holding ground required patience, skill, and stamina that tested a man's worth. The crew was assigned to work in pairs—Sam Hopson with Caleb Frye; Bill Bartlett with Len Tolbert, the cotton-haired greenhorn from Kansas; and Wyatt with Newt Hardy.

Wyatt had crossed the ridge from Castle Creek before daylight on Monday morning. He met the others on the rolling prairie that stretched south and westward until it butted up against the hills that surrounded much of the Keyhole range. He conferred briefly with Newt, then stood aside while the foreman issued assignments for each pair of riders. The holding ground was to be at Devil's Tank, a broad expanse of flatland where a geological phenomenon had unleashed the waters of underground springs eons ago to form a fifty-acre pond in a granite-walled crater.

As the riders fanned out to work in different sections, Wyatt and Newt had stayed behind to hunt for cattle along the banks of Castle Creek and eastward to the Lazy L boundary. Newt had followed Wyatt's instructions without question, but he was wise enough to guess the reason he had been sent to the Lazy L to steal a branding iron. Grinning, showing no surprise when Wyatt told him they were going to burn Naylor's brand on five calves with Keyhole mothers, Newt said, "This is one day's work I'm going to enjoy. I'm surprised Justin didn't do the same thing right off."

"Justin's too nice a man to fight dirt with dirt, but I'm

not," Wyatt said, laughing out loud for the first time in weeks.

By noon they had completed their task and driven the calves to the arroyo on Lazy L range. Afterward, he and Newt found four old steers, that they drove to Devil's Tank as evidence that they had been hard at work. They found Sam Hopson there, riding circles around about twenty head of cattle that the rest of the crew had hazed to the holding ground.

For almost three hours Wyatt and Newt gathered cattle, but they cut the day short. Following the plan Wyatt had devised beforehand, they all rode toward the Keyhole headquarters together. When they reached Castle Creek, Newt changed his mind about quitting early. He decided it might be a good idea if the riders crossed the creek to look for strays on Lazy L range. He pointed out the location of a particular arroyo where he had found strays in years past, and that was where Caleb Frye and Sam Hopson discovered the calves wearing Lazy L brands.

Wyatt had planted the seed of suspicion in Caleb's mind the night before, and the oldster was eager to announce the news. He returned from the arroyo shouting, "You were right, Wyatt! Naylor's trying to pull the same deal he accused Justin of doing."

It was obvious that Sam Hopson and Bill Bartlett did not share Caleb's shock and amazement. They remained quiet while Caleb told his story, eyeing Wyatt with knowing glances, but he ignored their skepticism. Now, a day later, the trap he had set for Herbert Naylor had been sprung, and secrecy was no longer important.

Caleb had gone for the sheriff before dawn. Mace had answered the summons, inspected the evidence, and Naylor had dropped his charge against Justin Kirk.

As he rode toward Devil's Tank, Wyatt forgot about Naylor's new threats long enough to chuckle to himself. The first phase of his retaliation against Naylor's harassment had worked to perfection, and he was eager to initiate the second step. He was less certain of its success, but it could be the overwhelming blow that would convince Naylor his vendetta against the Keyhole was a failure. It could also backfire. Naylor might be angry enough to abandon his war of nerves and resort to more aggressive methods to satisfy his mission of revenge.

The herd around Devil's Tank had grown to forty cows, and Wyatt found Newt Hardy keeping watch over them while the rest of the crew searched for more. Newt broke off his circling path when he saw Wyatt approaching and waited for him to ride up beside him.

"I thought you'd never get here," the foreman said anxiously. How'd it go?"

"Just like we planned. Justin will be home tonight. Naylor lost his head before I left and gave me an earful."

They kept their horses side by side while Wyatt repeated the information he had given Lester Mace. A cloud of worry settled over Newt's broad face and he shook his head in dismay.

"The man's lost his senses and I'm beginning to think you have, too." He swung a meaty hand in the direction of the cattle. "I know you need money, but there's no way we can gather four hundred head to sell by the middle of next week."

"Do the best you can," Wyatt said. "I need money and I'm ready to compete with Bert Naylor in dealing with a broker."

Newt did not like what he heard. "He'll compete, all right. If he hears we're planning a sale, he'll start a roundup of his own. He's got twice as many men as we have, and he'll get it done. Everybody around Rampart knows Justin has run the Keyhole into debt, and Naylor will make sure you don't make life easier for either of you. No matter what kind of price you offer the broker, Naylor will sell cheaper."

"Justin said the Lazy L pushed the price down to fifteen dollars a head the last time. That's my price this time."

Shifting in the saddle, the foreman looped his reins around the saddle horn and rubbed his eyes with his fingertips. "Any man who sells his cattle for nothing is a fool. You're going to end up with no cattle and no land. Naylor will lose four, five thousand of his own to make the Keyhole lose one. You'll be broke before he is and he knows it. I made a mistake coming back here."

"You did the right thing." Wyatt smiled coldly. "You're going to have the pleasure of watching Naylor look stupid. I'm sure he's got spies watching the Keyhole all the time. I want them to see what we're doing. This roundup is just bait. When Naylor bites we'll make a sucker out of him."

"Are you saying we're not serious about a cattle sale?"

Wyatt nodded. "It's a phony roundup for a phony sale.

If Naylor does what we think he will—if he cuts the price—we'll buy his cows. I've got enough money in the Drovers Trust Bank to swing the deal if he goes low enough."

Swearing under his breath, Newt Hardy let it be known that he did not like deception when he was the victim. He said, "Naylor's used to winning his fights with money. When he sees that ain't enough, he'll find other ways. I don't fancy riding my horse into the ground, tearing up my hands with rope burns, and sweating blood so you can force a showdown with the Lazy L."

"I ain't looking for a war," Wyatt said. "I made Lester Mace believe I've got a broker coming in to buy Keyhole cattle. If he don't gossip about it and spread the word, we will. I figure Naylor will look up my broker and beat my price. We'll buy his cattle cheap and sell them to a broker at market price. That'll turn enough profit to make a big dent in our bank debt."

Newt rolled his eyes. "It don't make sense. The broker will buy Naylor's cattle and leave ours standing. He'd be a fool not to grab such a bargain."

Wyatt grinned. "I don't have a broker yet. I'm going to invent one who's as phony as this roundup—somebody from our crew who can fool Naylor."

"It won't work. Naylor's got people going back and forth to Rampart all the time, picking up telegraph messages, sending out mail, buying supplies and just sniffing around. They've seen all our people and they'd spot your broker as a fake in a minute."

"Maybe not," Wyatt said thoughtfully. "I had Sam

Hopson in mind. He's got reasons to keep to himself. I don't think he's been seen much in town. If he's as smart as I think he is, he'll do."

"Hadn't thought of him. He signed on after I left and I don't know much about him. Maybe you've got your man."

After spending another ten minutes asking questions and offering suggestions to refine Wyatt's conspiracy, Newt was excited about the possibility of turning the tables on Herbert Naylor one more time. He was also aware of the risks.

"He strikes me as a man who won't stand for being outdone twice," Newt warned. "If you make a fool out of Naylor, he'll turn to Texas ways, all right. He'll kill you—or get Ward Chesser to hire somebody to do it. I'd bet Chesser knows where to find the right man."

"It might happen," Wyatt said. "Naylor hinted at something like that, but I'm hoping he'll worry about Bertetta ending up without a father while he's thinking about leaving Justin without a brother. Maybe he can find a faster gun, but I don't aim to die without taking somebody with me."

Newt Hardy measured the cold light in Wyatt's china-blue eyes for a moment and changed the subject. "These cows are pretty well settled here and I think they'll stay put. If we're going to have a phony roundup, let's do our part to make it look good. You might as well get some saddle sores as the rest of us."

Nudging his horse with his bootheel, the big foreman rode swiftly away from Devil's Tank. Wyatt sent his buckskin along behind him, heading toward a gap between two knolls where he could hear the high-pitched "Hi-yi-yi" of one of the cowboys who was trying to force a stubborn cow out of the brush.

Newt Hardy was still thinking about their conversation. As Wyatt drew close to him, the foreman turned in the saddle and shouted, "I read a paper that said you was the meanest man in Texas. I don't know how mean you are with a gun, but you've sure got a mean mind."

It was meant as a compliment, but Wyatt was not pleased by Newt Hardy's jocular comment. He was tired of hearing the words that had been written about his bounty-hunting days. He returned to the Keyhole to end those experiences, hoping he would never again have to draw his gun against another man. Herbert Naylor's threat lingered in his mind. The peaceful ranch life he had come home to enjoy was still beyond his reach, and his instincts told him he had not seen the last of gunfire and violent death.

EIGHTEEN

The rapid knocking on the front door of Wyatt's cabin at dawn the next morning was loud and insistent. He had grown accustomed to the solitude of Castle Creek Basin, and the interruption startled him. He had been up for an hour, had finished his breakfast, and was sipping his second cup of coffee at the kitchen table when he heard the sound.

His puzzled frown changed to a smile of anticipation. For a moment he speculated that his early-morning visitor might be Laurie Custer. His smile faded, but the fleeting thought made him aware of how much he longed to see her. Even if she was willing to make the first move toward renewing their relationship, Laurie would not leave her school to ride this way in midweek.

Wyatt's gunbelt with the pearl-handled Peacemaker in its holster was draped across the empty chair beside him. He strapped it on as he walked to the front door, then swung it open.

Justin Kirk stood on the porch, his face glowing with a smile. His Levi's showed no signs of wear, his blue flannel shirt had not been faded by the sun, and his tan Stetson looked almost new. During his visit to the jail, Wyatt had told Justin that if he went free, he would be expected to abandon his books and work like a cow-hand. Justin had come dressed for the occasion.

"It's my brother, the jailbird!" Wyatt said, laughing.

Had it been anyone else Justin might have been offended by the greeting, but he was accustomed to Wyatt's manner. Before sadness and tension changed both of their lives, Wyatt was usually carefree and light-hearted, often poking fun at his older brother. Justin was too happy to be home to let words bother him.

"You're a free man at last!" Wyatt added.

"Thanks to you." Justin grabbed Wyatt's hand and shook it vigorously. "I got home around midnight. The sheriff told me how you backed Naylor down. I didn't think about trying to frame him like he framed me. I've been afraid I'd start a fight with Naylor I couldn't handle. Nothing seems to scare you."

Shrugging off his brother's praise, Wyatt invited Justin inside. He walked to the kitchen with his arm across Justin's shoulder, relieved that one worry was off his mind.

"I've been scared plenty, but I don't let that hold me back," Wyatt said. "You know it's hard to make a life in this part of the country. If weather and disease don't whip you, there's somebody ready to fight you over land or water, or a personal grudge. Texas either makes you tough or beats the life out of you."

After Justin was seated at the table, Wyatt took a cup from the shelf beside the stove and poured coffee for both of them.

Justin traced his finger along the checks on the table's oilcloth cover. He looked at Wyatt with a meek expression. "I guess I counted too much on Pa to protect us. After you came to see me at the jail, I did a lot of thinking. The truth is, I'm depending on you to protect me now. While you were learning how to stand up against hard work and hard men, I was keeping to myself—trying to learn to be an executive. That was foolish. I've got to start over and learn how to be a rancher. I hope you can save the Keyhole."

"We'll do it together," Wyatt said, and Justin appeared pleased by his brother's confidence.

While they sipped their coffee, Wyatt told Justin what he had learned about Herbert Naylor's campaign of revenge and the motives behind it. He was able to skip many of the details. Justin had already questioned Lester Mace about the events that led to his release. Since it was family business, the sheriff felt free to relate what he had seen and heard at the Lazy L.

"It's hard to believe Naylor's after us because of what

happened to Bertetta Halsey," Justin murmured, shuddering.

"I can believe it." Wyatt rose and began clearing the table. He stacked the breakfast dishes in a pan of water to wait for washing at the end of the day. "He's lost someone very dear to him, and he's not going to let it pass without making us hurt as much as he does. That's the long and the short of it."

A pink tinge on the grass outside the kitchen window indicated that dawn was about to break through a red glow in the eastern sky. Wyatt was eager to start the day, but Justin seemed reluctant to move. He said, "We're going to get ourselves killed over something Pa did. I knew we'd all end up paying for his lust one of these days. I wish he had left that woman alone."

"It takes two," Wyatt snapped. "I'm tired of hearing everybody blame Pa. Bertetta was unfaithful to her husband, and it was Evan Halsey who cut her face up. Naylor can quote the Bible until he's blue in the face, but he's not putting any guilt on me. If he wants peace of mind he'll have to find it somewhere else. He's not going to get it by watching us go broke."

The excitement and energy born of his newfound freedom were gone from Justin's lean face and he appeared unnerved by the anger in Wyatt's voice. He remained in his chair, resting folded hands on the table, and Wyatt knew there was more on his mind.

"You're the boss now, Wyatt, but I didn't think you'd be selling cattle. That's a mistake I made, and the herd's pretty well run down."

"Didn't Newt Hardy tell you about that?"

"He told me to ask you about it. He said you wanted me to help with the roundup, but that's all. Newt doesn't like me much."

Wyatt smiled. "He'll get over it if you'll pull your load."

Daylight began to lighten the room and Wyatt snuffed out the wick of the lamp that had been burning in the center of the table. While Wyatt explained his reasons for the roundup, Justin's expression changed from worry to hope.

Finally, he rose from his chair and laughed. "If this goes right, we can work things out at the bank. We'll be able to walk with our heads up again. When this is over, I want our lawyer to change the papers on the ranch so we'll own it fifty-fifty."

Wyatt looked away, fearing that he might have promised more than he could deliver. "If we own it at all," he said.

He put on his hat and continued talking as they went outside. He told Justin their destination was Devil's Tank and mentioned that Lloyd Rocker had asked him to return to the bank during the week for a decision on the Keyhole's notes. He explained that he was going to postpone the trip for a few days until he knew how the Lazy L was going to react to the Keyhole's plan to sell cattle.

Wyatt shared Justin's optimism about Lloyd Rocker's attitude if they could make a substantial payment. The banker made his money from the interest he collected on loans. He was not in the business of selling land and cattle, and he preferred to keep it that way.

"He'll play it however is best for him," Wyatt said. "He wanted to take my money as a starter, but he'd still sell you out if we couldn't come up with more than that. I'd end up broke, with a new partner at the Keyhole, and you'd be out in the cold. That might happen yet. It all depends on us outsmarting Naylor."

Justin waited beside his horse at the front of the cabin while Wyatt saddled the buckskin. He was still standing on the ground when Wyatt rode up beside him, and he appeared preoccupied and uncomfortable.

"You ready?" Wyatt asked, trying to read the thoughts behind his brother's dour expression.

"Yeah," Justin said, but he made no move to mount his horse. Instead, he turned abruptly and blurted, "Wilma told me she thought about going to bed with you. That's how scared she was when you showed up at the ranch. She was afraid you'd beat me up and run us both off the place. It was the only thing she could think of that might get you to take it easy on us."

At last Wyatt understood the reason for the changing moods he had observed in Justin's manner since he arrived at the cabin. Wilma had been more honest with her husband than Wyatt expected, and her confession weighed heavily on Justin's mind. He wanted to watch his brother's face for signs of guilt when he told Wyatt how Wilma had described their meeting.

Instinctively, Wyatt knew the quickest way to relieve Justin's mind was to treat the incident as a trifle. He laughed and said, "That's a woman for you. Maybe Wilma thinks you're losing interest in her and she's trying to make you jealous. I never know what's in a woman's mind, but it didn't happen."

Justin grinned with an obvious lift in his spirits. "I know that, but I thought I'd tell you what she said. Wilma doesn't keep secrets from me. She's got to love me a lot to think about going that far to help me."

"I reckon she does," Wyatt said. As they rode away from the cabin he glanced occasionally at his brother's contented face, feeling a sense of admiration for Justin's trust in his wife. He would be more content himself, he thought, if he had shown as much trust in Laurie Custer.

Keyhole cattle were grazing in scattered bunches within a few hundred yards of the water hole at Devil's Tank when Wyatt and Justin reached the holding grounds. During the time Wyatt had ridden with the crew the day before, they had added twenty more steers to the herd, and the number had not grown since. There was good grass and ample water here, and the cattle were satisfied with their surroundings. A circle rider was no longer needed to keep them in place, and none of the crew was in sight.

The sun was barely above the horizon, but Wyatt could feel its heat burning the back of his neck. Dew-wet grass, mingled with the smell of fresh cattle droppings, filled the air with an earthy scent. Insects hummed in the boot-high grass, birds chirped in the saplings around the water hole, steers bawled at each other, and the earth came alive with rangeland sounds. Wyatt was back in the world he had missed so much while he was a bounty hunter, and he never wanted to leave it again.

The brothers sat their horses side by side and scanned

the rolling prairie, looking for dust swirls and listening for voices that would help them locate the Keyhole crew.

"What do we do now?" Justin asked.

"Try to run down Newt and get our orders," Wyatt answered.

He appeared calm and confident, but inwardly he was tense and impatient, distressed by the fact that he had been unable to think of any other tactic that would save the Keyhole if the cattle-sale scheme ended in failure.

They did not have to spend much time before they joined the roundup crew. As he and Justin circled the southern edge of the water hole, three longhorns trotted into view over a gentle rise a hundred yards away. Close behind them, swinging ropes and clucking their tongues, came Newt Hardy and Sam Hopson. They changed directions and trotted their horses up beside Wyatt and Justin.

"Afternoon," Newt drawled. "You're keeping late hours."

"Privilege of ownership." Wyatt laughed. Despite his worries, he could relax when he was with working cowhands. "The roundup ought to move faster today," he told Newt Hardy. "I've brought you another top hand."

With an exaggerated scowl, Newt ran his eyes over Justin as though he were meeting him for the first time. "I ain't too sure about that. This here feller is all scrawny and pale-faced and he's got soft hands. He'll probably die of blisters and sunburn before the day's out."

Newt's critical appraisal was a peace offering. He did not waste words on people he disliked, and his teasing was a way of saying the hard feelings that existed before he quit the Keyhole were forgotten.

"I'll ride with Justin to get him started," Wyatt said.

Newt Hardy shook his head. "You ride with Sam. I'll take Justin. I want to see if he remembers what I learned him."

Sam Hopson sat his saddle and listened to the exchange between Newt and Justin without comment. Wyatt could not decide whether the man was shy, disinterested, or embarrassed because Newt Hardy had succeeded him as foreman during Justin's absence. His thoughts were hidden by the unchanging lines of his swarthy face and the steady gaze of his black eyes.

Not wanting to ignore the man, Justin spoke to him, and Sam Hopson said, "Good to see you out and about again."

With the greetings finished Wyatt said, "Let's go hunt cows."

"That's my line of work," Sam Hopson replied, and reined his horse around to ride at Wyatt's side.

For that day and many more to come, Wyatt and Sam Hopson were riding partners. Wyatt found the man to be a skilled and tireless cowhand. When they joined the others each day at sunset, they usually drove the most cattle in front of them. Although they spent hours within sight of each other, there was not much talk between them. At times Wyatt thought about discussing his plans to assign Sam Hopson to play the role of a cattle broker, but he decided such talk was premature. Nothing was going to happen unless Herbert Naylor took the bait Wyatt had laid out for him.

Two at a time, a dozen at a time, the Keyhole riders drove cattle across the range, and by the end of the week the herd at Devil's Tank had grown to a hundred head. The cowhands were weary and irritable. Each man had covered scores of miles on horseback, circling, back-tracking, sometimes spending an hour to persuade a single steer to walk in a direct line to the holding grounds. They worked from sunrise to sunset, and by Saturday their bones ached and their tempers were short. They snapped at each other and glared at Newt Hardy while they awaited the next day's orders.

A half-hearted cheer rose from the crew when Newt announced they would not be required to work the next day. He would check on the herd, but the others would be free to do as they pleased.

"Tomorrow's Sunday and I know you hombres will want to go to church," the big foreman told them, and walked away chuckling.

The riders headed for their horses, eager to get back to the ranch for some rest before supper.

Except for a few minutes each morning, Wyatt had not seen much of his brother. Justin walked up to him now, grimacing with each step. Newt's prediction had come true. The fiery Texas sun had turned Justin's face beet-red, his nose was beginning to peel, and he held his hands open at his sides to ease the pain from the raw blisters on his palms.

"You must be getting tired of your own cooking," Justin said, smiling. "Wilma told me to invite you for supper. She's changed a lot lately. She's doing her own cooking, and it's pretty good. She's been holding back a cured ham we bought in better times, and she thought you'd like a change from beef. You want to come?"

It was a tempting offer, but Wyatt was not in the mood for company or a conversation that might lead to an argument over Justin's mistakes. He thanked his brother, and declined the invitation.

"I'm about as bad off as you are," he said. "I've used muscles that haven't been called on in three years. I'm going home and soak my bones in Castle Creek for at least an hour."

"Maybe you can come another time." Justin backed away, mounted his horse, and followed the others toward the Keyhole headquarters.

The memory of a sniper's bullets screaming around him once before was always in Wyatt's mind when he traveled the trail to his cabin. Dusk kept the day alive, and it was not yet dark when he came within sight of Castle Creek.

He could see patches of yellow sky through the pines and cottonwoods along the stream, but the shadows beneath them were deep enough to conceal a rifleman. He wanted to believe the intermittent gunfire from the hills around the ranch was more harassing than dangerous, but he was no longer sure Herbert Naylor would be satisfied with simple annoyances. He rode low in the saddle, his body stiff with tension as he peered around him and listened for suspicious sounds.

He reached his cabin without incident. He stepped down in the yard with a hard sigh, feeling mentally and physically drained. He took a step toward the cabin, stopped and said aloud, "What the hell," and went toward the creek instead.

The basin was a remote area of the range, and he was alone. His horse would not mind standing with trailing reins for a while, and it would make no difference if Wyatt had his bath first and dressed later. The Lazy L might have a spy who would see him walk back to the house with his dirty clothes under his arm, but being seen naked by another man would not embarrass him.

From the front of the cabin it was a short trip to his favorite spot on Castle Creek. It was a cove that had been scooped out of the west bank where the stream took an elbow-turn eastward. Most of the creek was less than hip deep, but here the swirling current had carved out a deeper pool that offered Wyatt a choice of swimming or relaxing in the shallows near the shore.

Wyatt was hot and tired, and sweat had left cakes of dust in the black stubble on his full cheeks. He piled his clothes on a flat rock, slipped through the saplings, and dived into the water. Enjoying the refreshing coolness, he swam leisurely from bank to bank a few times, then stood erect with the water lapping around his chest.

He ducked his head, washed his hair, and floated on his back for a while. Above him the sky had darkened, and the shadows beneath the trees were so deep he could not see beyond them. He spent half an hour at the creek, and wanted to stay longer, but the day was gone and he still had to care for his horse.

As he turned to wade toward the shore, he was

gripped by an uneasy feeling that he was no longer alone. An alien sound sifted through the sloshing noise of his own movements. It sounded like a splash somewhere around the sharp bend of the stream, like a heavy object falling into the water.

Wyatt felt the fine hairs stir on the back of his neck and fear hushed his breath. If someone was trying to bushwhack him, they had chosen an ideal time. His gun was thirty feet away, wrapped in the shell belt that he had piled atop his clothes. He took a step sideways, wondering if it would be safer to move slowly and quietly or risk drawing attention by the splashing of a rapid swim toward the bank.

He did not have to make a choice. He shifted his feet again, and his muscles froze. He stared in amazement as a slender white shape sped toward him beneath the surface of the water.

NINETEEN

Almost immediately Wyatt recognized the approaching figure as an underwater swimmer. He had only enough time to observe that the body was too small and graceful to belong to a man before Laurie Custer bobbed up in front of him.

Surprise sent Wyatt stumbling backward. He caught his balance and stammered, "What the—Laurie! What're you doing here?"

She rubbed her hands across her face and tossed her shoulder-length blond hair to shake the water out of it. "Going for a swim. Can't you see? I figured if I caught you this way you wouldn't be so quick to run me off again."

Wyatt shook his head in disbelief. "You scared the hell out of me for a minute. Where did you come from?"

She talked so fast she was almost breathless, apparently afraid he would turn away before she finished. She had been waiting in his cabin when she saw Wyatt stop at the tie-rail. When he left his horse and headed for the creek she assumed he was going for a swim, and she followed him.

"I decided if you were too stubborn to come to me I'd come to you. You didn't give me time to talk before, but I'm going to talk now. There's nothing between me and Ward Chesser. I met him one day when he came up the basin looking for strays, and I told Wilma about him. She asked me to make friends with him and see if I could learn more about the Lazy L. I thought she'd tell you."

"Wilma's been too upset to think about anything except her husband," Wyatt said. "She didn't even tell me you were using my cabin on weekends. I was mad at everybody and myself, too, the day I saw you with Ward Chesser. I wanted to hurt somebody. I'm glad I whipped him, but I'm sorry I hurt you."

She came closer to him and put her hands on his arms. She had removed her outer garments, and was wearing frilly knee-length pantalets topped by a cotton camisole. Wyatt found himself admiring the outlines of her firm, high breasts and the curve of her hips where dampness had pasted her underwear against her skin.

He looked into her upturned face and forgot about

Ward Chesser, Herbert Naylor, and the Keyhole's troubles. He reached for her and Laurie came eagerly into his arms. Her lips moved hungrily under the crush of his kiss, and Wyatt's blood pulsed with desire. He felt the warmth of her skin through the wet cloth as she pressed against him. She backed toward the shore, pulling him along with her.

They moved in unison, holding each other close. Laurie did not stop until the water was knee deep, then she fell backward into the shallows. She drew him down with her and clung to him while he kissed her again. He felt her spine tremble, then she pushed him away and stood up.

She said. "Let's don't go too far with this. One minute I feel like you've never been gone, and the next I feel like I don't know you anymore."

Wyatt squeezed her hand. "My feelings for you haven't changed."

Smiling, she led him back to deeper water. Darkness closed around them while they swam together, laughing and cavorting like children at play. The fingernail moon was above the trees, dimpling the water with its silvery light by the time they stopped and waded toward the creekbank. In his excitement over Laurie's arrival, Wyatt had given no thought to the fact that he was naked. As they approached shallow water again, however, he lingered a few steps behind her.

She looked back at him, laughing at his crouching stance. "I left my clothes up here," she said, pointing upstream. "It's one thing to swim with a skinny-dipper, but I don't fancy walking around with a naked man. I

235

brought you some clean Levi's from your room. I hope you don't mind."

"I'm tickled to death. I feel liked a plucked chicken."

He stayed in waist-deep water until Laurie went farther into the brush along the creek and returned to leave the Levi's with his other clothing.

"When we get back to the cabin, I'll fix us some supper while you take care of your horse," she called as she retraced her steps to put on dry clothing. "You must be hungry and tired."

Wyatt smiled, enjoying a pleasant exhaustion. "I feel better than I've felt in years. I've missed you, Laurie. We have a lot to talk about."

"We'll have time for that. I plan to spend the night, if it's all right with you."

"Wouldn't have it any other way," Wyatt said.

For an hour after supper they sat together on the mohair sofa in the cabin's parlor and talked about old times—reminiscing about the experiences they had shared and laughing about the schoolyard fights Wyatt had started when he felt some young man was paying Laurie too much attention.

She talked about her college days, how her interest in writing had been encouraged by her professors, and told him she had just been notified that *Harper's Weekly* had accepted one of her poems for publication. This led to the subject both had purposely avoided while they tried to close off the outside world to enjoy a renewal of their friendship.

"Did Ward Chesser's help have anything to do with that piece of good luck?" Wyatt asked.

236

His tone brought a frown to Laurie's face. "He might have. He's been very good about finding flaws in my work and telling me how to improve it. Ward would make a fine teacher, but he thinks that's not a man's work. He thinks a real man is someone who rises to a position of authority because he can outfight and out-shoot everyone else. I think he wants to be like a friend he talks about—a gunman named Burdine Fisher. He—"

"I've heard that name," Wyatt cut in. "Do you know anything about him?"

"Nothing except what Ward says. His eyes light up when he talks about Fisher, says the man is an artist with a gun. He claims he's seen him kill men before they could blink an eye, much less draw their gun. He knows I don't like to talk about guns and dead people, but he does it anyway. I should have known there was a mean streak behind all his smooth talk, and yesterday he—he—"

Laurie's voice faded in a sobbing whisper and tears sparkled in the corners of her eyes. She shuddered and tried to turn away. Wyatt pulled her around to face him, sensing that Laurie's lighthearted manner had been a front to conceal her despair over something Ward Chesser had done or said.

"He did what?" Wyatt asked.

"He tried to rape me!" she cried angrily.

She looked at him and saw fury build fires in his eyes. She bit her lip, and looked away. Before he could say anything she began talking. Once she started, she seemed determined to tell her story in one breath, and

Wyatt did not interrupt her.

Chesser had been waiting for her at the hotel when she arrived from school. She had told him the good news from *Harper's Weekly,* and he appeared to share her joy over her success. He wanted to see the acceptance letter, and Laurie invited him to her room.

She was in such an exuberant mood it took her a while to recognize the change in Chesser's behavior. He had grasped her hand, and she thought it was a gesture of congratulations. His intentions were more personal. When Laurie tried to withdraw her hand, Chesser would not let her go. He pulled her close to him, pressing his body against hers, and tried to kiss her.

"I pushed him away and tried to make a joke out of it," Laurie said tearfully. "He got this—this strange look on his face and I knew I was in trouble. He said he had to have me before you did. He said he was crazy about me and that I'd feel the same way after I made love with him. I couldn't get loose and he started touching me all over. Finally I wrestled him around the room until I could reach one of the books I'd left on the table. I hit him in the face so hard it knocked him down."

Before the Lazy L foreman could regain his senses, Laurie had run to the lobby. She stayed there until he came sheepishly down the steps, but he did not leave without the final word.

Realizing her words were gushing out in a steady stream, Laurie paused and raised her head in a show of strength. She wiped her tears away and her voice grew stronger. "On his way out Ward had the nerve to lean over my shoulder and whisper that if he couldn't have me, you couldn't either. He warned me not to tell you what happened. He said if you started anything, you'd have to face either him or Burdine Fisher."

Wyatt stood up, his face dark and threatening. "I'll kill that son of a bitch! I should have done it the first time I saw him."

Leaping from the sofa, Laurie grabbed his arm as he started toward the door. "He didn't hurt me, Wyatt. Stay away from him! He's still smarting over the way you whipped him. He thinks he could have beaten you with a gun, and I can tell he'd like to have another chance. He's leaving in about a month and he'll be out of our way forever."

"He'll never leave as long as he can live a good life as Naylor's lapdog," Wyatt growled.

Laurie clung to his arm, pulling him back toward the sofa. "He doesn't have any choice. Ward told me at lunch one Sunday that Naylor's going back to Saint Joseph soon. He's offered Ward a superintendent's job in his wagon factory, and Ward wants to go with him. Let it end that way."

The anger inside Wyatt was slow to die, but he could not ignore the pleading note and the fear in her voice. She put her arms around his neck, leaned across his chest, and held him close. "Now that we're back together I don't want to lose you," she said softly. "I've heard your ranch is in trouble and that you believe the Lazy L has something to do with it, but don't make it a personal war with Ward Chesser."

In Wyatt's mind, there was a picture of Ward

Chesser's hands exploring the curves of Laurie's body, and it was hard to get rid of the image. As Laurie continued to talk, he succumbed to her persuasion, and began to think about other information that Chesser had passed on to her.

Most of what Laurie knew about the Keyhole's troubles had been gleaned from town gossip and conversations with Wilma Kirk. Maggie Gregg, the Keyhole's former housekeeper, had told her of Justin's release, but Maggie did not know how it was arranged.

With her head resting on his shoulder, Wyatt told Laurie of his visit to the Lazy L, how he had learned that Bertetta Halsey was Naylor's daughter, and of the Missourian's open admission that he had moved onto the Rampart range for the sole purpose of seeking revenge against the Kirk family.

Amid Laurie's gasps of astonishment, Wyatt said, "I can't believe Naylor will walk away from the Lazy L before he makes a last stab at destroying us."

"I guess he can't get another place close to the Keyhole," Laurie said. "He has to give up the Lazy L. According to Ward, Matt Latham didn't want to sell his ranch. Naylor had to make him a no-lose deal to get what he wanted. Ward says Naylor never meant to stay permanently, and he agreed to sell the ranch back to Latham in one year if Latham didn't like his new place. Naylor must have thought that was enough time for him to do whatever he had in mind. The year is up in less than a month, and Matt Latham has given notice that he wants his ranch back."

Wyatt was pleased that Matt Latham would be his

neighbor again, but he could not believe Herbert Naylor would give up his vow of vengeance and slink away in defeat. After a few minutes of thoughtful silence, Wyatt asked Laurie how much power Ward Chesser held at the Lazy L.

"All he wants," Laurie replied. "Naylor's used to having assistants to do his routine work. He lays out a broad picture of what he wants, and Ward decides how to get it done. Naylor must like the results. Ward says Naylor treats him like a son. He overstepped his bounds once, he told me, and almost lost his job. There was a problem with a family relative and Naylor didn't like the way Ward handled it. Ward laughs about it, like he pulled off a sly trick."

Lifting her head, Laurie looked at him with worry arching her eyebrows. "Why did you ask me that?"

"So I'll know what to look for. There'll be a show-down before Naylor leaves Rampart. He might not want a real fight, but if Chesser has as much power as you say, he'll feel free to take it into his own hands. He's more dangerous than Herbert Naylor."

He eased Laurie away from his chest and stood up. He paced restlessly to the window and looked out for no reason, then stopped in front of the gunbelt that hung on a peg beside the door. Lamplight glistened on the pearl-handled Peacemaker. He had not fired the gun since he was forced to put a slug in young Ken Holby's chest in a town far away, but his instincts told him he had better keep it oiled and ready for use.

"I'm sorry we got into this dreary discussion," Laurie said when he went back to stand near her. "I'll be worried about you until Herbert Naylor and Ward Chesser are gone."

He smiled down at her. "Don't make any funeral plans for me yet. I've been up against worse people. Let's forget about them and go to bed."

He went with her to his bedroom and picked up a pillow and some blankets. He no longer doubted Laurie's affection for him, but they had been apart for a long time and it was too soon for him to expect her to invite him into her bed. His long frame would not fit on the sofa, and he slept rolled up in his blankets on the floor, much as he would have done on the open range.

It was a night that Wyatt wanted to last forever, but it passed quickly. He awoke at dawn with the same knot of dread in his stomach that had been there since the day he returned to Rampart. Laurie's visit had given him moments of joy, but the things she had told him about Ward Chesser and the Lazy L gave him more to think about and filled him with a sense of foreboding.

Laurie left shortly after breakfast, telling him she wanted to spend the day with her parents before she returned to town to begin another week of teaching. Wyatt was quiet and preoccupied while he saddled her paint horse and tied down the soft leather valise that she had brought with her.

Laurie noticed his somber mood. She tried to cheer him up by promising to return on Friday and spend the weekend with him. Her eyes clouded when Wyatt told her not to come back until he sent for her. "I thought you understood about Ward and that we—"

"I love you, Laurie, and I don't want anything to

happen to you," Wyatt cut in hastily. "We might have some trouble and I don't want you in the middle of it."

Her face paled and she shifted in the saddle as though she might stay. "You promised not to go after Ward Chesser, but you're not telling me everything."

"I'm not going to start a fight, but I don't know what the Lazy L is going to do. Maybe nothing. If Naylor's agreement with Matt Latham is like you said, this mess will come to an end one way or another in a week or so."

Her eyes held to his face as if she were looking at him for the last time. She tossed her head and made her voice sound angry. "If you get yourself killed, Wyatt Kirk, I'll marry the ugliest man on this range."

Clinging to the saddle horn, she leaned down and kissed him on the cheek. Wyatt laughed aloud, and stood watching her until she went out of sight.

Monday morning was like others before it, and the roundup continued. Newt Hardy had volunteered to keep an eye on activities at the Lazy L and had been riding out each night after supper to scout different parts of the range. It was midweek when he reported the news Wyatt had been waiting to hear. Naylor was putting together a herd.

"I been looking in the wrong places." Newt called him aside to talk when Wyatt reported for work, but he still lowered his voice to a gruff whisper. "They've set up holding grounds on the north range. Ward Chesser and Jesse Estep was ridin' circle when I sneaked down an arroyo and took a look at 'em last night. I don't know how they got the word, but it looks like they've got at least four hundred head ready to drive."

Wyatt glanced toward the other riders who were standing around their horses, smoking and talking among themselves. "Now I've got to see what Sam Hopson thinks about setting himself up in town as a cattle broker."

Newt pressed his fingertips against his eyelids. "He's gun-shy about showing hisself in public. He might not go for it."

"We'll see," Wyatt said. "I've got my winning ways."

The Keyhole crew rode away from Devil's Tank in the usual pairs, with Sam Hopson as Wyatt's partner. Half a mile from the holding grounds, Wyatt guided his dun into the shade of a pin oak and stepped to the ground.

So far Sam Hopson's only words had been a quiet " 'Mornin', Wyatt" as they left the holding grounds. Now he put his hands on the saddle horn and leaned forward. "Somethin' wrong?"

"Something's good." Wyatt motioned for Hopson to dismount, and told him what he wanted him to do.

At first the swarthy cowboy refused to accept the assignment as a phony cattle broker. He was still uncertain about his status with the law, and did not want to risk being arrested as a result of the gunfight in New Mexico Territory that he had described to Wyatt earlier.

"I don't hang out in town," Hopson said. "You never know who you'll run into."

With some assurance from Wyatt, he changed his

mind. "I've seen a lot of flyers, Sam, and your picture wasn't on any of them," Wyatt told him. "I think you're worried about nothing, but I'll make you a promise. If you get in jail I'll get you out—even if we have to shoot our way out."

Hopson blinked in surprise, then grinned to show his gratitude for Wyatt's support. "I ought to have some better clothes for a job like that," he said, and Wyatt knew the decision was made.

"I'll get you some," Wyatt said. "You're Justin's size and he's got suits you can borrow."

Squatting on his haunches with Hopson hunkered down in a similar stance across from him, Wyatt explained his scheme so quickly and simply that the cowboy had no problem understanding their goal. Hopson was to check into the Sunset Hotel and talk freely about the purpose of his visit to Rampart. In the saloons, the restaurants, and along the boardwalks, Wyatt wanted him to initiate conversations and casually mention that he was waiting for the Keyhole Ranch to deliver him a herd.

"You can quote our price," Wyatt reminded him. "Keep talking and waiting until somebody from the Lazy L approaches you. If they offer to sell you four hundred head for less than fifteen dollars you get them as far below that as you can, then buy them. I'll call in our regular broker, Homer Utley, and we'll sell Naylor's cows to him. We'll laugh all the way to the bank and Naylor will tuck his tail like a whipped dog."

"If it works," Hopson murmured.

"It'll work if Naylor's as eager to show me up as I

think he is," Wyatt said. "You convince people you're a real broker and I'll do the rest."

Early the next morning, taking a circuitous route that made it appear that he was approaching Rampart from Caprock Junction, Sam Hopson rode his unbranded horse down Front Street and took a room at the Sunset Hotel. An hour later, Wyatt met with Lloyd Rocker at the Drovers Trust Bank.

He found the banker in an irritable mood. Rocker had expected him days earlier, and was worried that Wyatt had become as evasive and unreliable as Justin. It took all the humility and sincerity he could muster, accompanied by promises of a forthcoming payment, but Wyatt finally convinced the banker to allow him at least two weeks before he took any legal action against the Keyhole.

While he had the banker in a tolerant mood, he drew up a document that would allow Sam Hopson to draw against the money Wyatt had in his bank account.

Sam Hopson did his job well. When a business deal was pending, it was natural for the principals to confer and Wyatt wanted to be seen in town. During the next week, he made two trips to Rampart to meet with Sam Hopson.

"I'm beginnin' to enjoy actin' like a big shot," the cowboy had confessed. "People shine up to you. Your friend Lester Mace bought me a drink last night, and didn't give me no funny looks."

At their second meeting Hopson reported that the talking he had done in town was showing results. Ward Chesser had accosted him in front of the Sunset Hotel and offered to sell him as many cattle as he could handle.

"I told him I couldn't renege on my deal with you," Hopson told Wyatt. "He said his boss might beat your price."

"The pot's boiling," Wyatt had said. "He'll be back."

He was so confident of his prediction that he telegraphed a message to Homer Utley in Caprock Junction, inviting him to come to Rampart and look over a herd for sale.

Twelve days after Sam Hopson moved into the Sunset Hotel, he rode out to the Keyhole on the pretense of inspecting cattle. Ward Chesser had been back to see him at regular intervals, but Hopson had continued to stall and quibble over prices. On his fourth trip, Chesser became exasperated and declared he would deliver four hundred steers at eleven dollars a head.

Wyatt laughed, "I feel like a thief but I'll take them. Make the deal."

"Already told him to start driving the cows to the flat-lands outside of town," Hopson replied. "I wanted you to know I'm spendin' your money."

Wyatt and Newt Hardy were elated, but they were not yet ready to tell the Keyhole crew what was afoot. It was not the nature of cowhands to meddle in ranch affairs, and if they were curious about Sam Hopson's absence from the ranch they did not mention it.

The cattle purchase was finalized the next day. Wyatt arrived in town in early afternoon. He killed time playing checkers with Del Avery at the blacksmith shop while he waited for Sam Hopson to meet with Ward

Chesser at the bank and complete the transaction. They had estimated that the exchange of money for a bill of sale would be accomplished by two o'clock. Wyatt had asked Hopson to meet him at the Wildfire Saloon to celebrate with a drink when the business was done.

"You play worse than Jesse Estep," Del Avery grumbled as Wyatt stood up to leave the blacksmith shop.

He teased Del Avery about cheating, shifted his gunbelt nervously, and at a quarter to two walked across the vacant field toward Front Street. Not long afterward, on a day when his future looked promising, Wyatt's past caught up with him.

TWENTY

As he walked down Rampart's main street, Wyatt did not look like a man on his way to celebrate a victory. Tension showed in the stiffness of his wide shoulders and the tight line of his mouth. Although he was pleased by the prospect of eliminating much of the Keyhole's debt, he had a premonition that something would go wrong before he left town. In freeing Justin from jail and finding a way to turn the Lazy L's price-cutting practices to his advantage, he had accomplished the goals he had set for himself, but he had made himself the target of dangerous enemies—Herbert Naylor and Ward Chesser.

Ironically, Wyatt was uneasy about his own success. So far, he had outdone Naylor at every turn. It seemed too easy. Naylor had dropped his charge against Justin Kirk with apparent indifference, but Wyatt knew the

248

Missourian's pride was wounded when he learned his wealth did not give him the same power in Texas that he had enjoyed elsewhere. Secrets did not last long in Rampart, and Wyatt feared the man's reaction when he learned the cattle he thought were being sold to a legitimate broker had ended up in Wyatt's possession.

Deep in thought, he was hardly aware of his surroundings until he heard a voice behind him. Sheriff Lester Mace had seen him as he passed in front of the jail and stepped out on the boardwalk. He called, "Hold up a minute," and strode up beside him when Wyatt stopped. "I been seein' you in town every few days lately," Mace said. "It makes me nervous. You could run into some fool lookin' to see if his gun's faster'n yours."

"I don't think anybody cares about that anymore. I've been trying to finish up some business. It's about done."

The sheriff was carrying a half-dozen sheets of paper in one hand. He held them out as though he was going to say something about them, then dropped his arm to his side. He pushed at his shirttail and studied Wyatt's face.

"Somethin's goin' on," Mace drawled. "I can smell that. There's been some happenin's around here that make me edgy. The Lazy L drove in some cattle yesterday and they're holdin' 'em on the open range along the stage road to Caprock Junction. Last week I met a broker name of Sam Hopson who told me he was here to buy Keyhole cattle. This mornin' I was havin' breakfast at the Silver Spoon Cafe and Ward Chesser was in there. He mentioned he was sellin' a herd to that same broker. He was growlin' because Naylor ordered him to let the herd go dirt cheap—eleven dollars a head. That's givin' beef away. Chesser knows that's bad for everybody on this range. I figure you've been beat out of your chance to raise money again, and I'm afraid you don't aim to take it layin' down."

Wyatt showed him a crafty smile. "You figure wrong. I'm right happy about the situation. Sam Hopson ain't a real broker. He's a Keyhole cowhand. He's buying those Lazy L cows for me."

"Hell's fire!" Mace exclaimed. "That's worse. Naylor and Chesser will be rip-roarin' mad. You've rubbed them wrong already, and they'll be after your hide."

Wyatt shrugged and turned to walk on, but the lawman stopped him. He waved the handful of papers and said, "I stopped you to talk about that Burdine Fisher feller. I've been diggin' around in letters and flyers that go back two, three years. If he's a hard-case, he's covered his trail good. Goin' by my records, nobody except Ward Chesser ever heard of him."

"Maybe he works under different names in different places."

"That's possible." The sheriff flipped through the papers in his hand. "I got notices here on people nobody's been able to track down—letters about hired guns, bushwhackers, and plain thieves. Some use a half-dozen different names, and one of 'em might be Burdine Fisher. The descriptions sound like any cowhand you'd meet on the street. You want to look at what I've got?"

Wyatt shook his head. "If you can't make anything out of it, I can't either. Burdine Fisher may be working at the Lazy L right now under another name. Who knows? If he's around, my guts tell me Ward Chesser's going to make sure I meet him."

Mace agreed. "I been thinkin' all along that this thing with you and the Lazy L won't end without a killin'. It's comin' to that and I don't know how to stop it. Naylor's goin' to feel like you cheated him, and he'll leave it up to Chesser to settle things for him. If this Burdine Fisher hombre is Ward's friend, I'd say he'll call on him when word gets out about what you've done."

"We'll see," Wyatt said, and walked away.

On weekdays there was little activity in Rampart. Only two or three people were moving about on Wyatt's side of the street, and it was so quiet the thudding of his boots echoed like footsteps in an empty room. Farther away, on the other side of the street, he saw the short, plump figure of Maggie Gregg swishing a broom around the entrance of the Sunset Hotel. Just ahead of him, an overalled man was putting a new coat of yellow paint on the shutters of the Opera House.

Wyatt had an errand to run before he went to the Wildfire Saloon to meet Sam Hopson. He stopped at the telegraph office, which occupied a small room in one corner of the Family Emporium, and found that his luck was still good. There was a reply to the request he had sent to Homer Utley. It said the broker would arrive in Rampart Friday on the noon stagecoach. That was two days away, and Wyatt's bank account at the Drovers Trust should soon grow to more than eight thousand dollars. With a payment that large, he was sure Lloyd Rocker would give him time

251

to pay the balance of the Keyhole debt.

A lone bay horse tied at the hitching rail with a bedroll lashed to the saddle rings was the only sign of life at the front of the Wildfire Saloon. The horse looked tired and underfed. It wore a brand Wyatt did not recognize and he assumed it belonged to a drifter who had paused for a drink while passing through town.

With a wariness born of his years as a bounty hunter, Wyatt pushed the batwing doors open and entered the saloon. He stopped after two steps, blinked to adjust his vision to the change in light, and looked around. Sam Hopson had not yet arrived, but the owner of the bay horse was there. He was standing at the bar, hunched forward on his elbows, and was rolling a whiskey glass between his hands. Only his back was visible, but that was enough to tell Wyatt something about him. His boots were scarred, run-over at the heels. Salty crusts of dried sweat rimmed the snakeskin band on his black Stetson. His Levi's were dirty and speckled along the seams with imbedded thorns.

Wyatt had no idea where the man had come from, but he knew he had ridden long and hard. He had avoided the convenience of established trails. His clothing told of rough travel through the brush and briars of the unin-habited back country favored by desperadoes who were hiding from the law.

With his right foot propped against the brass rail on the floor, the stranger's posture threw his black-handled Colt into prominent view. It was obvious that he attached more importance to the care of the weapon than he did to the rest of his dress. At some recent time he had wiped the gun clean and polished the holster.

Experienced eyes could read such sign in seconds, and Wyatt did not like what he saw. Apprehension rippled the nerves along his spine. He was looking at a man on the run, and he wondered if the stranger's name might be Burdine Fisher.

Behind the bar, Walt Dorsey stood with his arms folded across the beer-stained apron that covered his paunchy middle. He had backed away as far as he could and was resting his shoulders against the shelves of whiskey bottles on the rear wall. A wooden matchstick slanted from one corner of his mouth and he chewed at it nervously. Sweat glistened along the bartender's receding hairline and he looked uncomfortable in the stranger's presence.

There was no one else in the saloon. Empty chairs and empty tables threw long shadows across the planked floor where sunlight streamed through the front windows. It was so still, Wyatt could hear a dog barking somewhere in the distance, and he was aware that he was trying to silence his own breathing.

He had too much at stake on this day to lose his life, and his instincts warned him he would face that risk if he stayed here. In a move barely noticeable he lifted the pearl-handled Peacemaker with his forefinger and dropped it back in place, making sure it was loose in the holster. The precaution was born of habit, but he had no business here without Sam Hopson. The paperwork at the bank was taking longer than they had expected, and he could meet Hopson just as easily outside.

He was turning to leave when Walt Dorsey called,

"Hey, Wyatt! Don't run off so quick. This feller's been asking about you—says he's a friend of yours."

The proprietor of the Wildfire looked relieved to see a familiar face, and now it was Wyatt's turn to feel uncomfortable. He knew what was coming. It had happened before. Someone who knew his name, knew his reputation and his habits, stopped in a place to inquire about him. They claimed to be a friend, a relative, or the bearer of an important message, but they always turned out to be a gunman with a craving for fame or a score to settle.

A ragged sigh and a shudder shook Wyatt's shoulders. Like a cat shifting positions to stalk a bird, he faced forward again, the china-blue eyes gleaming against bronze skin, arms dropping limply to his sides while he stared at the stranger's back.

"He's not a friend," Wyatt said. "I don't know him."

"I know you, mister!" The stranger put down his whiskey glass and wheeled around, his right hand resting against his polished holster. "You're the man who got my brother killed. I'm Alvin Beemer—Ray Beemer's brother. You remember Ray, don't you?"

Alvin Beemer was older than the outlaw Wyatt had turned over to Deputy Jim Colley in Clayfield, but there was a family resemblance—the same sharp chin, pointed nose, and close-set eyes.

"I never forget a back-shooter," Wyatt said coldly. "I remember Ray Beemer. He was alive when I left him."

"He's dead now," Alvin Beemer snarled. "That's your fault. Wasn't for you taking him in, Ray would be riding free somewhere. I visited Ray in jail enough to learn something about you, things he overheard when you was talking to Jim Colley—enough to know where to find you. I had to kill that deputy to break Ray out, but they got up a posse and come after us. They killed Ray, shot him to pieces, but the Lord saved me to come after you."

Driven by hate and fury, the words poured from Alvin Beemer's throat in a whining screech.

"You killed Jim Colley?" Wyatt asked grimly.

"That's your fault, too. You set it all up by what you done. Ray and Colley are in hell, and I'm sending you to join them!"

Alvin Beemer had more nerve than his brother. He had cheated, stolen, and killed, and lived to tell about it. His survival had given him confidence, and he was not afraid of Wyatt Kirk. He took a step away from the bar and spread his feet. The crooked grin on his face was evidence that he thought he would survive again.

Had the man been less sure of himself, there might have been time for Wyatt to reason with him, to convince him that he would die here if he reached for his gun. There was no time left. As the last word fell from his lips, Alvin Beemer's hand streaked toward his holster.

Two swift hands moved down and up. Two guns boomed. The quiet saloon vibrated with the roar of exploding powder. Splinters flew from the floor a foot in front of Wyatt's boots. The slug came from a dead man's gun. Alvin Beemer's gun cleared the holster, but it was a split second too late. The life left his arm as Wyatt's bullet bored a red hole in his forehead. He was thrown against the bar as though blown by a wind gust. His arm drooped and the reflex action of his trigger finger fired his gun for the last time. He slipped down until his head lodged on the footrail.

In the aftermath of times like this, Wyatt felt numb and disoriented. It was like he had died and been reborn, and it took him a while to come back to reality. The saloon seemed even quieter than before, muted by the presence of death. For a few seconds he stood with the pearl-handled Peacemaker still extended, then slowly put it back in the holster. The acrid odor of gunpowder mingled with the smells of stale tobacco and whiskey mash. He blamed the heavy air for the nausea that rumbled in his stomach.

Walt Dorsey's voice broke the silence. "My God, he almost beat you," the bartender murmured, stretching his neck to peer over the bar at Alvin Beemer's body.

Wyatt's chest sagged as he let out a long breath. "He came close. They all come pretty close."

The saloon began to fill up with people. Boards rattled under booted feet, voices rose in an unintelligible chorus, and the batwing doors moved in and out as nearby shopkeepers who had heard the shots rushed into the Wildfire. They were followed by the few pedestrians who had been on the boardwalks. Most of them stopped abruptly midway across the floor, growing silent as their gaze went from Wyatt to the dead man in front of the bar.

Wyatt did not turn his head until he heard Lester Mace's bass voice ordering people to stand aside. He saw the sheriff coming toward him, his big shoulders weaving to nudge people out of his way. Mace's breath was hissing in and out in short gasps as he went past Wyatt and knelt beside Alvin Beemer's body. He grasped the man's waistband and pulled him forward so his head could rest flat on the floor. He picked up Beemer's Stetson, which had slid away from the body, and placed it over the man's staring eyes.

He stood up, hitched at his belt, and looked at Wyatt. His jaw sagged with sadness. "It finally happened," he said quietly. "Did you know him?"

Wyatt's throat was dry and he had to swallow twice before he was sure of his voice. He said, "I'd never seen him before, but he told me who he was. He was a brother to that back-shooter I turned over to Deputy Jim Colley down in Clayfield a while back. He wanted to kill me to even the score."

"He force you to draw on him?"

Wyatt nodded, and looked at the crowd for the first time. He saw Sam Hopson standing near the front window, and beside him, with a thin, pointless grin on his face, was Ward Chesser. He was not surprised to see them together. Chesser was Herbert Naylor's representative for the cattle sale, and Wyatt knew he would be the one to meet Hopson at the bank to close the deal. Apparently they had done so.

"I need to know what happened," Lester Mace growled when he saw that Wyatt was distracted.

Wyatt was thinking about what had happened in Laurie Custer's hotel room when Ward Chesser tried to force her to submit to his advances. A knot of muscle jumped along his jawline and his face grew darker.

Without taking his eyes off Chesser's face, he said, "You know I had to be forced into it, Lester. Let Walt Dorsey tell you about it. He heard it all."

He looked once more at Alvin Beemer's still form, grimaced, and added, "I got to get out of here. You know where to find me."

"I reckon," Mace murmured. "I got to get the undertaker over here, then send a telegraph to Jim Colley and see if he knows where to send the body."

Wyatt was already striding in Sam Hopson's direction. He stopped and looked back at the sheriff. "Jim Colley's dead. Beemer killed him. Walt can tell you about that, too."

As he walked away he heard the sheriff mumbling behind his back, "Damn the scum we get in this country. I reckon we need people like Wyatt Kirk sometimes."

Dressed in Justin Kirk's blue suit with a white collar and string tie, Sam Hopson lounged against the front wall and appeared calm and unmoved by the nervous chatter around him. Wyatt stopped in front of him, and made an attempt to continue his deception of the Lazy L with a show of anger.

Ward Chesser was an arm's length away, and Wyatt wanted to be sure the man heard his words. He said, "Word's all over town that you're buying Herbert Naylor's cows Instead of mine, Hopson. I don't like a man who don't keep his word."

Sam Hopson shifted uncomfortably and tried to give a signal by rolling his dark eyes toward Ward Chesser. Wyatt scowled, unable to find any meaning in Hopson's gesture until Ward Chesser took a step forward and said, "You've made a fool out of me, Kirk, but you won't get by with it. I'll—I'll—"

Chesser's words came out between choking breaths. His body shook with fury, and splotches of red broke through the tan of his lean, handsome face. In contrast to Hopson's appearance, Chesser wore work-worn Levi's, a faded shirt, and scuffed boots.

Ignoring the Lazy L manager, Wyatt kept his eyes on Sam Hopson. He shrugged and asked, "What's he raving about?"

"He knows," Hopson said uneasily. "He knows I'm a Keyhole man and not a broker. It all came out while we was at the bank."

"Have you got a bill of sale?"

"Chesser's got your money and I've got the bill of sale in my pocket," Sam Hopson replied. "Lloyd Rocker put the writing on the back that transfers it to you."

Wyatt had felt a moment of panic, but now he relaxed. He faced Chesser with a cold smile. "You can whine all you want, mister, but you're stuck. You and Naylor thought you were smart enough to keep me broke, but you've bailed me out of trouble instead. Now you and Naylor will know how Justin felt when Naylor forced him to close his stores."

Shifting his attention to Sam Hopson, Wyatt said, "Let's get some fresh air. We've got things to talk about."

He was turning away when Ward Chesser grabbed his arm. Wyatt shook off the man's grip and his hand went swiftly to the butt of his Peacemaker as he wheeled around.

"Don't ever touch me again!" The warning was voiced between grinding teeth. "Laurie told me what you did to her, and I'm trying to keep from killing you. Don't make it easy for me."

Chesser did not back away. He glared at Wyatt through round gray eyes that bulged in their sockets. "Naylor trusted me to beat you down, and you tricked me into giving his cattle away. He'll blame me for a bad mistake, but I'll square things. You'll never make a dime out of the Lazy L herd. I'm not through with you!"

"You're through," Wyatt said. "You just don't know it."

Words were still sputtering on Chesser's tongue as Wyatt headed for the door with Sam Hopson beside him. Wyatt was not listening. He was disappointed that events had taken a bad turn at the bank. Despite his apparent disregard for Chesser's threats, Wyatt was nagged by anxiety. Lloyd Rocker was demanding some action on the Keyhole's debts, and Wyatt could not satisfy him unless he could sell the Lazy L herd to Homer Utley for a profit. He knew Ward Chesser would try to keep that from happening.

Sam Hopson knew it, too. As soon as they stepped out on the boardwalk he said, "Chesser's more afraid of bein' laughed at than he is about anything Herbert Naylor might say. That eats at a man and makes him dangerous. When I first met him I thought he was a smart-talkin' dude, but he ain't. Get him in a corner, and he'll be as tough as they come. He ain't figured out what he's goin' to do to stop you, but he'll do somethin'."

"I know." Wyatt pulled his hatbrim closer to his eyes and squinted against the sunlight. "I was counting on getting Homer Utley's money in my hand before the Lazy L knew what was going on. Why in hell did you give me away?"

Sam Hopson's ruddy face sobered and he looked offended. There was a knot of people outside the saloon, and Hopson pulled Wyatt a few feet away so they could not be overheard.

"Hell, I ain't a fool," he said. "Your banker wouldn't let me draw on your account until I convinced him you could put it back and more with it. He said the money you had was his only security, and he was thinkin' about seizin' it as a payment on the Keyhole note. We left Chesser in the office and talked in the hall. The banker was right pleased when I explained what you was goin' to do. After the deal was closed, Rocker told Chesser everything I told him. He was gloatin' over it, laughin' under his breath and pokin' fun at Chesser. I think what it boils down to is that he likes you and despises the Lazy L bunch."

Wyatt sighed. "Lloyd Rocker thought a heap of my pa. Maybe he was trying to say he's proud of me, but he didn't do me any favors. It's almost two days before Homer Utley gets here. That gives the Lazy L time to make a move against us."

"Goin' by what I saw a while ago, I'd say you can handle it."

A surge of regret dulled Wyatt's eyes. "I don't want to

261

talk about that. Somebody was going to kill Alvin Beemer sooner or later, but I ain't proud it was me."

"I understand," Hopson said solemnly. "Chances are you'll have to do it again before you sell that herd."

"We'll see," Wyatt said, and the two of them moved farther away from the crowd.

TWENTY-ONE

Front Street hummed with the sound of voices and hurried feet as word of the gunfight spread through the town. There were more people in Rampart than Wyatt had estimated. Some had heard the gunshots and their rush toward the saloon drew the attention of others who followed. Shopkeepers stepped from doorways, spotted the crowd on the boardwalk, and hastened to join them.

Two women crossed in front of Wyatt and he heard one of them say, "Something bad has happened and my man will want me to tell him about it when I get home."

Sweat dripped from Wyatt's eyebrows and his stomach was still queasy. Twenty feet from the crowd, he stopped beneath the wooden awning that shaded the windows of Maybelle's Dress Shoppe. He took tobacco and papers from his pocket and rolled a cigarette. His shaking hands made the simple task difficult. Sam Hopson scratched a match alive on the butt of his six-gun and lighted the cigarette for him. The wiry cowhand's fingers were also shaking.

During the pause, Hopson gave him the bill of sale for the cattle, which Wyatt folded and slipped into his hip pocket. It was a reminder that he had to forget about the gunfight and keep his mind on business. He took two deep drags on the cigarette, tossed it away, and suggested that it was time for them to ride out to the holding grounds and take control of the Lazy L herd.

"You told me last week to see if I could find some help in case this thing went through," Sam Hopson said. "I found some. Chesser told me yesterday he was goin' to send his crew home before he met me at the bank, but the cattle are in good hands. I ran into a couple of cowhands who're on their way to the Colorado range. They're in no hurry to get there and glad to get some work along the way. It'll cost you a dollar a day for each man. They're with the cattle now."

"I hope to hell they're not rustlers. Can you trust them?"

"Think so." Sam Hopson wriggled his shoulders inside Justin Kirk's borrowed suit and made a wry face. "Don't matter much. I'm goin' to get out of these fancy duds and check out of the hotel. I'll get my horse from the livery and join the fellers I hired. If it suits you, I'll stay with the herd until the broker gets here. He might want them two waddies to help him drive the cattle to Caprock."

Wyatt nodded approvingly. "You won't need me, then. Justin don't get along too well with Lloyd Rocker, and he wanted to stay out of sight until this thing is done. He asked me to come straight home and tell him how it went. I'll do that and come back Friday to meet Homer Utley's stage."

"I'll be here."

Sam Hopson had volunteered to pay his own

expenses until his assignment was finished. Now that he was moving to camp with the herd, Wyatt offered to reimburse him from the money he had collected for the capture of Ray Beemer.

"Hell, I've got more money than the Keyhole," Sam Hopson said, backing away. "I ain't been anywhere to spend money and I've saved my wages for two years. Them cattle ain't been sold yet. You can pay me when you get paid."

Wyatt put his hand on the cowhand's shoulder. "You've done good by me, Sam. I appreciate it."

"You've done as good by me. You made me stop hidin' and get out among folks. I don't see no sign of anybody lookin' for me and I feel free again."

Smiling, Wyatt said, "Maybe we'll all come out ahead."

"Maybe. That depends on how Herbert Naylor takes it when he finds out he's been hornswoggled."

"Yeah." Wyatt's voice was barely audible.

They moved out of the awning's shade, heading in different directions. As he neared the corner where he could turn to reach the back street that led to Charlie Blake's livery stable, Wyatt turned for another look at the crowd at the Wildfire. His eyes searched for a particular small, shapely figure. Laurie Custer's school day was not yet over, but he was afraid the furor might cause her to leave early. She was not among the spectators.

He was about to leave Front Street when he heard a familiar voice calling his name. His shoulders slumped when he saw Maggie Gregg running toward him, her white apron fanning away from her round stomach as she increased her pace to a dogtrot.

"Wait, Wyatt! Wait! I have to talk to you."

He dismissed her with an impatient wave. "Not now, Maggie. I'll see you later."

A quick stride took him around the corner and out of her sight. He stopped abruptly, unable to ignore the crushed look that swept across Maggie's face. Maggie was like family, and he could not turn his back on her. He assumed his reputation as a gunfighter would be the talk of the town again, and he might as well let Maggie ask the first questions. He came back to Front Street and waited for her.

Maggie's cheeks were flushed and she was out of breath. She stopped in front of Wyatt, her bosom heaving. Her smiling face gave no indication that she was displeased with him. Either she did not know of the incident at the Wildfire, or she considered it none of her business. Holding one hand on her chest, she fumbled in her apron pocket and withdrew a pink envelope.

"Lordy, I was afraid you'd get away from me," she gasped. "I—I got a letter from Bertetta Halsey. It came on the noon stage, and I knew you'd want to know—"

"A letter from Bertetta?" Wyatt interrupted incredulously. "I thought she . . . I thought her mind was ruined—that she was past speaking or knowing what was going on around her."

"She's come out of it," Maggie crowed joyously. "I'm so glad, so happy for her!" She pushed the envelope into his hand. "Here, read it for yourself. Bertetta says the last thing she remembers was hearing her pa say he was going to reward me for helping her. That's where my money came from! Her pa is Herbert Naylor . . . I didn't know that."

"Lester Mace should've told you," Wyatt said. "We both knew."

"It don't matter," Maggie said. "Bertetta's getting well and that's what I care about. Read the letter!"

The uneven lines and wavering pen strokes suggested a hand grown clumsy from inactivity, but the words were legible. It was a long letter, and Wyatt's eyes were moist when he finished with it.

Bertetta spoke of months and years lost in a dark void. The words reflected a sad tone when she tried to convey the mystery of a mind and body frozen by shock and horror, of deadened senses refusing to acknowledge sights or sounds, or the touch of a comforting hand.

She called her recovery a miracle—a slow, then sudden, awakening while she was walking one day in the gardens around the rest home. A young man was holding her hand, leading her around the flowers and shrubbery and speaking gently to her all the while. He was dark and slender, and wearing a cleric's collar. Later, she learned he was the pastor of a Saint Joseph church, who had learned about her illness and had visited her every day for months. He had talked constantly to her, read to her, and taken her daily into the fresh air and sunshine. Despite her apparent oblivion to his presence, he had persisted until his voice and touch broke through the shell that had shielded her from reality.

Many of her phrases were a celebration of joy, and they stuck in Wyatt's mind. "Stacks of letters from my mother that I hadn't read, don't remember receiving . . .

nurses tell me she's been visiting me once a month . . . Daddy's been so sad . . . didn't know they'd moved to Texas . . . writing this same day to tell them to come home . . . you were very kind to me, Maggie . . . I recall Daddy saying he'd do something for you in return . . . it was all my fault and I think that made me sick . . . don't know what happened to my husband—never want to see him . . . the pastor is so nice, so handsome . . . maybe I'm in love again . . ."

Folding the letter thoughtfully, Wyatt handed it back to Maggie Gregg and said, "I'm glad she's all right. I don't like Herbert Naylor but I feel sorry for him. He loves his daughter, and it's been hard for him."

"Fathers and daughters," Maggie mused as she put the letter in her pocket and patted her apron. "They're always close."

"Yeah." Wyatt pulled his hatbrim close to his eyes and shuffled his feet restlessly. "I got to be going."

"I knew you'd want to know about Bertetta," Maggie said.

"I did. I'm glad I waited for you."

Maggie gave him a maternal pat and went around the corner to Front Street.

Charlie Blake was peering through the skinned poles of the rambling fence that encircled the barn and feed-lots when Wyatt arrived at the livery stable. The liveryman started talking while he was still swinging open the gate to let Wyatt inside, his short legs jabbing the ground in prancing little steps.

"People been runnin' around and yellin' and cuttin' a fit down on the main drag." Blake's flop-brimmed hat with its shapeless crown was a foot below Wyatt's chin. He tilted his head between his shoulders to watch the taller man's face. His mouth was full of tobacco juice and he sounded like a man trying to speak underwater. "What in tarnation is goin' on?"

"There was a shooting at the Wildfire Saloon. You'll hear about it."

Charlie Blake swore. "A shootin', you say? Danged long time since we've had a shootin' in Rampart. Anybody killed? Who—"

"You'll hear about it." Wyatt's tone left Charlie Blake's mouth hanging open in silence. He shoved his hands into the pockets of his baggy Levi's and stared uneasily at the cold sheen of Wyatt's eyes.

He cleared his throat and changed the subject. "I reckon you want that buckskin. It'll be two bits for day board."

Wyatt handed him a coin, and the liveryman said, "You want me to get him ready for you?"

"No. I handle my own saddle."

"Last stall at the back on the other side of the barn," Blake murmured, and retreated to stare again toward Front Street.

The slobbering of horses and the scuffing of hoofs in nearby stalls were the only sounds at the rear of the rambling barn. Beneath the tall roof the air was cool and dank, seasoned by the herblike aroma of cured hay, intermingled with the odors of leather harness and fresh manure. Wyatt welcomed the stillness and the brief escape from the burning sun. It gave him time to think.

He had much to be pleased about. He had participated

in another gunfight and was still alive. Unless Ward Chesser was able to enforce his threats, Wyatt would double his investment in the Lazy L cattle, and reduce the Keyhole's debt to a figure that would satisfy Lloyd Rocker until the next roundup. The time was drawing near, Wyatt told himself, when he would be rid of the two men who had tortured the Kirk family with so much trouble and uncertainty.

Matt Latham would return soon to reclaim the Lazy L Ranch, and Herbert Naylor would leave the Texas range forever. Now that Bertetta Halsey showed signs of regaining her mental faculties, Wyatt was sure her letter would hasten her father's departure.

If the hopes Ward Chesser had confided to Laura Custer materialized, the Lazy L foreman would follow his boss to Missouri and assist in the management of Naylor's wagon factory. It was possible, however, that Chesser would not go before he settled a score with Wyatt Kirk. He had been chagrined and belligerent when Wyatt left him at the saloon. He wanted to regain his pride and settle a personal grudge, but Wyatt was counting on Herbert Naylor to keep his foreman in check.

Naylor's motive for revenge would be tempered by Bertetta's recovery, and Wyatt doubted the Missourian would have the stomach to continue a vendetta that was beginning to backfire on him.

As he reviewed the events of the past weeks, Wyatt felt better about himself and his future. Gradually, the emotional impact of the violence at the Wildfire Saloon lessened its grip on him. By the time he finished saddling the buckskin he had convinced himself that most of his worries were over. He was still disturbed by the memory of Alvin Beemer's death, but perhaps the incident had served a purpose aside from silencing a dangerous killer. Walt Dorsey would tell many tales about Wyatt's gunspeed, and the talk might persuade Ward Chesser to go away with Herbert Naylor without causing any more trouble.

Wyatt led his horse outside with a growing sense of satisfaction, feeling relaxed for the first time since he arrived at the Keyhole. It was a short-lived sensation.

He came into the open at the same moment that Ward Chesser stepped into view. He came from the rear of the barn, which was twenty feet beyond the stall entrance. Chesser was walking on tiptoes, apparently attempting to sneak up on Wyatt while he was still inside. For the space of a heartbeat, both men stood paralyzed, each surprised to see the other.

Wyatt reacted first. He dropped the reins, jabbed an elbow against the buckskin to keep it moving, and was left with an unobstructed view of the Lazy L foreman. The afternoon sun threw the shadow of Chesser's hatbrim across his face, but Wyatt could see that his eyes were contracted to pinpoints. Rage deformed his face, cutting harsh lines around his wide mouth and juggling his Adam's apple.

"You're not getting away!" Chesser's voice was shrill. "You won't get the drop on me before I can get to my gun this time. It's an even play, and it's the last one you'll ever make."

Wyatt was puzzled by his shifting emotions.

Strangely, he felt no hate for Chesser at this moment. The Keyhole was on the threshold of surviving its difficulties, and Laurie Custer had escaped unharmed from his unwelcome advances.

Wyatt weighed these things in his mind, thinking of his desire to be known among his neighbors as a peaceful rancher rather than a bounty hunter. He cringed inwardly at the prospect of another gunfight. Despite his misgivings, he felt a surge of warmth through his arms and legs as he always did when he anticipated that he might have to fight for his life. His arms dangled limply at his sides, his right hand exactly the distance from the Peacemaker Colt that he wanted it to be.

"You surprise me," Wyatt said tightly. "I figured if you wanted me dead you'd call on your friend Burdine Fisher."

Chesser's laugh was wild and irrational. "Burdine Fisher? So you've heard about Burdine Fisher. Hell, there ain't no Burdine Fisher. I made him up out of thin air to keep out of trouble with Mr. Naylor. First thing he did when he came to Texas was send me looking for Evan Halsey—wanted me to bring him back so he could cut him up like Halsey cut Bertetta. He was going to hurt him some, then turn him over to the law."

The keen voice sank to a hoarse whisper, and Chesser spoke like a man betraying a secret. "Halsey wasn't too hard to find. I checked on towns that had been without a doctor and turned him up down in Rumford. I watched him for a while and learned his habits. He stayed in his office till dark every day, then got in his buggy and drove to his cabin out on the flats. One night—"

"You waylaid him and shot him in the back," Wyatt cut in icily.

"You got it, mister." Chesser laughed again, thrusting his chin toward Wyatt. "I didn't fancy standing guard over him for a hundred-mile ride, and I wanted to put an end to the job I was sent for. Mr. Naylor don't like killing, though. I figured he'd raise hell if I told him the truth, so I made up a story. I told him I got a friend to help me, a gunman named Burdine Fisher, and that Fisher killed Doc Halsey before I could stop him. I kept the name alive so the Lazy L crew would show me some respect and you'd be afraid to cross me."

Chesser clamped his mouth shut. His shoulders twitched and he shuffled his feet nervously. "I know what you're doing—you figure if you keep me talking I'll back down and let you go."

"Talking beats shooting," Wyatt said earnestly. "I don't hold with bushwhacking, but Evan Halsey killed my father and I can't mourn for the man who did that. You lived to tell the story, and you can keep on living if you're smart. Chances are Naylor's going to leave me alone and get out of Texas as fast as he can. He wouldn't want you doing anything stupid at this point. There's been some developments you ought to know about."

"I know about them." The shrill tone was gone now, and Chesser's voice was guttural and threatening. "That little old lady who works at the Sunset Hotel has been running all over town talking about the letter she got from Bertetta. I was waiting in Lloyd Rocker's office for Sam Hopson when she showed up there. She was wondering if she ought to give Mr. Naylor's money back to him. The banker told her to keep it. Jesse Estep rode in with me to pick up the mail, and Mr. Naylor has his letter by now. I know what that means."

"It means this feud is over," Wyatt said flatly.

"It means I've lost out on the best deal I've ever had," Chesser snarled. "I've got to tell Mr. Naylor how you hoodwinked me on the cattle sale. He's a smart man, and he wants smart people as his assistants. He won't take me to Missouri with him. He'll think I'm dumb and he'll fire me."

"You don't know that until you talk to him."

"I know!" The color drained from Chesser's face and a vein throbbed on the side of his neck. "You've ruined my life, Kirk. You've taken my girl away from me, you've cost me my job, and you've made me look like a fool. There's only one thing that might get me back in Mr. Naylor's good graces. He hates you as much as I do, and he could go home feeling good if he knew you were dead!"

The talk was over. Ward Chesser had followed Wyatt to the livery to kill him. He would not leave until his mission was accomplished. While Wyatt talked with Sam Hopson and Maggie Gregg, Chesser had circled through the brush and trees on the back side of the feed-lots and waited for Wyatt to come for his horse. The wait was over. Chesser did not expect Wyatt to live through the day or he would not have admitted that he was the man who bushwhacked Dr. Evan Halsey.

The way Chesser's jaws clamped tight with his final words told Wyatt his efforts at persuasion were futile.

He kept his eyes on Chesser's face, watching for the telltale signals that telegraphed a man's thoughts at the moment of a desperate decision. He saw enough to alert him.

Shoulders stiffened, eyelids flickered, and Chesser's hand swept toward his oak-handled Colt.

TWENTY-TWO

Experience and instinct were in Wyatt's favor. The Peacemaker rocked in his hand, spewing fire and lead. Ward Chesser had lifted his gun waisthigh when Wyatt's bullet drilled a hole through the man's flannel shirt and punctured his heart.

The impact of the slug drove Chesser backward. His gun dropped from a limp hand. He turned half-around, his body flopping out of control until he ran into the wall of the barn. He slid to the ground in a sitting position with his hat jammed between the back of his head and the wall, his legs jutting forward to expose the soles of his boots. His mouth hung agape, his eyes wide and glassy. Blood trickled from the corner of his mouth and a circle of crimson stained his shirt. The face that had been so handsome in life was ugly in death.

Wyatt stared at the body for a few seconds, then turned his head. He holstered the Peacemaker and sat down on an empty crate farther along the wall. He was still there when Charlie Blake came up in front of him.

The liveryman was sweating and wheezing as he sucked in his breath. He ran over to look at the dead man, then back to Wyatt. "My God, you've killed Ward

274

Chesser! Where'd he come—"

"Go get the sheriff," Wyatt said quietly.

"I heard the shot, but I never dreamt—"

"Now!" Wyatt said sternly. The liveryman nodded, and hastened toward the front of the barn.

Fifteen minutes passed before Sheriff Lester Mace arrived, moving across the lot in calm, unhurried strides. Years as a lawman had brought him to the scenes of many deaths and he was in no hurry to gaze upon another one. He stopped in front of Ward Chesser's body, glanced at the man's oak-handled Colt lying in the dirt a few feet away, and walked over to stare at the back of Wyatt's bowed head.

"You going to kill everybody in town before you leave today?" he asked bluntly.

Wyatt drew a deep breath and stood up. He did not like Mace's disgruntled tone. "I'm trying to get home alive if I can," he said in a measured voice. "It ain't been easy."

Without waiting for Mace's questions he described how Chesser had forced him into a gunfight, driven by his own hate and the hope of winning favor with Herbert Naylor. It was a familiar story, the pattern of many frontier showdowns. The sheriff listened indifferently until Wyatt told him that Ward Chesser admitted he had bushwhacked Dr. Evan Halsey and his reasons for blaming it on a nonexistent gunman named Burdine Fisher.

The sheriff whistled softly between his teeth. "I knew there was somethin' fishy about Burdine Fisher."

Wyatt wanted to get everything off his chest before

Mace heard an embellished version of his other activities from the town gossips. He spoke frankly about his dealings at the Drovers Trust Bank, and related the main points of the letter that Maggie Gregg had shown him.

The lawman was pleased by the news of Bertetta Halsey's recovery, and chuckled aloud when Wyatt told him the result of Herbert Naylor's attempt to undercut the Keyhole cattle prices.

Mace's good humor faded quickly. He pushed at his shirttail, and his craggy face was unhappy. He said, "The day you showed up here, I had a feelin' my quiet little town was goin' to change. You've cleared up a lot of dirt, but you've brought a lot with you. I saw where Chesser's gun fell. I reckon it was a fair fight, but I don't like what's happenin' to Rampart. Looks like your reputation ain't keepin' anybody from drawin' on you."

Mace put his steely gaze on Wyatt's face and it was met by the glare of china-blue eyes that were just as unyielding. "Chesser wasn't looking for a reputation," Wyatt said. "He had personal grudges to settle."

A muttered curse, a hitch at his gunbelt, and a look toward the heavens told of Mace's frustration. "Dead is dead, no matter what. I'd just finished gettin' business settled on the other corpse when Charlie Blake come for me. I didn't want Charlie up here runnin' his mouth and I left him at the gate. I'll need to send him after somebody to move Chesser's body. You're sure keepin' the undertaker busy. How long is this goin' to go on?"

"It's over. I'll sell the cattle day after tomorrow. Naylor's learned that making sons pay for the sins of their father ain't as easy to pull off as he thought. He's got nothing to keep him here, and he'll want to see his daughter. The fight's over."

The hard lines did not leave Mace's face. "Maybe it's over, maybe not. Only God knows what might happen between now and the time your broker gets here. Come Friday, I'll be keepin' my eyes on everything that moves in town. If there's any more killin' to be done in Rampart, I'll do it."

Wyatt did not see Lester Mace again until almost four o'clock on Friday afternoon, but Homer Utley arrived on time. The broker brought with him a fine saddle, a bedroll, and a small valise.

"You've growed some since I saw you last," he said as he stepped down from the noon stage and shook hands. "My horse is getting too old for long hauls. I figured I'd buy something from Charlie Blake to ride home on if I take your cattle."

Wyatt helped the cattle broker carry his belongings to a room at the Sunset Hotel, and afterward they sat in the lobby and talked business. Homer Utley was a man without pretensions. He spoke plainly and dressed plainly, arriving in wrinkled Levi's, flannel shirt, and a cowhide vest. He was known as a sharp trader, but an honest one.

"Last time I was over this way I bought cows for fifteen dollars," Utley began. "I'm looking for another good deal."

"That was Herbert Naylor's way of using his wealth to keep Justin in debt," Wyatt said evenly. "I bought

Naylor's cattle this time. I want market price—twenty-five dollars a head."

It was a bargaining point, and Wyatt expected it to change. He had quoted the price for cattle delivered in Caprock Junction. Homer Utley made his money from the spread between what he paid for cattle and what the Chicago packers paid for them. His profit was further reduced by the expense of driving a herd to the railhead. Wyatt did not have Utley's business contacts, and there was too much work to be done at the Keyhole for him to spare half his crew on a two-week round trip to Caprock Junction. He needed cash and Homer Utley needed cattle, but dickering over prices was part of the process.

Finally, Homer Utley pushed back his Stetson and rubbed a hand through his thick white hair. He set a finger beside his sharp nose and squinted speculatively.

"I'll look at what you've got," he said. "I don't get many spring cattle and there's a demand for them. If they're prime I'll give you twenty-two dollars a head."

It was the figure that Wyatt had fixed in his mind at the beginning, and he quickly accepted the offer. They shook hands and went outside. Wyatt walked back to the Overland office and stood beside his buckskin while Homer Utley carried his saddle to Charlie Blake's livery and returned shortly on a rented horse.

Two hours later Homer Utley gave Wyatt a bank draft for eighty-eight hundred dollars. Wyatt took it directly to the Drovers Trust, and paid Lloyd Rocker eight thousand. Satisfied, the banker praised him for keeping his word, assuring Wyatt he would arrange a long-term schedule for further payments. After withdrawing five hundred in cash so he could pay the Keyhole crew, Wyatt left the bank in a happy mood.

He found Sam Hopson pacing back and forth beside his horse outside. The herd had been left in the care of the two Colorado-bound cowhands, who agreed to accompany Homer Utley on the drive to the railhead. Hopson had packed his bedroll and ridden back to town with Wyatt and the broker, but he did not want to leave until he could carry a message to Justin Kirk and the others at the Keyhole Ranch.

"It's all done," Wyatt told him. Hopson leaped immediately into his saddle. He cried, "Hi-yi-yi," as he spurred his horse out of town, leaving behind the echoes of his Texas war whoop.

Wyatt looked down the street and saw Homer Utley sitting alone on one of the benches beside the entrance to the Sunset Hotel. Wyatt planned to wait in the same spot for the next hour, and it would be good to have the broker's company. Laurie Custer would dismiss her classes before long, spend some time grading papers, then come to her room at the Sunset. Wyatt looked forward to telling her peace had come to the Keyhole, and that she had nothing to fear if she wanted to ride back with him to the cabin on Castle Creek.

Halfway between the bank and the hotel Wyatt was intercepted by Sheriff Lester Mace. The lawman's face wore a complacent expression, unlike the tight-lipped countenance Wyatt had witnessed at their last meeting.

"I can tell by lookin' that you got it done." Mace's voice was again the mellow drawl Wyatt had known since boyhood. "I meant to stay close to you today, but I've been tied up with Herbert Naylor. After he showed up I got a pretty good notion the Lazy L wasn't goin' to try to stop you, and it put my mind to rest."

Naylor's visit was to inquire about the sheriff's investigation of the gunfight that had left Ward Chesser dead. Mace had told the rancher what he observed at the scene, and of Wyatt's account of the killing. He also told him about Ward Chesser's admission that it was he—not anyone called Burdine Fisher—who had murdered Naylor's son-in-law.

"Naylor's pullin' out and leavin' it up to the bank to handle the money end of turnin' the Lazy L back to Matt Latham," Mace said. "He's pretty down in the mouth. He figures it's his fault that his foreman got killed, and he ain't blamin' you none. He can't wait to see Bertetta, but he's stayin' around to see that Chesser gets a big funeral and a proper burial. It's tomorrow at the Baptist church. You comin'?"

Wyatt scowled, unable to tell if the question was intended to be serious or ironic. "I'll pass on it," he said evenly. "Chesser might have kin who'll want to take up his fight. I'm going to stay out of sight awhile. This business of my reputation worries me. I don't want to face up to that for the rest of my life."

Mace gave him a fatherly pat on the shoulder and grinned. "Time and old age will take care of that. Make yourself a name as a good neighbor and the best rancher in these parts, and people will forget about your gun."

"Hope so," Wyatt muttered, and went on to join Homer Utley.

Good friends did not need constant conversation to enjoy companionship. Wyatt exchanged only a few words with the broker while they sat side by side on the bench and watched the traffic along the street. They rolled cigarettes and smoked quietly, raising their eyebrows or nodding to each other when they noticed something unusual or interesting about the pedestrians who passed in front of them.

Presently, Utley said, "I think I'll go in and wash some of this trail dust off me before supper. You're as hard a nut to crack as your pa, Wyatt, but it's been a good day. You made some money, I'll make some money."

He was half standing, his knees still bent, when he glanced across the street, then sat down hard on the bench. "What's that?"

Wyatt turned his head to follow Homer Utley's gaze. A small man on a pinto horse was drawing rein at the hitching rail in front of the Wildfire Saloon. He kicked free of the stirrups, looked down, and held to the saddle horn to soften the impact of his landing as he slid to the ground.

"He's going to need a ladder to get back on that bronc," Utley said, chuckling.

"He's going to need a bodyguard if he keeps wearing that getup," Wyatt ventured.

The brim of the newcomer's white hat was so wide it dwarfed his narrow shoulders. His Levi's were the dark blue of unwashed denim, his shirt a gaudy plaid with a red neckerchief circling the collar. Goathide chaps, worn with the hair side out, flapped around his stubby legs as he tethered his horse and went through the batwing doors of the Wildfire. Before he disappeared from sight, sunlight drew Wyatt's attention to the man's weapon as it flashed on the nickel-plated six-gun in the cutaway holster tied above the goathide on his right leg.

"I been reading some and hearing a lot about you, Wyatt," Utley said solemnly. "I'd say that feller's after you. If you want to keep your reputation, you'd better run for your life."

"I'll chance it," Wyatt said, and they laughed again.

Incredibly, Homer Utley's remark turned out to be more of a prophecy than a joke. The man in the wooly chaps returned to his horse, freed the reins, and led the pinto up the street. When he reached the hotel, he stopped in the powdery dust and studied the two men on the slatted bench.

He was not as young as he looked at a distance. Egg-shaped pouches bulged beneath his eyes. The skin sagged slightly along his narrow jaw, and points of black beard gave his reddish-brown complexion a sooty look. The lines on his forehead and below his cheeks belonged to a man in his forties.

"You're Wyatt Kirk," the man declared. "A gentleman at the saloon pointed you out to me."

"That was good of him," Wyatt said dryly. "Who're you?"

"Mark Wright. I heard you'd returned home, and I've been trying to find this place for a week. You don't know me, but I write for a newspaper called *The Prairie Scout* down in—"

"I know you," Wyatt snapped. He stood up, stretching

his height to its full six feet four inches. "I don't like you, and I'm not giving out any stories for you to turn into lies."

Mark Wright dropped his horse's reins and took a step to the side. "Oh, I'm not here for that. I've been fascinated by your fame. I'd like to be just as well-known in the West. People look down on little people, and it's important for us to do something big to gain respect. I've been thinking of challenging you for a long time. I finally made up my mind, and I came looking for you."

Wyatt and Homer Utley exchanged glances, both stunned. Wyatt stepped down from the boardwalk and faced the newspaperman. "Are you saying you want to fight me?"

"Yes sir. I've been practicing, counting seconds to myself when I draw, and I think I can beat you."

Wyatt sighed, and shook his head, finding it hard to believe what he was hearing. "You've read too many dime novels, mister. I'm not going to draw on you."

Standing with his arms folded, a half grin on his face, Homer Utley still believed it was a joke. He said, "Accommodate the man, Wyatt. Go ahead and kill the little squirt."

"There you go making fun of my size," Mark Wright said, his voice quavering as he glared at the cattle broker. He turned his attention again to Wyatt. "We must have a showdown. I've come a long way for this, and I won't back down. I understand the customary shooting distance is twenty paces. Pick your spot."

A cagey, cautious gleam replaced the amusement in Wyatt's eyes. He had learned long ago that it was a mistake to judge a man's ability by his appearance. It would be ironic, he thought, if he died at the hands of the little man in the oversized hat after overcoming the threats of such hard-nosed Texans as Alvin Beemer and Ward Chesser.

Any man with a loaded gun posed a danger, and Wyatt considered his next move carefully. With words and an active imagination, Mark Wright had complicated Wyatt's life, and he disliked the man intensely. He could not draw against him, but he could not let him leave without learning a lesson about the character of men who made their own rules to survive on the Western frontier.

"Twenty paces," Mark Wright repeated. "I could back away some or you could—"

"That's too far," Wyatt said.

Two long strides took him closer to the newspaperman, and Mark Wright looked puzzled. He took a step backward, settling his hand on the butt of the nickel-plated six-gun. He licked his lips and cried, "You must go for your gun and give me a chance—"

Wyatt kept walking until he was almost toe-to-toe with Mark Wright. He swung his arm and slapped the little man's cheek with his open palm. It was a fierce blow, backed by the muscles of heavy shoulders and the force of a rope-hardened hand. Mark Wright fell like a man struck by lightning. He rose on one elbow, bobbed his head to clear his senses, and looked up at Wyatt in disbelief.

He opened his mouth to speak, but the words were never uttered. Wyatt took another step. He raised his foot and kicked Mark Wright squarely in the face. Blood spurted from the newspaperman's nose. His face was smudged with dirt from Wyatt's boot, and his mouth looked like a crushed mushroom.

This was the man whose exaggerated writings had saddled Wyatt with a reputation that put his life in constant danger. The anger that had seethed within him since the first story he read about himself pressed Wyatt to keep punishing the man. He picked Wright up by the shirtfront, hit him in the jaw, and lost his grip on him. He reached down to lift him from the ground so he could batter him again with his fists, then straightened and left him where he was as better judgment prevailed.

Mark Wright lay cowering in the dust, one arm crooked to protect his face. When he saw Wyatt back away, he struggled to a sitting position. He retrieved his hat and dabbed at his bleeding face with the tip of his neckerchief.

"You—you're not the brave and fearless man I wrote about," he whimpered. "You're a mean and vicious roughneck who declines to fight fairly. I'm going to tell the world about you. You're a—"

"Get up!" Wyatt growled. "Get up and get out of town while you're still alive."

Wyatt moved toward him. Mark Wright sprang to his feet and hurried to the side of the pinto, that had skittered a few yards away. After missing two attempts to get his foot high enough to reach the stirrup, he hopped up and down on one leg and tried to reach the saddle horn to pull himself into the saddle.

Shrugging, Wyatt walked up behind him. He grabbed

Wright's shirt-collar with one hand and the seat of his pants with the other, hoisting him into the saddle like a sack of flour. He handed him the reins, slapped the pinto's rump, and said, "Get!"

The horse galloped away. Wyatt watched until he saw Mark Wright leave town and head toward the open range. The altercation had not lasted long enough to attract attention, and Wyatt was glad there would be no talk about him because of it.

"If you're sure that's the last show of the day, I'm going to go inside," Homer Utley said when Wyatt returned to his seat on the bench. "You staying over tonight?"

Wyatt shook his head. "I'm waiting for a friend to show up, and then I'll be riding home."

"Luck to you," Utley said.

Afterward, Wyatt moved to another bench where he could rest his back against the building. He smoked a cigarette and reflected on his confrontation with Mark Wright. He had treated the man brutally, and it was for a purpose. There would be no more stories in *The Prairie Scout* glamorizing the art of gunfighting. He suspected that Mark Wright would change his views on the violence that erupted often in this untamed land, and do all he could to destroy Wyatt's reputation as an idealistic gunfighter. That possibility made the fight worthwhile.

For the first time since he had come home, Wyatt's mind was not burdened by concerns over Herbert Naylor, Ward Chesser, or past-due debts. He was free to think about more pleasant matters—about a ranch that would grow prosperous in a few years, and the words he would speak when he asked the girl he loved to marry him.

The air around him seemed cooler and more invigorating. He looked at the sky. A line of clouds had floated in from the southwest, blotting out the sun. He swung his gaze idly along the street. Far down the boardwalk he saw a trim blond woman with her arms full of books coming toward the hotel. He hastened to meet her. It had been a long time since Wyatt had carried a girl's schoolbooks, but it was only one of the small things he hoped to do for Laurie Custer during their lifetime together.

Center Point Publishing
600 Brooks Road ● PO Box 1
Thorndike ME 04986-0001 USA

(207) 568-3717

US & Canada:
1 800 929-9108

3